Wewukiye tugged her hand, drawing her closer. His warm breath puffed against her ear.

"You need only think of me and you will have strength."

His soft silky voice floated through her body like a hot drink.

Dove swallowed the lump in her throat and asked, "When will I see you again?" The thought of sleeping on the hard ground next to the fire in Crazy One's dwelling didn't sound near as inviting as using his lap to rest her head.

The days and nights grew colder; to be wrapped in his arms would warm her through and through.

"You will find me at the meadow every day when the sun is directly overhead." He brushed his lips against her ear.

She closed her eyes, relishing the silky feel of his lips and the heat of his touch.

"Think of me," whispered through her head.

Dove opened her eyes. She stood alone. Her palm still warm from their clasped hands, her ear ringing with his whisper.

Praise for *SPIRIT OF THE MOUNTAIN*

"Paty Jager has written a beautiful tale of love in a time when people were governed by their dreams and their prayers."
~Tony/Paul Reviews

Spirit
of the Lake

by

Paty Jager

Spirit of the Lake

Cover Art by *Rae Monet, Inc. Design*

The Wild Rose Press
PO Box 706
Adams Basin, NY 14410-0706
Visit us at www.thewildrosepress.com

Publishing History
First Faery Rose Edition, 2011
Print ISBN 1-60154-924-5

Published in the United States of America

Dedication

To my husband, who puts up with
all my travels and my writer's quirks,
to my editor Kelly Schaub
for believing in my stories,
and to Jade Black Eagle and Red Wolf
for their insights.

Disclaimer:

The daily activities and beliefs of the Nimiipuu in this book are factual—the spirits, other characters, and situations that evolve are only factual in the imagination of this writer/storyteller.

Ná-qc
(1)

Wallowa Country 1867

Wewukiye stared at a fully clothed Nimiipuu maiden walking into the lake. Her measured steps continued as the water rose around her. Why was she clothed if she planned to bathe? Before he could conjure up a reason, her head disappeared below the surface of the water, and his chest tightened. She wished to leave this earth. He pivoted away from his sister and loped in his elk form to the edge of the lake.

If not for his powers, he would not have seen the maiden on such a moonless night.

He was on this earth to protect the Nimiipuu. Why did this maiden wish to disgrace herself and her family? Raising his face to the sky, he asked for his man form. A form he had not used in many seasons.

Once the smoke around him settled, he plunged into his watery home. As the spirit of the lake, he resided in elk form at the bottom of the lake when not roaming the Nimiipuu country.

He found the maiden's limp body and wrapped an arm around her, drawing her out of the icy mountain runoff. Her cold body folded over his arm. He walked out of the lake, water running off him and the maiden. Her body convulsed. She choked and sucked in a great gulp of air.

She fought the air with more effort than she fought the water. Why?

1

He placed her on the soft summer grass, stomach down, and pushed on her back. She clawed at the ground trying to drag her body away. Her head raised, her face pointed toward the lake Nimiipuu village. A moan escaped her throat, and she collapsed unmoving but for the great draws of air filling her.

Wewukiye sat back, and she scrambled to her hands and knees, moving away from him. He captured her ankle, holding her in place. In her weak condition it didn't take but a couple gentle tugs and she collapsed.

"You will not dishonor yourself or your family," he said.

"Let—me—go," the maiden panted, struggling against his hold.

Wewukiye raised her from the ground and held her face to make her look at him.

Panic widened her eyes, and her body shook harder.

"Do not fear me. I am only keeping you from harm," Wewukiye said, willing her to look into his eyes. As a spirit his eyes had a calming effect on mortals.

Her wide brown eyes gazed into his. The tremors lessened, her body relaxed, and her breathing, though raspy from swallowing water, slowed.

He loosened his grip, giving her more space.

"Do not...take me to...the village. The cave...up there." The maiden raised a shaky hand and pointed up the mountain.

Wewukiye gazed along her outstretched arm to the area beyond. "I know this place."

The woman's body slumped in his arms, slipping into unconsciousness.

He stared at the maiden. Her strange request baffled as much as her attempt to drown herself. He would do as she asked. He gathered her in his arms and set off up the side of the mountain to a cave his brother had once shown him. It was the only one on this side of the mountain. He would take her there and learn why she refused to go to the village and wished to end her life.

At the cave he found a blanket, basket of water, and a basket of herbs neatly placed against one wall. She must live here. Why was she not at the village?

The maiden shivered and her teeth chattered. He may have saved her from ending her life, but unless he got her warm and watched her closely, he could lose her to sickness. The wet dress must come off, and her body must be warmed. He held her in his arms, and bent to grasp the folded blanket. With some effort, he managed to spread the covering upon the ground.

He knelt, placing the maiden on the blanket, and slipping her dress up her body. She sat, leaning against his bent leg with her dress over her head. Tugging on her deerskin garment, he finally pulled it free. Her arms slid from the sleeves, one slapped against her body, the other draped over his leg. He glanced down to see if his rough actions awakened her.

Her dark lashes fluttered on her cheeks, but her eyes remained closed, and her breathing rattled from the water within her. He tossed the wet dress toward the opening and gently lowered her to the blanket. He wrapped the other side of the blanket over her naked body, noticing bruising on her upper legs, inside her thighs, and on her breasts. What could she have done to leave such marks? He tucked the blanket around the maiden and sat back, watching her sleep.

Good fortune had brought him and his sister Saqan to the lake to visit. His sister's keen eagle eyes had noticed the maiden walking into the lake. At first he thought the maiden only stepped into the water to wash her feet, but when her determined steps carried her farther and farther into the lake, he knew she planned to walk into the water and end her life.

The dark circles under her eyes told him she had not been resting well. The bruises...he shook his head. He knew of no way those bruises could be made. No way by accident.

Where was this woman's man? Why was she alone in a cave? He had not heard of any men being lost to the Lake Nimiipuu. Perhaps she did not have a man. Was there something about her—craziness or such that prevented a warrior from wanting her as a wife?

Was that the reason she tried to end her life? If so, it was foolish. From what he knew of mortals, he found her pleasing to look at. Her wide hips and full breasts would produce many healthy children. If she were crazy, herbs and a firm hand took care of such things. No, there must be some other reason she had not been taken for a wife.

Wewukiye stared out the entrance of the cave. The night would soon be over, and his man form would vanish. He glanced at the woman. If she did not awake soon, he would have to leave. He couldn't care for her as an elk, and he couldn't allow her to know he was not a mortal.

Moaning and the scratch of the blanket turned his attention back inside the cave. Her head slowly moved back and forth as if she dreamed bad thoughts.

"Are you waking?" he asked, edging closer to the woman. "I wonder why you would try to end your life and bring shame to your family, and why you wished to not go to the village."

Her eyelids flew open, and her head jerked, turning her gaze on him. The fear in her dark eyes

4

reminded him of a cornered animal.

"Do not fear me. I will not harm you." Why were mortals so fearful?

She started to sit up. The blanket fell, revealing her ample breasts. Shame clouded her eyes and gripped his heart with compassion. Something had brought her to taking her life. His gut told him it had to do with the bruises.

She clutched the blanket and scooted away from him. He witnessed the terror and humiliation on her face. To gain her trust he would need to keep his distance just as with an injured animal. He shifted his body farther away from her, giving her the space her frantic gaze sought.

"I know it was wrong to have undressed you, but your clothes were wet and you were shivering from the cold. I did not want you to get the sickness."

She coughed and her body shook. His first reaction was to reach out to her, but the suspicion darkening her eyes kept his hands on his thighs and his body in place.

When the coughing stopped, he continued, "I cannot stay any longer, but I will return later with food." He stood, stepping toward the entrance of the cave. "I would like to find you here when I return."

The blank stare in her eyes, gave him little hope she would be here when he returned.

Dove watched the retreating back of the man who interfered with her decision to end her shame. After being marked a troublemaker and sent to live with the old women for telling lies which were the truth, she no longer wished to live.

In her nineteen summers, she had never once caused anyone to be upset with her. How could they not listen to her words now? The Wallowa Nimiipuu trying to tread softly and not cause trouble with the *so-yá-po*, White man, hurt the people more than if they came out and said how they really felt. They could not go on ignoring the badness brought by the *so-yá-po* in hopes of keeping peace.

Her stomach growled. She stared at her dress in a wet pile near the door. It would need to dry before she could roam the mountain for food. She stood and the cave blurred, her body swayed. The ordeal had weakened her already spent body. She put a hand on the cave wall to steady herself. If she did not eat and remained in the cave, her troubles would soon be over. *If she had the strength to not seek food or water.*

She had the strength to walk into the lake and shame herself and her family when no one seemed to care. Her heart ached. But now that the stranger had pulled her from the water and knew of her thoughts...the shame ripped her heart twofold.

The words of the warrior who hauled her out of the lake rang in her ears. "You will shame yourself and your family." She had already done that. How could taking her life shame her any more than what had already been done? Had she followed through, the others would believe she had fallen in the lake and drowned. Now that someone knew of her attempt, she couldn't shake the feeling she was a coward.

Cautiously, Dove bent, picking up her dress. She walked to the entrance and hung the garment on a bush where the sun would dry it. Without thinking, she peered down the mountain to the shimmering lake below.

Guilt sliced through her heart. She did love the lake and the Nimiipuu country surrounding it. Taking her life would bring as much shame as it lifted from her family, but it also would take her from the country which made her heart beat with pride. In a moment of rashness, she'd believed taking her life provided a way to bring an end to her torment.

She searched the memories of her childhood, her

heart grew sad. Should she go through with her plan, she would no longer walk this earth, and no longer voice her objections of Evil Eyes, who all the others listened to with tainted ears.

But to remain on this earth, she would be alone. Unless she relinquished and lived with the old women who would relentlessly work at making her see things the way of the blindfolded leaders. No warrior would want her after what Evil Eyes did. She shivered remembering that awful afternoon she strayed from the others picking berries and Evil Eyes came upon her.

How would she survive alone? She would not become so pathetic to follow along behind the band as they moved from camp to camp.

Her stomach growled, but she returned to the cave and curled into a ball on the hard ground. Her eyes fluttered closed, and she tried to forget her troubles for a little while.

****

Wewukiye could not get the maiden off his mind as he wandered the mountain in his elk form. His broad chest pushed him through the bushes in his path as visions of the bruised maiden and the fear in her eyes tormented him. He'd had very little contact over the years with mortals other than his brother, who became mortal to marry a Nimiipuu maiden, and the family they made.

He snorted. How his brother could bring himself down so low as to become mortal for a woman was the highest form of foolishness to Wewukiye. Spirits were needed to make sure the Nimiipuu were cared for. He had wondered many times over the years how his brother could give up his mountain and his status to join the ranks of the average.

The mid-morning sun beat down on him as he shouldered his way out of the brush. He found himself outside the cave. The maiden's dress hung on a bush. If her clothing remained, she must still be in the cave.

Mortals needed food. He would find her some nourishment and come back to ask all the questions banging around in his head.

He returned to the trees and headed up the slope. Several suns back he had encountered a bear rummaging through a patch of huckleberries. The patch was not far from the cave. He could pick enough for the mortal in little time.

Wewukiye hurried to the berry patch. He stood beside the bushes and realized though his elk form was regal and moved him about the mountain with speed, he would have to change into man form to pick and deliver the berries. He rarely used the man form, feeling uncomfortable and awkward in the two-legged vessel.

Realizing the maiden's intentions last night, he'd changed into a man knowing of no other way to get her out of the water and to safety without her discovering he was a Nimiipuu spirit.

He raised his face to the sky and asked for the man form. Smoke swirled around, covering the world in a gray veil before vanishing and leaving him as a man. He snatched a piece of bark from the ground and picked the small, round, dark berries piling them on the bark. When he could place no more without them rolling off, he walked quickly back to the cave, juggling the bark to keep from losing any berries.

The dress no longer hung from the bush. Disappointment squeezed his heart. Had the maiden dressed and left? He hoped not. Unraveling mysteries was one of his pastimes, and even if he did say so himself, he had a knack for it.

He stepped into the cave and heard the maiden's raspy breathing. She remained. He spotted her sitting cross-legged beside the basket of water.

"I have brought you something to eat," he said, approaching her slowly. Suspicion replaced the fear in her eyes.

"Why do you bother with me?" she asked. Her gaze clung to the berries he held out to her.

She did not reach up to take the offering. He placed the food in her lap and sat down across from her.

"Because life should not be thrown away."

The color darkening her cheeks told him she knew this. And yet, she tried to throw away her life.

Her hand fluttered over the berries as though she fought with herself to take one.

"Go ahead. You need to eat to build up your strength. Having swallowed so much water, you have weakened your body."

Her dark eyes stared at him. "My wish was to leave this earth."

"Why? There is nothing so bad you should want to fall in disfavor with the Creator or your family."

Anger sparked in her eyes as her lip curled into a snarl. "When your body has been taken from you, and your family does not believe you, there is nothing left to live for." Large tears rolled down her cheeks.

He reached out to pat her hand, she jerked it back.

"How was your body taken from you, and what is it your family does not believe?"

She rubbed the tears from her cheeks. Her angry gaze stared into his eyes never wavering.

"I have witnessed the evil which creeps into our valley."

Lepít
(2)

"What is the evil you have seen?" Wewukiye asked, leaning back from the intensity in her eyes.

"The *so-yá-po*. He is evil. He takes everything in this valley he admires." She wrapped her arms around her body as though to keep it from being pulled from her.

"He is not good for the Nimiipuu, this I also believe." He had yet to see the good of allowing the men the color of antelope to enter the valley. They grazed their animals and set up camps and eventually homes.

Her eyes took on a gleam, hatred shooting from their dark depths. "Our leaders do not see this. They say, 'do not make trouble.'" She sat up. "I have never made trouble nor said a cruel word against anyone, yet they hold me as a troublemaker for telling them the truth."

"What is the truth?" The minute he asked, the anger in her eyes faded to fear.

"I do not wish to remember." Her voice lost its tenacity and her shoulders drooped. She pulled the blanket tighter, shutting him out.

Knowing she did not wish to be touched, he nonetheless reached out, tipping her face up to peer into his eyes. "Are the bruises on your body the reason you do not wish to remember?"

Her cheeks darkened, shame and revulsion sprang into her eyes. She tried to pull her face from his scrutiny, but he held firm.

"You do not have to tell me what happened.

Only who is the man who would do such to a maiden."

"Evil Eyes." She spat the words.

"He is a White man?"

She nodded her head slightly.

"Which one?"

"The one they call Two Eyes, who takes meals at the fire of our chief. The one who says he can give the Nimiipuu fair trade for their horses. The one who secretly plans to take over the Nimiipuu country."

Wewukiye had not seen a man take meals with Joseph, but had heard of a *so-yá-po* making himself friends with the Lake Nimiipuu.

"This man. How does he look?"

"His hair is the color of dead grass."

Wewukiye stared into her eyes. "Is that why you fought me so hard at first? You thought I was he?" Her cheeks colored, and he knew he touched on the truth. "I do not hold that against you. He was not kind."

The fear faded in her eyes. She stared at him. "Your hair is the color of moonbeams. Now in the light of day, I do not see the slightest resemblance."

His heart quickened at her kind words. Why, he didn't know. Emotions such as these were unknown in his spirit world. Her words should not have moved him.

"And your eyes...are different." She closed hers and swallowed. "I will never be able to look at another such as he and not see the evil." Her eyelids opened. "You can tell he is evil looking into his different eyes."

"How are they different?"

She shivered. "One is brown and one is blue."

Hatred, something he rarely harbored, flashed hot and bright in his gut. A man such as she described matched a spirit he dealt with many,

many summers past. Back in the time before horses and anyone had seen a man with light skin. Surely this could not be the same spirit. Why would he return to this earth as a *so-yá-po*? And why would he want the Nimiipuu valley?

He shook off the coincidence and watched the maiden whose name he didn't know.

"I am Wewukiye, and you are?" he prompted.

"Dove." She bent her head and peeked up at him. "How is it I have not seen you around the village?"

Ah, the question he had dreaded. To lie or tell her the truth. He knew the Creator would not like him telling her his true identity.

"I am of another band of Nimiipuu. I was passing through and saw you." She blushed at the mention of their meeting.

"Then you will be moving on?" Did he catch disappointment in her voice?

"When I have completed my mission." He hated telling half-truths to Dove, but he could not tell her he was the spirit of the lake. He was forbidden to let a mortal know of his presence.

He wished to keep the conversation light, but he needed to learn more about Evil Eyes, and why her people would not listen to her.

"I do not wish to bring you more discomfort, but I must know all about Evil Eyes and why you are living alone in this cave." She glanced down at her wringing hands. "It is the only way I can find a way to help." Her head jerked up, and she watched him, her eyes seeking acceptance.

"Do you wish to be back with your people?" he asked. He created a spectacular sight as a bull elk, but knew his man form while less elegant, still remained regal and domineering. He knew these qualities would get him the answers he sought and hopefully help the maiden watching him through sad eyes.

"My people and the country we live in warms my heart and feeds my existence." Her spine stiffened and the conviction in her words left little doubt to her reverence.

"Then why were you determined to end your life?"

His blunt question nearly knocked Dove backward. Why indeed was she so determined to end her life? Jutting out her chin, she peered into his soft blue eyes.

"If what I live for no longer has faith in me, and my country will soon be taken from me and my people, why would I wish to exist in such a place?" She watched him, struggling to read the emotions hidden in the planes of his face. He had practiced well the art of not letting others read his emotions.

Tendrils of heat spiraled through her the longer her gaze lingered on his form. His blue eyes, straight nose, high cheekbones, and square chin showed his strength of character. His full bottom lip and curved upper lip softened his look. Giving one to think he would laugh easily.

"To fight the ones pushing you from your home. To prove to your people you are faithful only to them."

His words shrunk her confidence. She had run from her obligations, hiding from her people. Due to her impulsive behavior, she had taken the cowardly way out. For this, shame would forever clothe her.

Tears burned at the back of her eyes. Why had she not thought of these things? *Because you act before thinking.*

He reached toward her.

She leaned back. Her encounter with Evil Eyes remained too fresh in her memory to allow a man close. Even one she instinctively knew would not harm her.

"I did not mean to make you sad. You must become strong. If you are the only one who knows Evil Eyes's plans, you must find a way to reveal it to the leaders."

Dove nodded her head. She knew this was so, but how? "How do I do such a thing? When I told them"—she choked on the bitterness bobbing in her throat—"they would not listen. They said I made it up."

Anger gave her purpose. "The bruises on my body are proof I did not make this up." She hit her stomach. "The evil seed growing within me is not made up." The day she should have gone to the menstruation lodge she knew Evil Eyes had placed a seed within her. What warrior would want her, knowing she carried the seed of an evil *so-yá-po*?

Wewukiye stepped forward. "You are sure there is a seed growing?" His curiosity and acceptance rather than revulsion surprised her.

"Y-yes. My time has not come as it should." A woman did not speak of this matter with a man, yet he stood calmly in front of her, watching her as though they talked of the seasons.

"There is your proof." He stated, pointing to her belly.

"I do not understand?"

"When the baby comes out with hair the color of dead grass and two different colored eyes, your people cannot disbelieve you. The proof will be in front of them."

His announcement skittered excitement across her skin.

Would the child growing within her vindicate her? Could she endure the stares and the accusations labeling her a troublemaker until the child was born?

"How?" Could she survive living among the nonbelievers and suffer the birth alone?

"How what?"

"How can I live that long on my own and bring the child forth by myself?" A thought hit her. "What if he does not come out with hair the color of dead grass and different eyes? What if he looks like me?" Could she carry this child knowing how it was conceived? Her body shook remembering the pain and roughness of the man's hands on her. "How can I bring a healthy child into the world when I feel nothing but revulsion at it?"

"If this man is as evil as you say, his difference will be his undoing. You will not be alone. I have a friend in the village who will take you in."

"Who? I thought you were just passing through, how do you know someone of my village?"

"We are family."

"Who is your family?"

"Pe`tuqu`swise."

"Crazy One?" Here she thought this man could help her. If he believed Crazy One capable of helping her, he must be as mad as the old woman.

"She is as quick as in her younger days," he said, defending the woman.

"She walks around picking at people and muttering questions."

"Have you stopped to listen to those questions? They carry great insight."

Dove shook her head. She wanted a better option than living with a crazy woman. But could think of none other than what she had already tried.

"You only have to live with her until the child is born," he said as though reading her thoughts. "Once you have proof, your family will take you back."

Even though at this moment she did not wish for a mate, she could not help the sadness which filled her knowing she would never be loved by another. She did not want to exist with a man to be used for children and to take care of him. She yearned for a mate who would hold her and create safety, something she had lost since the attack.

He tipped her head up. She had not realized how tall he stood until this moment. Her head tipped back, and she gazed up into his eyes. The blue darkened as his gaze explored her face.

"Do not be fearful,," he said, his touch soft as a feather against her skin.

She closed her eyes. The concern in his weakened her. Once Evil Eyes was exposed, she could hope her life would go back to normal. But did anyone ever get over being violated and bringing a child you did not want into the world?

This man would not understand. How could he? He would never bear an unwanted child nor be forced to shame. His strength and gender kept him safe and invincible.

She swallowed the resentment crawling up her throat and opened her eyes. "I know I will never have the life I had before. Not only the child growing within me will change who I am, but the facts I will tell the leaders will also change me." She pulled back from his warm hand and glared at him. "It will be hard to sway the leaders without proof of Evil Eyes's deeds. However, you have given me no choice by pulling me from the lake and making me understand things clearly."

For the first time since they met his lips curved into a smile, and his eyes flickered with humor for a brief moment.

"Good, use anger to move you forward. The battle should not be with yourself, but with those who are harming the Nimiipuu." His smiled vanished. "You do realize it will be a battle? The Lake Nimiipuu leaders have tried to keep peace with the *so-yá-po* to instill the safety of the people. Bringing out the evil in the one they trust will not be easy."

He took her hand, dropping it hastily when she flinched. "I will help you disgrace the Evil Eyes and with the coming of your child." He peered into her eyes. "You will not be alone through this."

Mita
(3)

Dove's heart quickened. He would not let her do this alone. His statement and unguarded affirmation in his eyes lifted her spirits.

"*Qe`ci`yew`yew*. Thank you," she whispered, overcome with gratitude.

Wewukiye's heart pattered in his chest. He liked being alone, but having told this woman he would not leave her had lightened her load. He had helped mortals over the years at a distance. His existence was for that purpose alone. Helping this mortal first hand and experiencing her gratitude humbled him beyond words.

"Come. Crazy One will be waiting for us." He reached out for her hand.

Dove pulled her hand back. "How do you know she is waiting for us?"

"We have been meeting at this time since I have arrived."

She cast suspicious eyes to him. "Why do you not go to the village?"

"It is by her request we meet outside the village." He shrugged, biding for time to decide how to explain his relationship to Crazy One. She was his niece, yet as a mortal she had aged while, though he was hundreds of years old, he looked younger than Crazy One. "As my elder I do as she wishes."

He reached to help her up, fear and distrust flickered in her eyes. He pulled his hand back allowing her to stand on her own. Time would have to pass before she would feel comfortable being touched by a man. His blood boiled thinking of the pain and torment the *so-yá-po* gave her. He doubted he'd be able to contain his anger should he meet this man.

He followed the small woman out of the cave and wondered at her ability to survive such an ordeal. Her strength glowed in her determination to end her life and her vengeance to make her people see the *so-yá-po* for the truth. How could she believe taking her life would help anything? He and Crazy One would help her see her worth.

She stopped. "Why do I lead when I do not know where I am going?" Her baffled expression made him laugh.

"I do not know. You left the cave ahead of me, so I followed."

She motioned with her hand for him to pass. He tipped his head and walked by, directing his feet to the meadow where he and Crazy One met on a regular basis. She was the last of his brother's children.

He entered the meadow and held his breath. Though he trusted Crazy One, she did not know his identity was unknown to the woman behind him.

"How is my uncle?" she asked as he walked up and embraced her.

"Fine."

"Why is this maiden with you? Does she know?" The old woman's gnarled fingers plucked at imaginary objects on his shoulder.

Wewukiye watched Dove scan the woman and listen intently.

"No," he said, gazing into Crazy One's eyes and speaking with more than his voice.

The woman nodded and tipped her head toward Dove. "Is she staying away from the village?"

"I have come to ask if you would keep her in your lodge."

Dove stepped sideways out of his vision, but he sensed her retreat. She would not tolerate forceful restraint. He peered into her eyes, holding her with his gaze.

"Dove has learned something important and is being kept silent to preserve peace." He never took his gaze from the young woman staring back at him. Fear and uncertainty swirled in her eyes, but he wouldn't let her go. She must remain, not only for her people, but for herself.

"Is it of the *so-yá-po*?" Crazy One stepped beside Dove, slipping her arm around the maiden's arm. Wewukiye mentally thanked his niece.

"Yes." He watched Dove. "Crazy One needs to know everything to be able to help." The shame and uncertainty in Dove's eyes angered him. He could not fathom how one man could touch a woman and bring fear to her.

"You are with child?" Crazy One nodded her head, picking at nothing on Dove's dress. They both stared at the old woman.

"How do you know?" Dove asked, trying to pull away.

"Are they starting rumors?" Crazy One shook her head. "Are you running from shame?" The old woman's eyes glistened. "Am I believing the words of those who hide or the words of a good girl?"

Dove sobbed and threw her arms around the woman. Crazy or not, the woman believed in her. She finally found someone who did not look at her as though she were the evil instead of the man who brought all this upon her.

"Will you help her? Be her friend and listen to her truths and believe?" Wewukiye asked.

The sincerity in his eyes and the husky concern in his voice warmed Dove's heart and told her she had two people who believed in her.

"Am I not crazy?" The old woman laughed

loudly, opening her mouth and showing the dark spaces where her teeth once stood.

Dove studied the woman and wondered if given the old woman's name she was stable enough to help. Her thoughts must have penetrated the old woman's laughter.

"Can I keep you safe? Can I feed you? Can I help with the child?" She nodded her head. The woman put her arm around Dove and walked them both out of the meadow.

"Crazy One knows how to contact me. If you need anything, I will be around." Wewukiye's strong voice followed her down the trail back to the village.

How would she face her family and the rest? What would they think when she returned with Crazy One to live in her lodge? A shiver of doubt rippled across her skin.

"Are you well?" the woman asked, walking determinedly down the mountain to the village.

Dove's throat tightened. She couldn't utter a word for the anxiety tightening her muscles and wearing away at her good sense.

"What will we find?" the woman said. "What does it matter? Are you going to prove them wrong? Am I going to help?" The old woman squeezed her shoulders, and they stepped out of the trees.

Teepees and lodges dotted the ground all the way to the edge of the lake where the sweat lodge stood. Dove glanced around at her summer home. Chills of apprehension knotted her stomach. The last time she set foot in her village no one would listen to what she said. Everyone, even her family, looked upon her as though she'd tried to stab them with a knife.

She shook away her doubts and boldly stepped toward the village. A few women glanced up from tanning hides and drying fish. When they spotted Crazy One at her side, they started nudging one another with elbows. Crazy One led her past her family's lodge. Dove dared not look. If she saw any recrimination on her mother's face, she knew her newfound courage would zip away like the dragonfly.

"Dove?" Her mother's voice stopped her feet. What was she to say or do? Her mother had sided with the leaders, even after seeing the bruises on her body. No one believed her about the White man. Willow had glared at her daughter with disapproval.

"How are you walking?" Crazy One said, tugging on Dove's arm, pulling her from her family's sight.

She wanted to watch her mother and see sorrow and a plea of forgiveness for not believing her daughter. But what if that wasn't what her eyes said? What if she still had doubts? Dove put her feet soundly one in front of the other and walked beside Crazy One to her lodge.

"What do you want to do?" The old woman pointed to the lake then glanced at the villagers watching. How did this woman know she had tried to end things in the lake? A chill slid down her back from the woman's knowledge and her escape from death.

Without a backward glance, Dove ducked into the lodge and out of sight of the curious eyes.

"How do you know what I tried to do last night?" she asked, walking around the small dwelling. An extra sleeping spot lay on the far side of the fire. Did the woman know she would have a guest?

"Am I the only one to have visions?" The woman sat down and motioned for Dove to do the same.

"You know what I tried to do and you knew Wewukiye would ask you to let me live with you." Dove sat cross-legged beside the woman, studying her neatly braided gray hair and the creases of time etched in her dry sagging skin.

"How would I know it was you?" She waved her hands. "Who was it I saw?" Tapping her head, she continued, "Were you the one to walk into the lake with such determined steps? Did not my uncle carry you from the dark end?" She motioned to the sleeping area. "When would I find company?" Anger deepened the creases of her face and sparked in her eyes. "How do they treat me? Do they believe me stupid?" The dull eyes took on a glow. "Should they ask me questions?" She took Dove's hand. "Do we know the truth?" Her head nodded as she stared into Dove's eyes.

Energy to fight the battle ahead seeped into Dove's body. She had the acceptance and encouragement of this woman and the man who pulled her from the lake. With it, she believed she could make a difference for their people. But how to make the leaders hear her words?

"Does it not take time?" Crazy One asked.

"How do you know what I am thinking?" Dove asked, becoming accustomed to the strange woman.

"Do you think I do not talk right? How foolish does that make me look?" She shrugged. "Can others think I am dim-witted? Is it not their loss?"

"Yes, it is definitely their loss to not see the wisdom in you." Dove hugged the woman and received a warm, toothless grin.

The sound of many feet approached the lodge. Dove peered at the woman for guidance.

"How you must sit?" she said, pushing to her feet and approaching the opening.

Had the whole village come to throw her out? She had never known anyone to be banished. But no one had been labeled a traitor to her knowledge.

"What is it you want?" she heard Crazy One ask.

"I would like to speak with Dove."

Unease settled in her belly. Thunder Traveling to Distant Mountains had come to talk with her. She had taken her concerns about Evil Eyes to Old Joseph. He had listened and then dismissed her.

After she told the other maidens to watch out for Evil Eyes, she had been called to Old Joseph's lodge. Thunder Traveling to Distant Mountains and his wife had talked with her.

"Is she wishing to speak with you?" Crazy One asked, turning and questioning Dove.

Dove nodded. She had to know what the council thought.

Crazy One stepped aside. Thunder Traveling to Distant Mountains entered. The old woman picked at his shirt. Crazy One stood by the opening, holding the flaps tight. She chanted loud enough to cover what was said.

Dove smiled at the old woman. She would never underestimate her.

Thunder Traveling to Distant Mountains stood, looming over her. He was the calmer, more compassionate of Joseph's sons.

"Why did you leave?" he asked. "Many wondered at your departure."

"I could not live among people who did not believe me." Her heart galloped in her chest. She knew these were not the words he wanted to hear.

"But you have come back. Does this mean we were right?"

Her heart sunk. What was she to say?

"Is the truth now what you wish to live by?" chanted Crazy One.

Dove stood and stared straight into Thunder Traveling to Distant Mountains's eyes. "I have come back to prove my truth and save my people from Evil Eyes."

Thunder Traveling to Distant Mountains watched her a moment. He pivoted, walked away, then back. "We cannot give the *so-yá-po* a reason to kill our people."

"But you will allow him to take your women brutally? If one of our own had done this to me he would be whipped. Why does the *so-yá-po* not get whipped? He will think you agree with his treatment of your maidens."

Thunder Traveling to Distant Mountains shook his head, and his eyes blazed with anger. "Hold your tongue. We do not condone his behavior. It is your word against his."

"And you wish to believe the *so-yá-po* over a Nimiipuu?" She flinched at the angry twist to his features.

"I cannot go to Agent William with your accusations. There is only your word against Two Eyes. Who will they believe?" He slapped a fist into his hand. "And who will they harm for the insult?"

"I will tell you this now. When the child from the *so-yá-po*'s evil seed comes into this world, it will prove my words. Until then I will find what will sway not only our people, but his people as well." She stared unflinching into his dark eyes.

Thunder Traveling to Distant Mountains's eyes never wavered. "This is not wise for you or the people."

"Is it wise to let the *so-yá-po* take away our way of life? We have lived here before the fathers of our fathers. They cannot come in and push us out. Not without a fight."

"We cannot lose our people to anger." He placed his hands on her shoulders, peering deep into her eyes. "Do not stir up trouble. I do not want to remove you from this lodge to the lodge of the old women."

She ducked out from under his hands, crossing her arms. "Women who will hold their words about what I say, and let the *so-yá-po* walk on us." Her anger grew brighter and hotter each time he insisted she keep quiet.

He stalked to the opening and grasped the flap from Crazy One. "Do not stir up the warriors or you will have their blood on your hands."

Pí-lep
(4)

Wewukiye stood on the ridge above a small cabin. The building huddled in a canyon two ridges toward the setting sun from the Nimiipuu Lake. He'd learned the man living here spent time at the lodge of Joseph. One look would tell him if it was the man who hurt Dove.

Several White men rode up to the cabin, dismounted, and broke into livid conversations. The door to the cabin swung opened. A large man with hair the color of dead grass stormed out. Wewukiye snorted. The hair meant nothing—it was the man's eyes he must see. But how?

He raised his nose to the blue summer sky and bugled. The men turned and pointed to the ridge where he stood silhouetted against the summer sky. He snickered. No man could resist a specimen such as him. The man he wished to see grasped one of the horses tied in front of his cabin and swung up onto its back. With a holler he and another set off galloping toward Wewukiye.

The chase was on.

Wewukiye waited with his head down pretending to eat. He snickered at the men and horses crashing through the brush. Any other elk would bolt from the noise of the approaching men. He lifted his head, sniffed for their direction, trotted away from the men and horses, creating noise by hooking his massive antlers in the brush and snapping limbs.

He caught sight of the men. They separated and

he stopped thrashing about in the woods, to silently follow the man with the light-colored hair. Wewukiye crept as close as he dare get while the man sat atop the horse peering into the trees.

The man took off his hat and wiped at the sweat beading on his forehead. Without the hat shading his face, Wewukiye saw the man's eyes.

Anger shook his body. If not for Dove needing this man alive to renew her honor with her people, he would have rammed the horse and gored the man with his antlers. The moment the thought struck, he shook his head. Where had the anger come from? During his existence through the ages, emotions had never surfaced in him like they had since saving Dove from death. Why did he carry this new sensation of anger and protectiveness toward one mortal? Why did he center his thoughts on helping Dove and giving her what she wanted; to be respected by her band and family?

He now knew where the man lived and could watch him to find out his secrets. Wewukiye moved away from Evil Eyes. The White man would not put a bullet through a great bull elk this day. Wewukiye circled both men and made his way back down to the cabin. He wished to hear what the others waiting for the hunters had to say.

With great stealth, he walked through the trees and stood behind a bush. He could get no closer without being seen. It frustrated him to only hear snippets of the conversation.

"Jasper'll get them Injuns—" A man laughed.

Another added, "They won't know—" When the man stopped talking the others all laughed raucously. The thundering sound of rapid approaching hooves quieted the men.

Evil Eyes slid his horse to a stop in front of the cabin. He yanked the animal's head around and slammed his feet to the ground as he dismounted.

Anger radiated from his movements.

"Where's that monster elk you were going to bring back?" one man asked.

Evil Eyes grabbed the man's shirt front, lifting him off the ground. The man's eyes bulged, and his face deepened in color.

Wewukiye didn't hear the words. The face of the man being dangled above the ground drained to white and the others shuffled their feet. This man who hurt Dove embodied hate and venom. How she survived his torture was a miracle. For this man oozed evil.

The piercing scream of an eagle caught his attention, and he gazed to the sky. His sister called. With one last glance at the men, he set off at a run for their meeting place. Sa-qan rarely called a meeting. Something must have happened for her to have summoned him.

On the ledge, high up the mountain overlooking the Nimiipuu village, he walked out to his sister.

"Why have you called me?" he asked, standing in front of the tall, elegant bald eagle.

"What became of the woman you carried from the lake?" she asked as her beady yellow eyes searched his.

"She is staying with Pe`tuqu`awise."

"Why did she wish to end her life?" Sa-qan walked to the edge of the rock and glanced down.

"She was violated by a *so-yá-po* the leaders of her band believe to be a friend." Anger again overcame him. This new emotion toward a mortal unraveled him. Never had such fury for one creature, human or otherwise festered in his being. Resentment for Dove's people for not believing her had him talking harsher than usual. "They are not listening to her. Afraid they will bring trouble to the band if they accuse a *so-yá-po* of such evil."

Sa-qan peered at him. "How is it you have such

strong feelings toward this injustice?"

He should have known she would see past the words to the truth. "The woman has made a very strong accusation. One I believe to be true."

"Why do you believe this?"

Heat shot through him thinking of Dove as he undressed her. At the time, it was necessary to get her warm, and his body had remained aloof. Now, having learned of Dove's plight and gazing into her eyes, the thought of her unclothed body sent heat coursing through him. He swallowed the lump rising in his throat and tried to avoid the direct question and seeking eyes of his sister.

"I have seen the marks the *so-yá-po* made upon her body. She needs time to heal from the physical and emotional assault."

Sa-qan watched him closely. "You must stay your distance."

"I have told her I will be with her until she can prove the *so-yá-po* is not a friend of the Nimiipuu."

"That is not a good idea." Sa-qan moved closer to him. "You should have pulled her from the lake and left her for someone to find. Not taken on her troubles."

"You would not have left her either had you been the one to carry her out. The fear and shame on her face clearly showed, she did not wish to die. She had no one to talk over the problem. Once Dove realized the foolishness of her actions and thought through the actions she needs to take, she is willing to live."

"And what is she living for now?"

"Honor and revenge."

"Do you find this noble?"

Wewukiye dropped his head to stare at the ground. "Honor, yes. Revenge, no, but it is what has given her the strength to continue living." He studied his sister. "With my guidance she will see revenge brings nothing but sorrow. Honor can bring great riches."

"Why must it be you?"

Again, his sister saw far deeper than his words.

"She trusts me."

"Do not miss-use that trust." Sa-qan stared at the village below then faced him.

"There are White men on the north edge of the Lake Nimiipuu territory. It would be wise to see what they are doing." She opened her wings. "And keep you away from this mortal." With a thrust of her wings, she leaped toward the blue sky.

"I will go there, but do not expect it to keep me from helping Dove," he said, watching his sister fly high into the summer sky.

****

Dove spent as much time in the lodge as possible. The stares and disapproval of her village made her skin prickle. She did not think she could take the disrespect until this child arrived. That was many moons from now when they would be traveling from the winter home back to their summer home. As her belly grew what would the people whisper among themselves? Fear twisted in her stomach nearly making her dizzy.

"Do you need to sit?" Crazy One asked, holding her under her arms the moment Dove's legs gave way. She sank to the ground outside the lodge.

She glanced around. Had anyone noticed her frailty? If so would anyone care?

"Who do you seek?" Crazy One asked, picking at Dove's shoulder, taking unseen objects from her dress.

"No one." She stared at the woman. "Do you think I could see Wewukiye? To visit with another would be a nice change."

A smile crept across the woman's face, shining in her eyes and crinkling the creases of age. "Do I know where to find my uncle?" She nodded her head and disappeared into the lodge.

Strength seeped back into her legs and her heart. To talk with someone who did not talk in questions would be a relief. The woman was wonderful, attentive, and kind, but listening to her day in and day out would make *her* crazy.

Her legs gained strength thinking of Wewukiye. She took tentative steps. She no longer wobbled on newborn legs. Dove entered the lodge. Crazy One stood by the fire. She held a wolf fang dangling on a leather string above her head. Her lips moved, but no sound did she utter.

Dove waited until the woman opened her eyes and slipped the leather around her neck, dropping the fang inside her dress.

"Did he meet us in the meadow?" She stepped to the door and motioned to Dove.

"How do you know?" The woman she lived with had many rituals she did every day. Dove found them comforting, yet, wondered at her power. No one had ever spoken of Crazy One as anything other than crazy. Living with her, Dove had seen strength, love of the land and the people, and a surprising spiritual aura about her.

"Does he not speak to me?" She took hold of Dove's hand. "Are you well? Do you feel weak, losing light?" The worry etched on the old woman's face scared Dove. Was carrying Evil Eyes's seed harming her body?

"I have not been feeling well. But I wish to see Wewukiye." She had not seen the warrior in seven suns. His face had drifted in and out of her dreams ever since he left her with the old woman.

She had believed he was gone. But if he could meet them in the meadow he could not be that far. Which brought her back to how had Crazy One spoken with him?

"How is it you can speak to Wewukiye without seeing him?" Dove stepped out of the lodge. Her legs were wobbly again, but she wanted to see the warrior with moonbeam hair and blue eyes which gave her strength.

"Are we not family?" The old woman took her arm, giving her support as they walked out of the village.

Dove scanned the village wondering what they thought of her and Crazy One leaving without anything to carry back food supplies. Her gaze met Thunder Traveling to Distant Mountains's where he sat beside his father near their lodge. Did she see sympathy? Maybe for the briefest moment before he returned a blank stare.

She knew help would not come from him or any of his family. Without their backing, she had to fight this battle alone, for everyone sided with Joseph and his sons.

They entered the trees and began a slow ascent of the mountain. Her heart grew lighter, and her legs gained a renewed strength with each step. The farther she traveled from the village, her cloud of dismay lifted. Soon she would see the warrior who made her see her life held more importance than letting Evil Eyes win.

Crazy One stood back and motioned for Dove to enter the meadow alone.

"You must come, too," she said, watching the old woman sit on a log.

"Should I stand between you?" The old woman shook her head and remained seated.

Dove had no idea what the woman meant. Her heart fluttered in her chest with each step she took into the meadow. Would he be here? She glanced around the meadow and found him standing in the middle waiting for her.

She wanted to run to him, drink in the sight of

him, and feel secure in an embrace. But her fears of being handled roughly had not yet vanished enough to allow such closeness.

Slowly, on wobbly legs, she advanced. She blinked once to open her eyes and find his strong form beside her.

"Sit," he commanded, taking hold of her and lowering her to the sweet bed of grass.

Panic choked her. Evil Eyes had taken her in a meadow much like this. She started to fight the hands at her waist.

He withdrew his hands and sat back on his heels. The concern in his eyes brought shame to her heart.

"I'm sorry," she said, brushing back the tears of humiliation. This man would never harm her. He had saved her. Yet she could not shake the fear of a man's hands on her.

"No. Do not be sorry. My only thought was to sit you down before you fell. I did not think of what my actions would remind you of." He held up his hands in a submissive gesture. "I am sorry."

How could he even want to help her when she constantly reacted without trust?

"You are not doing well?" He leaned closer, gazing into her eyes.

"I cannot keep food down in the morning."

"Pe`tuqu`swise says this is normal." He moved to touch her cheek, dropping his hand before his finger met skin. "But not sleeping will not help."

Her eyes burned from fatigue and stirrings she found harder and harder to control. "When I close my eyes, I see only his cruel face. Such an image does not make me wish to sleep."

"Come." He stretched out on the sweet meadow grass and patted his stomach. "Place your head here and close your eyes."

She glared at him. Was this some kind of trap?

"I will not touch you other than your head resting upon me." He winked. "And Pe`tuqu`swise is just within shouting. You can call to her at any time."

His dark firm belly looked like a fine place to rest her head. And it would give her an excuse to see if he was as solid as he looked.

She swallowed, indecision tugging her thoughts in many directions. He placed his hands behind his head and closed his eyes. Was he playing with her? Did she dare give in to the weariness plaguing her?

His belly moved up and down in an even rhythm. He did look comfortable. Cautiously, she shifted, lying on her side, and placed her head upon his warm firm stomach. At first the touch of his hot skin and the firmness of his muscles sent energy coursing through her, filling her with a sense of belonging.

Warmth and eagerness drifted through her.

The stirrings of light, companionship, and security Wewukiye evoked weren't hurtful.

Her head moved up and down with the pattern of his breathing. The steady motion and the warmth of the sun beating down on them wrapped her in contentment. She drifted to sleep with warm thoughts.

Wewukiye did not sleep. He only pretended to get Dove to relax. Her breath finally came in even puffs, and her chest moved in rhythm. He opened his eyes and gazed down his body to the woman sleeping with her head on his stomach. Her face was even more beautiful when lax. Her lashes fluttered against her round cheeks as she dreamed. The smile curving her lips told him she dreamed of pleasant things.

That had been his wish when he asked her to place her head upon him. To take away bad dreams and allow her some much needed rest. The moment she had walked into the meadow, he thought she would collapse. Her sunken eyes with dark circles had scared him even before she stumbled.

Carrying the child was harder on her than he thought it would be. She appeared strong of body and able to carry many children through her lifetime. He had not thought about the way it was conceived nor the harshness of her people. Crazy One talked with him everyday. She was fearful Dove would not make it through the birth. After seeing her today, he had the same fears. What could they do to help her? Take away the pressure from the tribe, but how?

Dove moved, swinging her arm over his chest and murmuring. Her lashes fluttered up and down and her lips formed a grim line. She needed to sleep longer, but from her furrowed brows and down-turned lips, bad dreams came to her.

He cursed going against his word, but he placed a hand on her back creating soothing circles. He rubbed her back and chanted low, asking the Creator to bring her peaceful sleep so she may awaken feeling refreshed.

After a short time, she hugged him and snuggled closer, her lips curving upward into a contented smile. An ache in his lower regions stopped his hand.

Pá-xat
(5)

This region of his body had never stirred in the many seasons he walked this earth as a spirit. Why would it be doing so now? In the presence of a mere mortal? Wewukiye shifted, trying to relieve the ache.

Dove snuggled her head closer. Her soft hair tickled his skin and teased his senses. Need coursed through him, shaking his body and setting his skin on fire. He peered down the length of his body to see if his arousal awakened her. Her even breath whispered across his skin, and her lashes rested against her tawny cheeks.

Anxiety induced by arousal for this mortal nearly brought him to an upright position. He caught himself as his stomach tightened to sit and willed his muscles and nerves to relax. How could this have happened? He always kept his distance from mortals other than his brother's children.

He thought of the loss and grief he'd experienced when his brother, Himiin, became mortal. After Himiin's marriage to Wren, he and Wewukiye still met and talked. But Himiin immersed himself in the day to day lives of the Nimiipuu and his growing family. His children, all but Crazy One, had scattered to other bands through marriage. As Himiin's mortal body aged, they no longer took long runs over the mountain or sat up all night counting the stars and wondering how the Creator had chosen them.

"Is she sleeping?" Crazy One's voice broke into his disturbing thoughts. He glanced up to find the old woman standing over them. She gave no clue to her thoughts as she stared down at the woman sleeping on his stomach.

"Yes." He lowered his voice. "Do you know why she does not sleep well?"

She looked at him as though he were the one causing Dove's sleepless nights. "Why does she have a weakness from the child? Is it an evil seed that keeps her awake? Could it be the glances and whispers of her people?" The anger in Crazy One's eyes softened when her gaze traveled to Dove. "Is she not brave? Why does one so young have to defend herself to the leaders?"

She turned her gaze on him. "Why must she do this alone?"

"I told her I was here for her." The old woman's scolding bristled his usual good nature. He sought Evil Eyes to learn all he could about the man and decide how they could restore Dove's honor. He did this to help her, but he had kept his distance from the woman, knowing he had no resistance to her vulnerability.

And now, here he lay, chasing away her bad dreams and allowing the mortal to sleep on him. Her nearness drew urges and emotions from him that rivaled any he'd ever held. He should not have allowed Crazy One's pleas to talk with the woman overrule his good sense.

"Could she not see you every day? Could she not have you to talk to and plan?"

His heart skipped at the thought of seeing Dove every day. Sa-qan's warnings were doused by the joy it would bring him to talk with the woman regularly.

"I could talk with her every day. Here. In this meadow," he said, knowing Crazy One nudged him closer to the mortal when he should be fleeing.

"Why only the meadow?" she asked, crossing her arms and glaring at him.

"What do you mean?" Surely she did not want him to walk into the village with Dove. How was he to explain himself to the elders? He belonged to no tribe. He could bluff this distraught woman, but not the elders of her village. Dove had not asked hard questions. At least not yet.

"Could you not take her for a walk on the mountain and find her food, make her stronger?"

Dove rubbed her head on his belly and waves of heat shot through him. His face burned as if he stepped too close to a fire.

A knowing smile stretched across the old woman's face. "Is she not woman through and through?"

"I cannot have thoughts such as those. She is mortal and I—" He left it at that, not wanting the woman slowly rousing from her slumber to hear he was a spirit.

"Was not my father exactly as you and my mother exactly as she?" Crazy One's eyes danced with excitement. "Is it not time for the two worlds to come together once more?" She bent down and plucked at something on his shoulder. She straightened, walking away from him. "How should you find me when you bring her back to the village?"

She disappeared through the brush surrounding the meadow before he could utter a response.

Dove's arm slowly moved across his chest, hesitating at his nipple. Her fingers touched the tip, and he grit his teeth. Her drowsy exploration made it extremely hard to keep his thoughts off how much he wanted to explore her body as well. Afraid he would do something to lose her trust, he cleared his throat.

Her eyelashes rose slightly and settled on her cheeks several times with the effort of one trying to open tired eyes. Her lashes finally rose, revealing fear and uncertainty in her dark brown eyes. Her hand pushed against his body, shoving her from him. She sat back, staring. Her gaze quickly taking in all the details around her.

He drew his hands from behind his head and sat. "My hands stayed behind my head as you slept." The circles under her eyes had lightened in color.

She scanned the area around them. "Where is Crazy One?"

"She just headed back to the village. She saw you were sleeping well and asked me to bring you back when you woke." Her stomach growled and he added, "After I find you something to eat."

"It will not stay down." She placed her hands over her belly. "The evil seed in me has not allowed food to stay in my stomach. It is as if it wishes to die."

"Or you wish it to die?" Her gaze met his straight on, and he saw the truth shining before him. "If the child within dies, you would not have the proof you need to catch Evil Eyes in his lies." Wewukiye watched the parade of emotions marching through her eyes and across her face. "You will keep food down and bring this child forth." He gazed deep into her eyes and continued. "The thing you so despise is the one thing that can help set you free. I wish you to be free."

Her intake of breath and startled look in her eyes, told him she had not totally believed him before. Crazy One was right, he did need to spend more time with Dove to give her hope her future would not always be as a traitor to her people.

He stood, holding out a hand to her. She stared into his eyes and gradually raised her hand and allowed him to take it. He helped her to her feet. She swayed and he moved next to her. She stiffened, but did not pull away as he put an arm around her to steady her weak legs. Her acceptance of his touch and help was encouraging.

"I know of a patch of sweet, ripe berries not far from here," he said, walking at a pace she could easily handle. The slow pace would normally have irritated Wewukiye, but with this woman tucked against his body, he savored every minute of their unhurried steps.

At the berry bushes, he settled her on a downed tree and picked the small juicy strawberries a bear had yet to find.

"Why do you help me so?" she asked, as he dumped a handful in her lap.

He sat on his heels in front of her, making him the same height as the woman seated on the log. He stared into her eyes a moment, seeing no fear he placed a hand over hers. "Carrying you out of the lake I knew something terrible had happened to make a Nimiipuu try to take her life." He pushed a stray strand of hair out of her face and peered into her dark brown, guarded eyes. It pleased him she did not pull away from his touch or show fear in her eyes. "When I saw the bruises, I could think of no way you could have gotten them yourself." She flinched and half-heartedly tugged at the hand he still held. He squeezed and let go, knowing he would always have to let her go when she pulled away.

"After you told me of Evil Eyes and how your people responded, I could not walk away and let you face your future alone."

She turned her head, to hide the tears trickling down her cheeks.

"You will never be alone as long as you wish my help."

The warmth and caring in his deep voice drew Dove's gaze back to his. How could a man who had not met her until she tried to end her life, believe in her stronger than any who had known her since birth?

She brushed at the tears of hope tickling her

cheeks and studied the man watching her intently.

"We may never prove Evil Eyes's treachery."

He nodded and said, "But if we don't try, no one will ever know what he did to you and what he plans for our people."

"You want to go on, knowing we may never prove his disloyalty to the Lake Nimiipuu?" She found his resolve for her plight encouraging.

"If we do not try, we will never be able to lift our heads. By trying, we are showing courage and conviction. Bringing honor to ourselves and, if they listen, to the Lake Nimiipuu."

Dove pushed a berry between her lips. She rolled it around on her tongue, savoring the sweetness. Her stomach growled. Dare she swallow or would the food come up as it had in the last seven suns.

"Do not worry about what will happen. Savor the food and know it will make you strong, and we can begin gathering the information to set you free." Wewukiye moved off to pick more berries. His smooth gait and long legs carried him quickly away from her. Loose blond hair hid half of his long straight back. He carried his head with great pride. Not only was he pleasant to look at from the front, but the back as well.

Her face heated, and she reprimanded herself for such thoughts. He may know how she was violated and show compassion, but no man would ever want her for a wife. If so, it would only be as a worker and never to hold and care for. Her heart squeezed. All her life she'd dreamed of a man holding and caring for her. In return for his devotion, she could give him strong children.

The man picking berries only wanted to help her prove to her people the White man was not their friend. She would do well to remember this. To hold feelings for this man other than as a companion and helper would only cause her more pain. She needed to focus on the outcome of the birth of the child and gathering information that would show Evil Eyes's dark side to her leaders before it was too late.

She swallowed the berry and quickly poked several more in her mouth. Dove closed her eyes and dreamed of the day she could walk among her people, head held high, and embrace the honor of freeing them from Evil Eyes's spell. Her stomach clenched and churned rejecting the food.

Something brushed her face. She lashed out with her arms, striking a solid object and registered the slap of skin against buckskin. She opened her eyes. Wewukiye stood in front of her, gazing down, his brow furrowed.

"Lie down," he commanded.

Dove shook her head. Why would he want her to lie down?

He scooped up the berries still in her lap and pointed to the grass at her feet. His commanding presence did not scare her. He proved on enough occasions that he would not harm her.

"Lie down." He knelt and waved his hand above the grass beside the log. "I will help your body keep the food."

She continued to watch him carefully while slipping from the log and lying down on the ground. He placed the berries in her hands.

"Eat these as I chant."

She placed one in her mouth, never allowing her eyes to stray from his face.

He placed a hand on her stomach. The warmth and soft touch did not revolt like the touch of the Evil Eyes. She flinched when he started making circles with his hand.

"My touch will never cause you harm," he said as if reading her thoughts. Dove gazed into his eyes and knew he spoke the truth.

His voice floated to the sky as he chanted and swirled circles on her belly with his large hand. The gentle motion and warmth along with the deep tone of his voice soothed her stomach and her fears. One by one she placed the berries in her mouth and swallowed. With each piece of nourishment a new surge of energy filled her body.

His hand remained light, yet heat penetrated her deer skin dress warming her body. The last berry disappeared between her lips, and she swallowed its sweet goodness. She watched him. His long light lashes hovered on his dark high cheeks, hiding his eyes from her. His deep voice continued chanting. The long hard muscles of his arms bulged, contrasting with the gentleness of his touch.

"I have finished the berries," she whispered, fearful of disrupting his chant.

His eyes slowly opened, and he smiled down at her. "You must remain this way for a short time." His hand rested on her belly as he shifted to sit cross-legged beside her.

The intimacy of his touch scorched her cheeks.

"What if someone comes along? These actions will give people false ideas." She glanced at his hand and back to his eyes, shining with good humor.

"You would not like to have your name linked with mine? Am I so ugly or foul you do not wish others to know of me?" he said, a glimmer of mischief lighting his eyes.

"How will the elders believe Evil Eyes violated me if they see me with another? They will think the child growing within me is yours." Heat surged through her body at the thought of this man and his gentle touch giving her his seed. If it had been he, the event would be joyous.

"I have thought of this, too. It would take away the whispers of the village, but make the elders think you told untruths about the *so-yá-po*." He lifted his hand from her. "We will meet every time the sun is directly overhead. Here."

Her heart fluttered with hope. His help would surely get her through this hard time.

"Bring food, and I will help you keep it down. We will also make plans for Evil Eyes. I have found his lodge."

Dove sucked in her breath. She knew he lived in the valley, but had not known where. Did she want to? Anger took over her good sense. She wanted to know where the foul man lived. Perhaps she could find answers there.

"Where is this?" she asked, a little too forcefully.

Wewukiye's eyebrow raised. "You do not need to go near the man."

"We could learn things watching and listening."

"Do you speak their language?" He watched her as if she were a child.

"Yes. I have spent time at the mission. I do understand the *so-yá-po*'s tongue." Pride curved her lips into a smile as he watched her with admiration shining in his eyes.

"Can you read his words?"

Her elation drifted away like leaves on the wind. "Some. I have learned only a little of the meaning of their scratches."

"When I found his lodge several men rode up. As I continued to watch him they came and went for several suns." He scanned the trees beyond her and then back. "I have heard there are new White men at the northern border of the Nimiipuu land. I must go see what they are doing."

Her heart nearly stopped. "Then I will not see you for several days?"

"I said I would be here at every high sun."

"How? It takes nearly two suns to get there."

"Not if I travel day and night." He bestowed her with such a superior expression Dove could not take him serious.

"And you will sleep the whole time we are together." She laughed at his arrogance. He glared at her and stood.

"It is time to take you back to the village."

He reached down to help her up. Dove didn't hesitate to put her hand in his. Everything he had said and done to this point proved to her he would not hurt her. He pulled her to her feet as if she weighed no more than a summer flower. It pleased her he held her hand walking down the mountain.

His stiff posture and regal tilt to his head revealed her laughing at his insistence he could go to the edge of the Nimiipuu territory and back in one sun and moon wounded his pride.

To ease his annoyance, she stopped and faced him. "I can make it back to the village from here. I do not wish to hold you up from your travels."

"The short distance to the village will not make a difference."

"But it will make me feel better to know I am not keeping you."

"I will see you tomorrow." He gave her hand a gentle squeeze before letting go. He gazed upon her face a moment before walking away. His slow perusal filled her with warmth and hope.

"I will be there," she said to his departing back.

Dove continued to the village. Her heart floated and sung with goodness. For the first time since that awful day, hope replaced the despair. She did not want to ever relive that day. Two people believed her and would do whatever it took to prove her truths.

She stepped out of the trees and saw two saddled horses in front of Joseph's lodge. Curiosity and fear made her wonder which White men had come to visit, but at the same time she wished to get to Crazy One's lodge and not be seen.

Staying to the edge of the encampment, she

walked swiftly to Crazy One's tipi. The dwelling sat in the middle of the village. She wove her way through the lodges and the haze of smoke from the fires drying fish. Four steps from Crazy One's lodge she heard a commotion and stopped.

The men stepped out of Joseph's lodge.

Her feet would not move at the sight of the buckskin coat that had covered her head as her body was tortured. Anger and fear shook her body. How dare he come to her village and act as if he had done nothing wrong?

She watched with clenched teeth as Evil Eyes shook hands with Joseph and Thunder Traveling to Distant Mountains. The man with him also shook hands with the chief and his son. Evil Eyes glanced around the encampment.

Her heart pounded in her ears as his strange eyes stared straight at her.

`Oylá-qc
(6)

A lecherous grin spread across Evil Eyes's round face. Dove's stomach pitched and twisted. An icy chill ran through her body, and her feet became two heavy boulders.

He took a step toward her. Her hands shook. The man's form blurred. Her head buzzed like the nest of wasps in the old pine tree. Her mind screamed to run and hide. Her heart argued to stand and face the man. To prove to the man, the village, and herself, she would not cower to the likes of him.

An arm slipped around her shoulders, pulling her away from his evil gaze.

"How is he so welcome?" Crazy One said, pushing Dove through their lodge entrance.

In the lodge, Dove could no longer see the man, her anger seethed and swelled. How could he come to this village knowing he would see her? Did he think she had not said a word about his attack? Or did the chief tell him of her ranting and they had a good laugh?

She shook with rage and stared at the blanket covering the opening, half hoping the man would set foot inside so she could shout her accusations at him for all the village to hear.

"Was he not a coward to take a young woman? How could he think of following?" Crazy One handed her a carved, wooden bowl filled with a foul smelling liquid. "Won't you drink?" she motioned with her hand to drink it all at once.

The smell was enough to upset her stomach.

"Wewukiye helped me keep down some berries, but this"—she visibly gagged—"will make them all come up."

Crazy One crossed the small space between them and held Dove's nose. "How can I help you?"

Dove tipped back her head and swallowed the liquid. Her body shook with revulsion. The aftertaste finally left her mouth, and she blinked at the woman through teary eyes. "What was that? And what is it to do?"

"Why do you not sleep well? Is it bad dreams? Why not drink something to give you good dreams?"

"The sun has not disappeared. Why would I want to sleep now?"

A smile spread on the One's face. "Were you not sleeping on a man not long ago?"

Dove's face warmed with the memory. "That does not mean I wish to sleep now."

"Was that drink to make you sleep now? Will you have pleasant dreams when you sleep as the moon rises?" The old one nodded her head. "What is it you wish for? Revenge? Honor? Respect? Love?"

Dove stared at Crazy One. How did she always know what was in her heart?

"Why not dream of all things you wish?"

"Right now I wish I were strong enough to be with Wewukiye."

"Why?"

"He is headed to the north border of the Lake Nimiipuu land to see what the White men are doing there."

"Ah?" Crazy One's face scrunched up. "Was it not what Two Eyes talked to Joseph about?"

"What did he say?" Fear stabbed at Dove, wondering if Wewukiye would walk into trouble.

"Did not Two Eyes tell Joseph these men were passing through?" She shook her head. "What was Frog saying? Why were the men piling rocks? Why were they scratching on paper if just passing through?"

Making sense of the questions, Dove was pleased to know Frog, Joseph's youngest son, kept an eye on the White men. That would mean Wewukiye would not be alone if something happened. She could rest easily tonight and anticipate their meeting when the sun rose high in the summer sky. This may be the first night since her attack she would fall asleep with peaceful thoughts.

****

Wewukiye crept through the trees toward the voices. The invigorating run to the far end of the territory made his senses alert. Dove had questioned how he could go so far and be back for their meeting. As a mortal and unknowing of his status, she had no knowledge he could run forever and never have to stop. He did not require rest or nourishment. For her to learn these things, he would have to tell her he was a spirit. Then he would fall in disfavor with the Creator. In all the many seasons he resided within the lake, he had never done anything to gain the Creator's disapproval. A reprimand, maybe, he grinned thinking of some of the things he had done to irritate the lowly mortals while in elk form, but no one had ever discovered he was a spirit.

He thought of Dove. Her dark eyes, compact body, and strength. She could very well be his one weakness. Now he knew the power the mortal Wren had had over his brother Himiin. He pushed Dove from his thoughts and peered through a bush, spotting five white men stacking rocks. One man held a stick to one eye and pointed to the next rise. The canyon splitting the two high spots was deep, narrow, and grueling to navigate. From the man's gestures, the group planned to meet on the far rise.

He smiled. It would take the men at least two

days to get to that spot with their slow animals. The poor creatures carrying the supplies plodded slowly with their heads down—the image of weariness. One man pointed the opposite direction of the rise and all spun around to look.

Wewukiye surveyed the men and beyond. Nimiipuu warriors surrounded a pile of rocks on the far rise. He could see Frog mounted among those studying the mound of rocks.

Wewukiye grinned. Frog believed in action more than words. Wewukiye was not opposed to violence like Sa-qan. It would give him pleasure to watch Frog and his warriors have a clash with the intruding White men.

The warriors disappeared, and Wewukiye took up a spot where he would not be seen, yet could watch the encounter. His only regret—Evil Eyes was not here to get a thrashing.

The yellow-orange of the fading sun topped the rise, throwing long shadows and barely lighting the surroundings. The White men loaded their belongings and led their animals down the slope in the direction the man had looked through the stick.

Where were Frog and his men? Wewukiye found it hard to understand why the Nimiipuu had not contested the men being in Nimiipuu country.

He walked out to the pile of stones. The narrower top came to his chin while the base was the breadth of his chest. He stood in the gray light of the evening wondering why White men would pile rocks in such a manner. Standing in one spot wondering would tell him nothing. He followed the path of the White men down into the canyon.

The skitter of rocks behind him set his senses on alert. The other White men and their animals plodded ahead of him. Who could be coming up behind?

The steep canyon, dotted with rocks and

boulders had few trees to hide his massive elk form. He had to become smaller. He pointed his nose to the sky and shifted into man form.

"I told you there wouldn't be any trouble from that squaw." Two men rode into view as Wewukiye ducked behind a boulder. The horses breathed heavily and their earthy scent of horse sweat met his nostrils.

"How do you know she didn't go to Joseph and tell him what you did?" The smaller of the two men spoke. His voice crackled with contempt.

"I made it clear she wasn't to tell no one. Or I'd take her again and any other squaw I found out in the woods." The man laughed, lifting his face to the quarter moon. Wewukiye saw the light hair and different colored eyes.

Evil Eyes.

Why was he coming to the men piling rocks? Evil Eyes's callous talk of violating Dove flushed Wewukiye's body with rage. He clenched his fists and held the impulse to attack as the men rode by close enough for him to pounce.

"Joseph asked too many questions." The other White man's voice shook with uncertainty. "I think the squaw told him."

"These Injuns aren't going to do a thing. They're too scared of the government taking their land to let a little fun with one squaw make them try anything." Evil Eyes stopped his horse on the opposite side of the boulder Wewukiye hid behind.

The nearness of the man made it hard to stay hidden. He loathed the man. An emotion he'd only felt toward evil spirits until now. The vileness of the feeling only deepened his conviction to help Dove show this man for his true self. To do the most damage to Evil Eyes and save Dove's honor, he would gather information and keep his rage under control.

"If I can keep Joseph and his sons happy until I gain the Indian Agent position and get rid of that Injun-loving agent, there isn't anything they can do once I'm appointed." He rolled tobacco in a paper, lit it, and blew smoke toward the darkening sky. "I've got several families willin' to pay good money for a section of the valley." Evil Eyes leaned toward his companion. "And I plan to make a killin'." He laughed, jabbing his horse in the ribs and heading down into the canyon.

Wewukiye waited until he could no longer hear the clank of horseshoes on rock before stepping out from behind the boulder. His fists clenched in anger. The man used his friendship with the Nimiipuu to feed his greed. No one but Dove would believe the words he heard. They would find proof of this man's dishonesty. He gazed at the quarter moon nearing its highest point. To make his meeting with Dove, he must head back.

Changing into elk form, he charged up the canyon wall, leaving the trail and moving in a straight line for the lake. His heart raced with anticipation to see Dove. Together they would find a way to stop Evil Eyes.

****

Dove woke feeling rested for the first time since the attack. She peered through the smoke hole in the top of the dwelling. The sky gradually brightened as she thought about Wewukiye and his easy acceptance of her truth. Her heart ached for her family's trust, but Wewukiye's friendship lightened the pain.

She pondered her emotions as she combed her fingers through her hair and added fur adornments. Crazy One smiled, making Dove conscience she made too much of herself, knowing she would meet Wewukiye this day.

Frustrated with her confusing feelings toward

the man, she pulled the fur from her braids and helped Crazy One prepare their morning meal.

Seeing Evil Eyes the day before made her more determined to find out what he planned and make the leaders see his evil. How dare the man come to her village and act as if he did nothing. What angered her even more was Joseph still honoring the man at his fire. It stung like a slap to her face.

The fish soup Crazy One boiled filled the dwelling with sweltering warmth and nauseating smells.

"I am not hungry." Dove picked up a basket woven of dogbane and headed to the flap and fresh air.

A gnarled hand caught her arm. "Why are you not eating? Did not my uncle make you better?"

Dove smiled at the strange endearment Crazy One gave the man younger than herself. She shook her head. "I am not ready for food right now. Maybe after my walk." She smiled and patted the hand still clutching her arm and ducked out the opening.

The village bustled with life. Women bent over fires, cooking the morning meal. Girls replenished wood by the fires, and boys hurried off to check on the herds. The men strolled up from the lake and their morning bath. Dove fought a twinge of envy as she watched a cousin help her husband ready his hunting gear for the trip.

At nineteen summers, she was beyond the age to have a husband and a child. No one had asked for her hand out of respect to her father and his need to have her care for her mother. Now her aunts dealt with their chores and those of her father and mother.

Dove glanced at the dwelling of her father. He had not said a word when she told of Evil Eyes's treachery. Sadness settled in her stomach adding to her nausea. Her family had never been overly affectionate. It surprised her that her father had not added another wife to his dwelling since her mother could not handle the everyday chores and would never give him another child.

Others of the band looked upon their family with guarded eyes. To not bring more children to The People did not add to the strength of the band. Was that why they did not believe her accusations? They already believed her to be against The People because of her father's behavior?

She left the village, cautiously scanning the trees and underbrush. Her first trip alone in the forest after the attack, she had jumped at every crackle and whisper. The fear lessened with each walk.

One step into the canopy of pines, the cheerful songs of the birds let her know all was safe. Thinking back, she acknowledged what she had not that dreadful day. The forest had known evil lurked. She had not heeded the warnings. In her desire to gather more berries than the others, she had wandered farther from the group and not listened to the silence of the forest around her.

The lesson had been hard taught, but she would heed the earth and listen from now on.

She bent to pluck ripe red berries from the plants hugging mother earth. Her hand froze, and her heart thundered. Panic squeezed her chest.

Someone approached on hurrying feet.

`Uyne'-pt
(7)

Wewukiye witnessed Dove entering the forest as he topped the hill on the north side of the lake. Evil Eyes had not headed back this way, but he couldn't shake the need to keep her out of danger.

He pushed his body through the brush and veered around the lake, heading in the general area he believed Dove had disappeared. He sniffed and caught a scent. His hooves moved faster over the forest floor. Fear hung in the air.

Voices slowed his pace. He heard Dove's soft voice. Her shaky words explained the fear he caught in the wind.

Uncertain whether to proceed as an elk or slip into man form, he cautiously moved closer to hear the conversation.

"Why do you not believe me?" Dove questioned the man standing in front of her. Her hands clutched her basket, turning her knuckles white.

"Why do you wish to spread rumors and shame our family?" The man grasped her arm, jerking her closer to him.

"I have done nothing wrong." Her words did not come out as forcefully as they should to show this man she spoke the truth.

Wewukiye stared at the man. Who was he that he questioned her so?

"Your mother will not be of this earth much longer. I see it in her eyes. Do not send her to the earth believing her daughter tells stories."

Dove glared at the man. "Do not use my

mother's sickness to make me tell lies. I have told you, my mother, and those who lead us the truth. You will all perish at the hands of the *so-yá-po* if you do not heed my warnings." She pivoted to walk away.

"Do not walk away from me, daughter!" The man's voice wavered in the wake of his command.

Dove spun around, the hurt on her face revealed more to Wewukiye than her words. "I am no longer your daughter. I could not have come from someone who believes the words of the *so-yá-po* over a child of his loins. Go back to my mother and tell her I miss her, but I will not live with people who say my tongue is tainted."

The man stood still as Dove ran into the trees not far from where Wewukiye stood. He followed keeping enough distance between them she would not become concerned.

She collapsed in a small meadow. Wewukiye raised his face to the sky, closed his eyes, and changed into man form. When the smoke dissipated, he walked into the clearing.

Dove's shoulders shook. She may have stood strong against her father, but now that she stood alone, her defenses floated away like the fuzz of a cottonwood tree.

Wewukiye knelt beside her. He wished to put his arms around her and take away the hurt of her people. The reason for her anguish kept his arms tucked against his sides.

"Dove," he softly said, keeping just enough distance she wouldn't feel cornered, yet close enough his breath sent her loose hair dancing.

She started and sat up on her knees. Her dark eyes widened with fear, until she focused on him. The relief on her face and in her eyes made him smile.

"Why do you cry?" he asked, not letting on he

saw the meeting with her father.

"My father followed me from the village." She glanced down, plucking at the fringe of her dress.

Wewukiye tilted her face to gaze in her eyes. "What did your father have to say?"

She licked her lips. The sight of her delicate pink tongue tasting the tears trickling down her cheeks set off protective instincts in him. He never wanted to see this woman cry. Her heart should be light, her future happy.

"He says my lies will kill my mother." Her back snapped straight, and her nostrils flared. "My mother has been sickly since the day I came to this earth from her body. I know my father and my mother blame me for this. But to say I will cause her death…that is the same as saying the Lake Monster will take me for my lies."

Wewukiye flinched. *He* was the monster in the lake of which the legend was told. He'd never taken a child, but the parents had used his one appearance that was seen by a mortal to scare the children into obedience. And he did want to take Dove down into his watery home. But not for the reasons of the Nimiipuu tale.

"I have not lied. I tell only the truth, but no one wants to hear the truth. The elders prefer lies to let the *so-yá-po* walk all over us and take our home."

The fire and fight lighting her eyes made his heart sing. She would need this attitude to get through the seasons until her baby and her proof arrived.

"I know you have spoken the truth. Together we will prove your parents and the band wrong." He held out his hand. "Come, we will find you food and talk of our plans."

A small trill of triumph rippled through him as she took his hand without hesitation. A good sign. She accepted he would not harm her. He stood, drawing her to her feet. She swayed and her face paled.

"Are you still not eating?" He moved next to her to still her swaying body. Her body stiffened at his closeness.

"I try, but not all Crazy One gives me will stay down." Her voice trembled as she glanced up at him.

"Let me help you." He waited for her slight nod before tucking her closer, absorbing the tremors in her body. Her head came to the middle of his chest. "You will not lose this child. It is your truth."

Her wobbly legs stumbled. He peered into her eyes. "I will carry you."

She again nodded, her eyes hooded by her lashes. He scooped her up into his arms and headed up the mountain away from the village and anyone who might stumble upon them.

Hesitantly, Dove wound her arms around his strong neck. She knew he would not harm her. She listened to the steady beat of his heart where her head rested against his solid chest. Her heart beat in time to his.

She wiggled her fingers through his soft hair and sighed. His strength and gentleness calmed her. He believed in her. Her whole life everyone watched her with distrust as though her mother's ailments were a curse she'd placed upon her. This man, who had only known her a short time, believed in her.

The sweet scent of berries subduing the tang of pine brought a smile to her face. With care, Wewukiye set her feet on the ground and slowly stepped away. The brief rest in his arms helped. Her sight no longer blurred, and her legs remained solid. Her gaze fell upon bountiful bushes laden with the sweet summer berries.

"Eat these while I find you more nourishment." Wewukiye walked to an opening in the bushes.

Fear overtook her. They stood high on the side of

the mountain far from anyone, yet to be left alone tightened her stomach and rippled a nauseous wave.

"Berries are enough," she said, reaching out to stop him.

He took a step toward her. A smile tipped the corners of his lips. "You cannot eat only berries, though I see you have a fondness for sweet things."

Dove hated she relied on this man to keep her safe. She had to learn to walk the land of her people and feel secure. To rely on this man who could slip from her life at any moment proved as foolish as believing they could sway the Nimiipuu leaders about Evil Eyes. Closing her eyes, she swallowed and shoved the image of Evil Eyes from her mind.

"Go, I will be fine." She returned to the task of plucking ripe berries from their prickly stems.

His breath whispered warm across her neck. "No one will come upon you without my knowing."

She faced him, her body inches from his. Dove tipped her head back to gaze into his handsome face. "How will you know?" Still so many things she did not understand about this man lay hidden in his eyes.

"This is a part of the mountain few travel."

"How do you know this when you are not of our band?" This and many other questions plagued her about Wewukiye.

His face darkened. He glanced into the trees, avoiding her gaze.

"There are many things about you I do not understand. How is it you are family to Crazy One, yet, you do not wish those of my band to see you?"

He did not look at her. She grasped his chin, directing him to gaze upon her. Good humor no longer glistened in his eyes.

"There is much I wish to tell you, but I cannot."

He closed his eyes, ending her search for answers in their depths.

"You ask me to trust you and believe you will keep me safe and help me with the coming of the child, but you keep secrets." She glared at him. "You know everything about me, and I know nothing of you."

His eyes opened. They matched the color of the lake. Deep blue and glassy. His jaw twitched, and his hands clenched at his side.

Memories of her assault sent her arms up to ward off blows. The motion caught his attention. His jaw and hands relaxed, and his eyes lightened.

"Do not fear me." Wewukiye reached for her.

She couldn't stop the squeak of fear.

"I may keep secrets, but I would never hurt a woman." The tone and deep conviction in his voice startled her. "Do not measure me to the man who hurt you. He is no better than the trickster coyote who uses people to cause trouble."

Shame washed over her for believing the man who pulled her from the water would do her harm.

"I try to see you differently, and I try to control my fear."

"You should fear nothing. You are brave and honorable to stand up to the band. You want only what is good for the Nimiipuu. This is your strength."

His words warmed her like a winter fire.

"Eat the berries. I will return soon."

She no longer feared his departure. He would know if trouble lurked. How? She knew not, but she believed in him and craved his presence. His touch faded memories of her attack and sung medicine to her heart.

She popped berries into her mouth, chewed, and swallowed. Nausea squeezed her stomach. Evil Eyes had taken the joy of life from her. Juice from the berries in her hand trickled down her wrist. Why could she not control her swings of rage, delight, and despair? Staring at the berries she'd squashed, tears trickled down her cheek.

****

Wewukiye called Sa-qan. He stood on a rise where he could watch Dove. Though he told the woman he would bring her food, he was at a loss as to what he could offer her without killing an animal of the mountain.

"You called, brother," Sa-qan asked, settling on a tree limb. The branch swayed and creaked under her weight.

He didn't take his eyes from the woman in the patch below. "She is asking questions of me I cannot answer."

"You knew this would happen if you continued to see her." Her criticism-spiked words stung.

"Crazy One and I are all she has."

"She has a family and band who will take care of her." Sa-qan hopped off the branch, landing without a sound on the ground beside him.

"They don't believe her or care about the life inside her."

"They are her family. You are to oversee not interfere in their lives." Sa-qan ruffled her feathers.

Wewukiye crossed his arms, standing firmly in front of his sister. "You were the one who insisted I keep the woman from drowning. Do not tell me I am interfering. The information Dove and I bring forth could save the Nimiipuu from the *so-yá-po*'s assault on their land."

"You do not know they are here to claim the Nimiipuu land."

"You have gone to the land where the sun rises. You are the one who says more and more White men are coming this way. You have seen the others being pushed from their homes. Do not tell me the White men coming to Nimiipuu land aren't planning to push the Nimiipuu from their homes." The venom in his words did little to dull the glare of disapproval in Sa-qan's yellow eyes.

"It is true. I have seen the coming of the White man. The tribes the *so-yá-po* has pushed to the side have caused them trouble. The Nimiipuu live peaceful and harbor no ill feelings to the *so-yá-po* who have come."

"The Nimiipuu are fools to believe the *so-yá-po* will not push them out. I have heard the truth." Wewukiye glanced down. He'd left Dove alone too long, and he still had nothing to take back for her to eat.

"When?" Sa-qan hopped between him and the sight of Dove.

"I heard the *so-yá-po* who hurt Dove and another speak of this." He glowered at his sister. "They will not leave the Nimiipuu alone."

"We will help the Nimiipuu deal with the *so-yá-po*. You must not interfere. The Creator is not happy."

"How can this be? By helping Dove I help all the Nimiipuu."

"You are beginning to sound and act like our brother before he angered the Creator." The censure in her voice shocked Wewukiye.

"I would never become an inferior mortal." Wewukiye stomped a hoof. His chest squeezed not from exertion but from the fear of never seeing Dove again should he follow his arrogance.

`Oyma`tat
(8)

Sa-qan spread her wings, preparing to leave. "Be sure you heed your own words." She leapt into the air, taking flight, and disappearing over the tree tops.

Wewukiye stared at the woman picking berries below. He would help her back in favor with her people, and because she was a mortal would let her go. She required his superior thinking to help her through these trials. Even as he logically made sense of his connection with Dove, the memory of her scent and soft curves heated his body with need and desire.

Dove stood, clutching her stomach. The sweet berries should have settled her stomach. He would find her other nourishment later. He hurried down the mountain to the woman who consumed his thoughts.

****

Why did her body not like the berries? The scent made her mouth water, yet after eating a handful, her stomach twisted and pushed, forcing the fruit back out. Sweat beaded her clammy brow as her body shook. She winced and lowered to sit on a log. Was this worth bringing forth a child she knew she would not be able to look at fondly?

Would suffering a mutinous body and the disparaging looks of her family show her people the white man meant them harm? She closed her eyes and tried to think of something pleasant to take her mind off her squeamish stomach.

"You are not eating." The deep voice laced with concern spun her shivers into waves of heat.

She opened her eyes and studied the man standing in front of her. His broad shoulders blocked the sun. Even with his eyes filled with concern, the lines beside his eyes, which deepened when he smiled, remained. His full lips were perpetually tipped at the corners in mirth. The lightness he brought into her heart just by his presence she had not felt since realizing her family believed she brought the sickness to her mother. No one had ever gazed upon her with such favor.

He knelt beside her, glanced at her stomach, and questioned with his eyes.

She nodded.

He placed a hand on her stomach. "You must gain strength."

His encouraging words brought a smile to her face as his hand slowly moved in a circle. She studied his face, searching his eyes, skimming across his angular cheeks, ending at his full, inviting lips.

"I wish to take you to Evil Eyes's lodge."

The words ripped apart the tranquility his hands had bestowed.

Her mouth opened and closed in her effort to object. She did not wish to go anywhere near the vile White man.

"We will only go while he is gone. I know he will not be near his home for two suns."

"W-why must we go there?" She forced the words and started to stand.

"Shh." Still resting his hand on her stomach, he plucked a berry and held it in front of her lips. She opened her mouth, allowing him to place the nourishment on her tongue. His eyes continued to watch as she chewed. "You said you can make sense of the *so-yá-po*'s scribbles. We will go to his dwelling to find the truth to take to your leaders."

He placed another berry before her lips.

She shook her head. "What if we do not find anything?"

"Then I will follow him until there is proof."

Dove grabbed his hand. "You cannot put your life in danger for me."

"Your life and the Nimiipuu are worth anything I can give." He twisted his wrist capturing her hand in his. His palm sliding across hers flashed heat and sparks up her arm.

She pulled her hand back and stared at him. "You have such faith in proving my truths. But I cannot ask you to give of yourself to help. You are not of this band. Go back to your people and tell them of the *so-yá-po* and his lies."

"When I pulled you from the lake, you were a puzzle. One I wished to unravel."

Dove's face heated. Embarrassed he came upon her trying to take her life and knowing he puzzled over her, pushed conflicting emotions into her chest. Her heart tightened with shame and fluttered with anticipation.

She opened her mouth to argue. He placed a finger upon her lips. The soft pad touching her delicate skin tingled her body clear to her toes.

"I do not walk away from challenges. I also will not walk away from you and the people of this lake."

The conviction in his voice and the authority with which he said it brought to mind the presence of Chief Joseph at the last council. This man who helped her keep food down and promised to be with her through the birth held more power than a warrior.

He moved about the mountain as if he lived here, yet he said he was from the Upper Nimiipuu. The way he and Crazy One communicated and his easy acceptance of her knowledge of Evil Eyes made her wonder. He proved to be more than a warrior.

65

Could he be a shaman? Was that why his chants helped her keep food and her body and heart sensed he would not harm her?

"Who are you really?" she asked, as he placed another berry before her lips.

"A warrior who wishes to help you and your people." The glint in his eye as her lips covered the tip of his finger before she sucked the berry into her mouth made her wonder if he too felt the flash of heat each time they touched.

She opened her mouth to ask another question, and Crazy One emerged from the bushes.

"Where is it you two hide?" She handed Wewukiye a leaf wrapped package. "Did you not find food for Dove?"

His cheeks reddened as he took the package, drawing back the leaves. He handed Dove the mixture of smoked salmon and dried crushed kouse.

"*Qe`ci`yew`yew, Pe`tuqu`swise.*"

"Should you not save some for your trip?"

Dove stared at the old woman. Wewukiye touched her hand holding the salmon mixture, pushing it toward her mouth.

"How did you know we were going somewhere?" Dove asked.

Crazy One's gaze met and held Wewukiye's as Dove watched. The two communicated without saying anything. A whisper fluttered through her mind. *Trust them.*

"Eat," Wewukiye said, again pushing the food to her mouth. "We will leave once you have eaten."

She didn't want to think about where they were headed. "How do you know he"—she swallowed the fear crawling up her throat—"will be gone?"

Crazy One walked away.

"Where are you going?" Dove ignored her food.

"Do you need me? Do you want me to not tell the others?" She shook her head.

"We will be back by the time the moon rises tomorrow," Wewukiye told the old woman. He glanced down at Dove. "Eat so we can leave."

She poked a blob of the food in her mouth and watched the two walk away talking. How was it they knew each other so well if Wewukiye belonged to another band? And how did the old woman know what they did and planned? She shoved more of the mixture in her mouth studying Wewukiye as he walked back to her.

"Are you ready?"

Dove held the food out to him. "You should eat something as well."

"I am not hungry."

She wrapped the remainder of the food and stood, placing the package in the pouch on her belt.

Wewukiye studied Dove. Though she walked beside him without saying a word, her trepidation and questions followed them, and he ached to take the fear away from her. Dove sensed more than most mortals. She noticed the communication between he and his niece. They would have to be more cautious.

He wished he could travel in elk form. He would be to the dwelling by now. He glanced back at Dove. The slow pace had to do. Dove could not move any faster in her weakened condition.

"There is a passage we can take. It isn't far from here."

Dove stopped. She swiped at the wisps of hair sticking to her perspiring face. "How is it you know my country so well?"

Her questions disturbed him. He didn't like keeping secrets from her. But it pleased him she had an inquisitive mind and wished to learn. He had never thought of a mortal as wishing to know more than was necessary to survive.

"I know your country because as a child I spent much time here." He spoke the truth, though his youth took place many seasons before her coming to this earth. Wewukiye continued walking and sensed Dove fall into step behind him. He preferred she walk beside him. He slowed his pace to become even with her.

"Why is it we have not met before?" she asked.

He watched her silhouette as they walked around granite boulders and over downed logs.

"I would roam the mountain."

"By yourself? Where was your family?" She glanced his way. The sun highlighted her hair and accented her cheeks. He wanted to pull her into his arms and tell her everything. His body had never craved anything as it did to be near hers. If he didn't get these impulses under control he would not only frighten Dove, he would anger the Creator.

He ducked away from her inquiring eyes and found the gap he planned to travel through to put them near Evil Eyes's lodge.

"Here is the spot." Wewukiye stopped and waved his hand toward the crack in the mountain.

Dove stared at the solid rock walls. "Where does this go?" She took a step forward, placing a hand on either side of the entrance, and peering into the crevice.

"This will take us to the other side of the ridge." No mortal knew of this passage.

She stepped back. "Through the ridge? Why have I not heard tales of this?" Dove shook her head and backed away.

"A few animals use this to travel from one side to the other, but I've not witnessed sign of a mor— man."

She cocked her head, considering him. "What did you start to say?"

Heat surged across his face. This surprised him. A spirit didn't feel anything other than regard for the Creator and interest in the Nimiipuu. Since saving Dove, his emotions grew more complex and confusing.

"Man."

"But you are a man and you know of this." She took a step closer, peering into his eyes.

Would she run if he told her he was a spirit?

"I am the only man who knows of this. I found it on a quest."

He reached for her hand. "Come, we must get to the Evil Eyes's lodge and away before the moon rises tomorrow."

He led her to the opening. "I will have to walk in front of you. There is no room to walk side by side." With a gentle tug on her hand, he drew her into the narrow rock-lined crack in the earth.

The crevice darkened after the sun slid behind the mountain and night descended. His vision wasn't impaired by the dark. Dove shuffled her feet and her hands now and then groped his back. She had trouble navigating in the dark. They would have to stop until the sun filled the crevice with light.

"We will stop here." He stopped and she ran into his back.

He grasped her by her shoulders. Fatigue dulled her eyes. "Sit." He helped her to the ground. "Eat the remainder of your food."

She slowly pulled the packet of food from her pouch, offering him some.

He held up his hand. "I am not hungry."

"You haven't eaten." She continued to offer him the food.

"You are the one I worry about. You need the food and the rest. Eat."

"I would rather you eat it. It may not stay in me and would be a waste."

He wanted to console the fear in her voice. "I will help you keep the food."

She searched the dim light, peering into his face.

"You are not always around."

"I gave my word I would be with you until your child comes of this world. After that, I can give you no answers." He wanted to wrap an arm around her shoulders and draw her near for safety and warmth.

"Crazy One believes once I accept the child I will no longer have trouble eating." Tears slid down her cheeks. "I have tried to believe this child will never think evil thoughts and will grow as a strong Nimiipuu." She bit her lip. "If he looks like the man who made him, I fear, he will live a life much like my own." She turned her head and scrubbed the tears from her face.

"Your parents are wrong to believe you brought a curse to your mother causing her sickness." A child was never a curse when it came into the world. The Nimiipuu prided their band on its growing numbers. According to Crazy One, Dove's mother's illness was in her heart and not anything to do with Dove's birth.

He took the packet of food from her hand and fed it to Dove. He chanted and placed a hand on her stomach. His palm itched to explore other areas of her body. To touch her anywhere else would undo any trust he'd established.

Her eyes drooped with exhaustion and Wewukiye shifted. "Lean against me and sleep." She hesitated, but soon her body sagged. He tucked her close to his side with an arm draped around her. It would be a long night feeling her body next to his.

He leaned his head against the side of the crevice and closed his eyes.

****

Sunlight illuminated Dove's eyelids. Cold seeped into her back yet her front and tucked in arms were warm.

She moved her arms. Her hands encountered a hard lumpy surface. One which rose and fell like—

someone breathing.

She pushed with her arms and found a man's body under her. His arms lay to the side of him, not confining her in any way.

Dove rolled off and sat, mortified to have slept on a man. Her heart hammered in her chest, reliving the shape and hardness of his muscles under her hands.

Wewukiye sat up. A smile quivered at the corners of his mouth.

"Good morning."

Dove ducked her head. What must he think of her, sleeping upon him like he were nothing but dirt.

He tipped her chin up with one finger. "Did you not sleep well?" he asked, concern deepening his voice.

"I—" She had slept all night. A feat she had not done since the attack. "It was a good sleep."

His smile grew, and his eyes lit with pride. "I am pleased you slept well." He motioned to the pouch on her belt. "Finish the food. We will continue."

Her fingers fumbled with the pouch flap. Why did his eyes upon her make her clumsy?

His hand covered hers, steadying her fingers, sending bolts of heat up her arms.

"Let me help." He pulled the food from her pouch and placed it in her upturned hand.

With shaking hands, she unwrapped the meal. His presence no longer brought fear to her, but she didn't understand the awkwardness his presence brought. She spread the leaves upon her palm and offered the food to him.

He shook his head. "It is all for you."

"You have not eaten since yesterday. I will not eat if you do not." Her hand lowered to her lap, and she watched him. She knew warriors could go several days without eating when hunting or traveling. Then they had no food or time to eat. That was not the case right now.

"You are the one who needs the food. You are the one who can prove the *so-yá-po*'s lies."

She smiled on the inside at his noble sacrifice. Her stomach growled and he grinned.

"See, your stomach calls for the food. Eat." He pinched his fingers into the small mound of dried salmon and held it before her mouth.

Dove leaned forward, taking the food and watching him. His eyes closed, shutting her out from his emotions as she licked a stray piece of meat from his finger.

His intake of breath intrigued her. He was as aware of her as she of him.

She sat back. What were these flashes of heat he brought out in her?

"Eat. I will scout ahead," he said, abruptly standing and stalking off.

She watched his broad back and long legs carry him deeper into the crevice. With haste she finished the food and scurried after him.

"Wait, I am ready to continue," she said, running to keep up with his long strides.

He stopped and spun. "You have eaten the food?" Wewukiye searched her face as though he hunted for deceit.

"Yes."

"You did not throw it away?"

"No! Why do you not believe I ate the food?" She crossed her arms and glared at him. How dare he suggest she would waste food?

"Because you have run after me and do not look pale and as though you wish to be sick."

It was true. She felt fine. Her stomach did not squeeze with discontent.

She smiled. "This is a sign I should push forward to expose Evil Eyes." She brushed passed Wewukiye, walking briskly through the crevice.

She would no longer be the victim. Evil Eyes would be exposed and pay for all he'd done to her and what he planned for her people.

Ku`yc
(9)

Shortly after leaving the confines of the narrow passage in the mountain, Wewukiye led Dove to a dwelling made of logs. She huddled, hidden in the brush and watched him creep to the building and peer through a window. What if he was wrong and Evil Eyes was in the lodge? She shuddered and hoped Wewukiye proved correct in his insistence the man was gone.

Wewukiye stood and waved her forward. She took tentative steps, closing the space between herself and the building. Wewukiye would not put her in danger. Her feet and legs balked at her command to walk. Evil Eyes lived in this dwelling. Anything he touched would be vile.

Determination to prove the man's evil put one foot in front of the other until she stood beside Wewukiye. He pushed on the door of the cabin.

"He will know someone has been here." A tremor of fear snaked up her back.

"He will not know it was us. He will think it was one of his friends." Wewukiye placed a hand at her back, gently urging her into the dwelling.

Smoke, rancid food, and the odor of his body assaulted her nose. Dove shook her head, backing to the door. Memories of his weight, his smell, the pain—assaulted her. Panic clogged her throat. She could not breathe. Could not think.

"You are strong. You can do this." Wewukiye grasped her shoulders, keeping her from escaping the hateful memories.

"I cannot-it—he…" Closing her eyes, Evil Eyes's ugly face floated in front of her. She opened her eyes to run from the image and stared into the concerned handsome face of Wewukiye.

"What has scared you so?" He loosened his hold, but blocked her running out the door.

"It smells like him." Her gaze locked onto a face she had come to rely on. "It brings back—" The mismatched eyes and nasty yellow sneer spun in her mind. Pressing the heels of her hands against her head, she tried to banish the attack from her thoughts.

"He is not here. I am here. Have I ever hurt you?" He tipped her chin, making her peer at him.

His light touch and caring eyes—so different from the memories of the attack—her fear lessened. This man's touch warmed her skin and her heart.

"No. You have done nothing but honor me."

"Then you know no harm will come to you if you are with me." His gaze searched her face.

Heat, clarity, and confidence blossomed within her.

A smile grew on his face. "Come we will find his secrets and be gone." Wewukiye withdrew his hand and scanned the room.

Dove glanced around the room and shivered at the White man's smell hanging in the air. They must find proof of the man's evil toward the Nimiipuu.

A trunk by the bed drew her like a shiny rock. Her throat constricted at the thought of touching Evil Eyes belongings. She crossed the room and knelt in front of the trunk. Her heart raced, pounding in her ears when her hand touched the box. She lifted the lid. Air, old, stale, and filled with his odor puffed out. Her stomach clenched. She could not do this. Too many things…

Pots clanged. She glanced toward the noise. Wewukiye sent her a lopsided mischievous smile. He was with her. Nothing would happen. He had faith Evil Eyes would not return. They had to find the evidence to make the elders listen.

She inhaled deeply and peered into the trunk. A book sat on top of clothes. Dove grasped the object and sat on the floor, opening the pages in her lap.

The scribbles on the pages were just that. At the mission, the White man's scribbles stood square and even, easy to decipher. These scrawled across the page like the flight of an insect. She turned page after page and found only a scratch now and then she understood, but nothing that would help them.

"These scribbles mean nothing to me," she finally said. Hope sputtered. She'd failed in finding the truth.

Wewukiye glanced up from a paper he studied. "I have found drawings of the land." She put the book back in the trunk and stood by his side. "This is the lake." He pointed to a large elongated circle. "And this is where the cattle graze and up here the horses."

As he pointed out the lines, she, too, saw the area the Nimiipuu called their summer home.

"Why does he have a drawing of the Nimiipuu land?" She glanced at Wewukiye. He stared deep in thought.

"We will take these." He rolled the papers up. "You will give them to your leaders as proof this man is planning something."

A horse nickered. Fear raced through her like the icy winter wind. "He's back!"

Wewukiye hurried to the window. "It's not him. But a *so-yá-po*. Come." He handed her the papers and pulled her to a dark corner of the room. His mouth buzzed against her ear. "Do not move."

With the stealth of a cougar, he crossed the room and pressed his body against the wall beside the door. The thumping of her heart boomed in her head. She squeezed tighter into the corner. What if the man came into the dwelling? Did Wewukiye plan to kill him? If so, it would bring the White man's wrath down on the Nimiipuu.

She held her breath and listened. The horse stamped and snorted outside the door. Someone dropped to the ground with a thud. They did not land without a sound like a warrior. Heavy footsteps grew louder approaching the dwelling.

A knot bobbed in her throat. She feared he would hear her swallow.

Wewukiye wished at this moment Dove knew he was a spirit. He could change into smoke, drift under the door, and distract the White man headed toward them. If he'd had any idea someone would show up while they searched the cabin, he would never have brought her along. With Evil Eyes a great distance away and this cabin a good ride from any other, he did not think someone would visit.

The footsteps stopped in front of the door.

BAM. BAM. BAM. The man beat on the door.

"Jasper! Open this door, we need to talk," bellowed the man.

Wewukiye stilled his breathing and stared into the dark corner where Dove hid. Her eyes were wide and filled with fear. He willed her not to bolt like the frightened animal she resembled.

BAM. BAM. BAM. "Dammit, Jasper. We got to get going if we're gonna meet those men from the agency."

The door creaked and started to open. Wewukiye pressed against the wall. He would be behind the door if the man looked in, and behind the man, should he advance toward Dove. He glanced at Dove. She pressed deeper into the corner and closed her eyes.

The door stopped short of touching Wewukiye's body. The man grunted and closed the door. His steps retreated, but it did not sound like he mounted his horse.

Wewukiye motioned for Dove to drop to the floor and crawl to him. She covered the distance on her hands and knees. She pressed against his legs and sat on the floor. Her body shook.

He squatted next to her and whispered in her ear. "I will look out and see what he is doing. Do not move."

She nodded and he crept under a window. He edged to his feet alongside the window opening and peeked outside.

The man walked out of the building not far from the cabin. Wewukiye knew Evil Eyes used the other dwelling for his animals. The man scanned the trees and adjacent hill top. From his comments he expected Evil Eyes to be here.

Wewukiye knew Evil Eyes to be far north with the men who piled stacks of stones. He could be on his way back to his home. Evil Eyes did not travel as fast as his elk form and would not have left until the sun came up.

How long would the man wait for Evil Eyes? If he stayed until Evil Eyes returned they would be found. Wewukiye closed his eyes and mentally called to Sa-qan. He needed a distraction to get them away from here.

The screech of an eagle rent the air, sending the hair on his arm spiking. He smiled and peeked out the window. A great eagle swooped down, scaring the man's horse. The animal bolted for the trees, the man chasing after it.

Wewukiye grasped Dove's arm, pulled her from her crouched position, and flung the door open. The bright mid-day sun entered the cabin. He swung the woman into his arms and ran straight for the passage through the mountain. Fate had sent the horse running the opposite direction. He didn't fear the man coming across them as he ducked under tree branches and dodged boulders and bushes.

Dove clung to him, her head buried against his neck. Her body pressed tight to his, hindered his concentration. A limb skimmed by his head as his thoughts drifted to her curves.

"I can walk," she whispered a good distance from the cabin.

Wewukiye slowed his pace and reluctantly stopped, placing her on her feet. She no longer flinched at his touch. This reaction he had dreamed of often when not in her presence.

She clutched the drawings in her hand. "Did I hear an eagle before we left the dwelling?" Her gaze searched his face, seeking answers.

"Yes, an eagle scared the horse, giving us a chance to flee." A small elaboration would not harm anyone. "The Creator must believe in your cause to show the Nimiipuu leaders the *so-yá-po* is not their friend."

She scowled and watched him intently. "You believe the eagle coming when it did was a sign from the Creator?"

"Can you think of any other reason the eagle would scare a horse?"

She shook her head, her brow still wrinkled in thought.

He took her hand, leading her into the passage. If they hurried they would be on the other side and near her village by the time the moon rose in the sky.

"Do I tell the leaders we stole these papers from Evil Eyes?" Uncertainty shook her voice.

How could they bring forth the truth without him becoming entangled and still keep the leaders from thinking her vindictive?

"You cannot tell them of me."

She stopped, jerking his arm.

"Why can't I tell them of you? How will they believe just me?" She dropped his hand like a hot stone.

"I—" How could he explain his existence? He was not of any tribe. He was not mortal. "I am not of your band. They will be as doubtful of me as they are of you."

"How do I make them see Evil Eyes's plans to take over our home?" A tear glistened in the corner of her eye.

Wewukiye placed a hand on her shoulder. "Come, we must hurry. I will think as we walk."

She nodded and followed. He strode ahead of her through the crevice. Each step brought them closer to the village and the need to have a plan before they arrived. Dove's footsteps lagged and shuffled along the ground. Wewukiye slowed to return to her side. She wobbled and he mentally thumped himself. He'd not given her any nourishment since this morning.

"Come sit." He helped her to a sitting position and glanced along the sides of their narrow passageway. Nothing within these walls would fortify a living creature.

"Close your eyes and relax. I'll be right back." He gently shut her eyelids. Her lashes rested on her pale cheeks, and shallow puffs of air caused her chest to rise and fall in steady rhythm.

Wewukiye stood, hurrying along the crevice. At a slight bend, he glanced back to make sure he no longer saw Dove. He raised his face to the sky, calling for his form to change. Smoke swirled and energy buzzed through him, converting him into an elk.

Ahh. His preferred form. He stomped his hooves and shook, settling his hide around his frame. The clang of his antlers scraping the side of the rock formation echoed. He tilted his head back, resting his massive rack upon his back to keep them from catching on anything, and ran full speed down the passage. Exhilarated from the run, he burst from the opening and headed to a spot Nimiipuu women harvest roots.

He stopped in the meadow and pawed at the dirt with his hooves, digging up bulbs of *kouse* and *keeh-keet*. The bulbs hung from his mouth by their stems as he hurried back to the passage and Dove.

****

The sun beat down in the crevice. Sweat trickled between Dove's breasts and down her back. She opened her eyes. How could she fall asleep so easily when only days before sleep brought nothing but nightmares? Her muscles ached. She stretched, causing dizziness to drench her in white light.

Before Evil Eyes attacked her, she'd never experienced a weak body. Not only did he take her from her people, he took her from herself. Anger engulfed her. She stared at the drawing still clutched in her hand. This man would not harm her people. She would stop him even if she had to pierce his evil heart with a knife held in her own hand.

Smoke tickled her nose as brightness filled the cavern and faded. Why was there a fire in the cavern?

Pu`ti`m
(10)

Dove pushed against the wall of the narrow passage for leverage to stand. Her legs wobbled, but would carry her should she need to run. Fear for herself and Wewukiye trembled her body. Wewukiye could be in trouble. What good would her weak body be to him? She bit her bottom lip in concentration and stared into the passage.

Wewukiye walked toward her, roots clutched in his hands. Relief swamped her, sliding her to a sitting position on the ground. At her collapse, he ran to her.

"Sit and eat." He placed the plants on her lap.

"What was the light?" she asked, rubbing dirt from a *keeh-keet* bulb.

Hope and eagerness slid from his face. His gaze avoided hers. He shrugged and took one of the roots, peeling the outer skin. The sweet pungent aroma made her mouth water.

"I did not dream the flash of light and stench of smoke." She shook the food at him. He had to have seen the light. It flashed the same direction he walked from. She scowled at him and bit into the root.

He smiled and offered her the bulb he skinned. She chewed and swallowed the strong tasting bite.

"You should eat as well." Her stomach churned. One bite. She was pitiful. She squeezed her eyes shut. *I can't even keep one bite down.* Furious with the frailness of her body and her bleak future, tears squeezed under her clenched eyelids.

"Why are you crying?" Wewukiye's deep voice drew her from her self-pity. The softness of his fingers brushing away her tears, opened her eyes.

"Will I ever be as strong as before? How can I save my people from the *so-yá-po* if I cannot even save myself from one?"

"You are not doing this alone. I will help." He cradled her head in his hands. His thumbs moved back and forth across her cheek bones.

His soft touch and concerned words whisked away part of her fears. His gentle manner stirred desires. This man would never cause her harm. Could she...

An icy shard of reality ran down her spine. No man would want her after what Evil Eyes did to her. And though she enjoyed the comfort of Wewukiye's tender touch, she would never be able to tolerate mating. She hiccupped and pulled her head from his grasp.

"Eat, we must get you back to the village. You must give the drawing to the leaders."

Dove shuddered. "What if they ask how I came to have the drawing?" She stared at the paper on the ground beside her. "They will scold me for taking something which could start trouble." She fixed her gaze on Wewukiye. "I know they will find fault with me and not see it as Evil Eyes's plan to take over our summer home."

"I've thought about this. Show the drawing to Crazy One. Hide it in your lodge. When Evil Eyes visits, Crazy One can drop the drawing near his belongings. No one will suspect you, but the leaders will be suspicious of Evil Eyes."

Dove thought on his plan. It made sense. If Evil Eyes stayed in his routine it would not be long before he visited Joseph. She nodded her head. "This is a good plan." She raised another root to her lips, bit, chewed, swallowed, and waited to see if her body would accept the offering.

"Rest your head in my lap." Wewukiye patted his thigh and smiled. He could see her body still refused the food. Reluctance flashed in her eyes. He patted his thigh again, and she rested her head upon his lap. He placed a hand on her stomach, swirling circles and chanting to the Creator to give her good health.

In his haste to bring her the food, she almost caught him changing forms. He would have to remember to remain farther away from her during his transformation. It wouldn't do for her to learn the truth. Though her knowing he was not of this world would allow her to realize he would not be able to stay once the baby arrived.

He shook his head and picked up another root, peeling away the dirty outer layer. He would make her well and help her bring the child into the world to prove the White man's treachery. Once completed, he would slip out of her life and tuck the memory of her soft skin and brave heart to keep him company through the ages.

She finished eating the last bulb. Her eyelids drooped closed. They should hurry back to the village, but she also needed the rest. A brief rest would allow the food to strengthen her body.

Her chest moved with the slow even rhythm of sleep. Wewukiye used this opportunity to study her high cheek bones, wide nose, and small mouth. Her small body was compact and muscular. His hands itched to run over the curve of her hip and experience the soft swell of her breasts, but should his touch awaken her, she would fear him like she did Evil Eyes.

He leaned his head against the rock wall and closed his eyes. His body didn't need sleep, but he required closing his eyes and mind to the desires this mortal brought forth.

Now he knew the lure his brother fought all those summers past. Watching the creatures of the area over the ages he'd wondered at the peculiar attraction both animal and mortals had for a mate. He liked being alone, content to help the Nimiipuu and travel the countryside. The woman sleeping upon him conjured up thoughts of the two of them traveling together, becoming as one. How they came together had to be of the Creator's making. What they were to do about it, he had yet to discover.

Dove stirred, rubbing her head against his manhood and setting his body on fire. Her hand on his thigh clenched and unclenched. Her dream did not hold peaceful images.

He placed a hand on her arm.

"Dove, awake. We must continue." His voice scratched through his constricted throat. The contact of his hand upon her smooth skin sent more heat crashing through his body.

Her head stirred, again arousing his body in a way she would not like or understand.

"Dove, please, we must go." He needed to push to his feet, to lose contact with the woman and the arousal her touch ignited. Yet, he wished to never let go and vow to her he would cause her no harm.

Her eyelashes fluttered off her gaunt, pale cheeks. Her hand wiped across her face, and she slowly registered where she lay. Dove shoved abruptly to a sitting position. Her eyes rolled back and her eyelids closed. He wrapped his arms around her, stopping her from falling into the dirt.

"Take your time. Do not rush to your feet." Wewukiye smoothed a hand over her hair. So soft. He inhaled the sweet scent of chamomile. His arm holding her against his body settled at the underside of her breast. He tensed, halting his hand from sliding up the smooth deerskin dress.

Her limp body shuddered. He yearned to draw

her tighter against him, to hold her intimately. Muscle by muscle her body tensed. He believed her awake and strong enough to hold herself up. His hands slid around, edging her body away from him.

Dark brown eyes stared at him. He stared back, willing her to know he would never harm her. His gaze dropped to her quivering lips.

"I—I'm sorry to be such a nuisance." Her eyelashes shrouded her eyes as she peered at her hands clenched in her lap.

Wewukiye gently enclosed her small hands in his. "You are not a nuisance. I pledged to help you prove the *so-yá-po*'s dishonesty. It was my urging that made you see you must keep the child growing inside you. This makes it my undertaking as well."

She raised her head, staring into his eyes. The hope glistening in their depths sucked the air out of him. He had to do everything within his power to help her survive the birth and the ugliness of persuading the band the White man was not their friend.

He rose. "Come, you must get back to the village. The wind is colder and the clouds have turned angry." Wewukiye drew her to her feet. He stooped to retrieve the drawing and tucked the paper in the waistband of his breeches. Dove held out her hand. An act which swelled his heart. Her show of acceptance sped his heart and filled his chest with pride. He grasped her fingers and led her through the crevice.

****

Dove stood at the edge of the trees surrounding the village. The strength she garnered from Wewukiye's hand in hers overwhelmed her. She wanted to ignore the power and the excitement his touch brought. The realization a man could bring out emotions other than fear, hurt, and anger healed a small part of the wound Evil Eyes inflicted.

Wewukiye's declaration to be here for her through it all also restored her faith.

Watching the village from the trees she wished to never set foot among her people again. None gave her the confidence and strength of the man holding her hand.

"You must go. Crazy One is worried for your return." Wewukiye squeezed her hand.

"She should not worry. You told her when I would return." She faced him. Her breath caught at the sight of his majestic stance and the way his eyes scanned the village beyond the trees.

"You have been gone longer than I predicted. She worries something has happened." His gaze dropped to her. His eyes lit with a warm glow, and his wide mouth tipped into a secretive smile.

Rustling, like the leaves in a wind, tickled her insides. Heat started in her chest and spread throughout her body.

"S-she knows I am with you." She licked her lips. "No harm will come to me with you by my side."

His smile grew. "It is true. I am glad you have learned this."

He tugged her hand, drawing her closer. His warm breath puffed against her ear.

"You need only think of me and you will have strength."

His soft silky voice floated through her body like a hot drink.

She swallowed the lump in her throat and asked, "When will I see you again?" The thought of sleeping on the hard ground next to the fire in Crazy One's dwelling didn't sound near as inviting as using his lap to rest her head.

The days and nights grew colder; to be wrapped in his arms would warm her through and through.

"You will find me at the meadow every day when the sun is directly overhead." He brushed his lips

87

against her ear.

She closed her eyes, relishing the silky feel of his lips and the heat of his touch.

"Think of me," whispered through her head.

Dove opened her eyes. She stood alone. Her palm still warm from their clasped hands, her ear ringing with his whisper.

She scanned the trees for a trace of him. He'd vanished as quickly as the last summer breeze. She glanced at the village. Crazy One stood beside her dwelling staring straight at her, smiling.

What would the villagers say if they found out about Wewukiye? Would they believe him the father of her child? The idea wasn't as unpleasant as thinking of the real father. She cringed and her stomach rolled.

Thoughts of Wewukiye quieted her stomach and her mood lightened. She found her clue to surviving the birth. From now on she would only think of the child growing within as Wewukiye's.

Crazy One motioned to her, and she stepped out of the trees. New strength in her legs bubbled up a laugh and new found confidence. With Wewukiye guiding her she would save her people. Her arm scraped the drawing tucked in her belt. When had he placed the drawing on her? The breathless moments when he whispered in her ear and all thoughts fled, that had to be when. She covered it with her arm and hurried to Crazy One's dwelling. It would not be good to have someone see the evidence before it fell at the feet of Evil Eyes.

When that day happened, she wished to witness the scorn due him from the leaders.

Pú-timt wax ná-qt
(11)

Several days later, Dove hurried back to the village. The new long buckskin dress and knee-length moccasins Crazy One gave her that morning kept the cold winds from chilling her skin. Her visit with Wewukiye also had a lot to do with the warmth in her body.

She smiled and continued at a quick pace down the side of the mountain. Her meetings with him had brought back her health and her joy to live. Only the task ahead of them, to prove Evil Eyes's wrong doings marred her life, but it also gave her direction. Something she had lost.

Cold wind blew down her neck. The crisp fresh air carried the scent of snow. It would not be long and her tribe would move to the lower ground of the Imnaha until the season of root gathering came once again.

She stepped from the trees and stilled. Evil Eyes spoke, his arms flailing in the air in front of Chief Joseph. His anger reddened face and forceful actions sent her back to the day he attacked her. She couldn't move. Fear lanced her body to the spot.

Evil Eyes peered at each Nimiipuu around him. She knew the sting of his two-colored glare. Chief Joseph raised something...

Her heart stuttered. She recognized the drawing. Crazy One must have dropped it.

Dove scanned the area around the altercation for the old woman. Something tugged on her arm. She glanced at Crazy One. The old woman smiled and put a finger to her lips.

"Should we not take a walk?" Crazy One led her back into the trees, treading quietly inside the edge of the forest. She led them to the opposite side of the village.

"You dropped the drawing." Dove's chest expanded with new-found appreciation for the woman.

"Did I not know the perfect place?" She grinned showing the gaps between her teeth. "Did not Chief Joseph himself find it? Was it not in front of Evil Eyes's trading pouch?"

Dove hugged the woman. "You are so wonderful. They cannot blame me. I was not in the village. Many saw me leave and know I take a walk at this time each day."

They peeked through a bush still clinging to a few dried leaves. Chief Joseph held the drawing out, his expression unreadable. Evil Eyes had stopped his ranting. He refused to take the drawing from Chief Joseph's offered hand.

Dove snickered. To take it would prove it belonged to him. His rigid stance and fidgeting hands gave away his fear of reprisal.

He scanned the encampment and scowled, giving him an even fiercer expression. She stepped away from the bush, moving deeper into the trees. He could not see her. In her bones she believed he knew it was she who brought the map from his cabin. No other knew his evil or his plan to bring in more White men.

Without another word to the chief, Evil Eyes mounted his horse and rode away, his gait slow and his back straight. She glanced back at Chief Joseph. He and his sons studied the map.

A sense of achievement warmed her chest. She wished Wewukiye stood by her side to revel in their accomplishment. Perhaps this would make the leaders more cautious when dealing with Evil Eyes.

"Is it not past time?" Crazy One pulled on her hand, leading her into the village.

"Past time for what?" Dove noticed large baskets near the opening of their lodge.

"Do you not grow bigger?" Crazy One ducked into their dwelling.

"It's too early to confine me to the menstruation lodge." She ducked through the opening. She had witnessed woman ready to birth stayed in the lodge until the baby arrived. Crazy One had reassured her she would be with her at that time. Dove did not like the idea of not seeing Wewukiye, but it was the way. Men did not see the woman while she brought a life into the world. For him to be with her during that time would weaken him.

The old woman shook her head. "Do you not follow tradition?" She held up a wide length of buckskin.

Tears burned Dove's eyes. The bulge in her belly proved her attack was not a bad dream, and now the wearing of the buckskin belt to protect the child glaringly brought the fact to heart.

She raised the hem of her dress, displaying the slight bulge of her belly. Crazy One chanted to the Creator for good health to the child and mother, tying the wide strip around Dove's bulge.

From now on the band of buckskin would be another reminder of the life growing inside her.

She dropped her skirt, and a male voice called out to enter.

Dove stared at Crazy One.

The older woman smiled and drew the blanket covering back.

One Who Flies, an elder on the council, stepped into their dwelling. His watery gaze found her standing by the fire.

"Your family has held much respect for many

seasons."

She nodded, unsure why he spoke to her.

"Because of this respect your actions have been brushed aside—"

"You mean *I* have been brushed aside." Unheard of to talk disrespectfully to an elder and one of his stature, she still could not hold back the flaring anger.

The pity in his fading eyes dropped her heart to her toes.

"Because of this respect for your family, you are to come with me to our chief's dwelling." He nodded to Crazy One and disappeared through the opening.

She peered at Crazy One. "They cannot know I had anything to do with the drawing." What would they say when she told them of Wewukiye and stealing the drawing from Evil Eyes? She could not lie. To do so would only have them believe she did not tell the truth about Evil Eyes and the attack.

"Do you tell the truth?" Crazy One nodded. Her graying braids slid up and down the front of her beaded blanket dress.

"I will. But I fear it will not help their feeling toward me."

Dove wished with all her heart, Wewukiye could stand next to her as she told the leaders how the drawing arrived in their camp.

She exited the security of Crazy One's cozy dwelling and walked, her head held high, across the village to Chief Joseph's lodge. How did they come to know she brought the drawing?

Untruths did not slide from her tongue like honey. She would tell the truth and suffer the consequences. One Who Flies entered the Chief's lodge. She stopped, swallowed the lump of fear in her throat, closed her eyes, and asked the Creator to help her say the right thing.

Pú-timt wax lepít
(12)

Wewukiye moved through the forest in elk form sensing Dove's unease. Crazy One also entered his thoughts. Something had happened.

He raised his muzzle to the weakening sun. Soon the snow would fall and the Lake Nimiipuu would move to their encampment near the warm river. He bugled to Sa-qan.

His hooves stomped the ground, matching his restless body and thoughts. Dove needed him. The sensations of fear and apprehension swirled in his belly, leaving him helpless.

Air ruffled the hair on his back and the creak of a branch drew his attention.

"What puts distress in your voice, brother?" Sa-qan leaned down from her perch, her beady yellow gaze locking onto his.

"I believe Dove is in trouble. I wish to help her. It would mean revealing my man form to the Lake Nimiipuu."

Sa-qan drew back as though he struck her. "You know the Creator disapproves of such notions."

"Dove and Crazy One call to me. There is trouble brewing. I am the only one who can help Dove."

"Why must it be you who helps this woman?" She leaned down closer, her eyes searching.

"I fear it has to do with the day you helped us leave the *so-yá-po*'s dwelling."

She straightened, walked the limb to the tree trunk and back. Her shiny white head shook, and her feathers ruffed up, then settled. "What, dear brother, gives you reason to believe the woman's trouble is due to the visit to the *so-yá-po*'s lodge?"

Wewukiye dug the toe of his hoof into the dirt avoiding his sister's eyes. "We went there for proof against the *so-yá-po*."

"And?"

"We took a drawing of the Lake Nimiipuu country the *so-yá-po* had drawn." He peered into her eyes. She had to understand.

Sa-qan had helped them escape the White man's lodge, but she did not know he took one of the man's possessions with him.

"You what?" She pointed a wing at him. "You are a spirit. You help keep peace and tranquility between the Nimiipuu, the land, and the animals. You do not start bloodshed." She paced the length of the limb again. "You will not bring us to more disfavor with the Creator. You will not be like our father."

Wewukiye's back hair bristled. "I am not our father! I have done nothing cowardly or deceitful. It is the *so-yá-po*. The Lake Nimiipuu must learn of this man's deceit."

"You cannot go around stealing from the *so-yá-po*. He will seek revenge on the Lake Nimiipuu for your actions. You must do everything in your power to avoid a confrontation." She spread her wings. "I must speak with the Creator on this." She sprang off the limb and into the air, flying away.

Dove's distress filled his thoughts. He set out for the village. He did not know how he would explain his presence, but he must take the wrath from Dove.

****

Dove sucked in air when Frog exited the lodge. By the surprise in his eyes she knew he had been sent to find her thinking she had run from the summons. He motioned her forward. She swallowed, but her dry mouth did little to help slide the knot of fear down her throat.

She entered the dwelling, keeping her eyes downcast so as not to upset them further.

"Do you know of this drawing?" Chief Joseph asked, his voice weary.

She raised her gaze enough to see the drawing she and Wewukiye took from Evil Eyes. Her stomach clenched, and she nearly doubled over from the pain of regret. Should her actions start a war with the White men she doubted they would let her remain among them.

"I have seen the drawing." Her voice cracked. Now was not the time to become weak. She reprimanded herself and dug deep within to find strength and bravery in front of the council.

Commotion outside the lodge caught the attention of the elders. Thunder Traveling to Distant Mountains motioned to the warrior standing near the door, and he ducked out the opening.

Her heart pounded in her chest and echoed in her ears. The minor delay gave her time to think about her words carefully.

The flap of the lodge flopped open. Her gaze flew to the entrance. Her heart stopped.

Wewukiye stepped through the opening. His golden hair shone like sunlight. His blue eyes scanned the interior before settling on her. He did not smile, but his presence wrapped around her as solid as the mountain.

The councilmen mumbled and many faces wrinkled in uncertainty.

"Who are you?" Thunder Traveling to Distant Mountains stepped forward.

"I am Wewukiye of the Upper Nimiipuu."

His deep, confident words hailed her confidence. She remained with her eyes downcast maintaining their custom. Her back straightened, and her strength ebbed.

"You are Nimiipuu?" Thunder Traveling to Distant Mountains walked closer.

"Yes. You know the legend of the Nimiipuu with sun colored hair? I am of that band." Wewukiye wanted to capture Dove's hand and instill his calm and strength upon her, but to be so forward in front of the council would not help their cause.

Voices murmured around them.

"We had another with hair the color of yours many seasons back. He was Crazy One's father," an elder said, peering at him through narrowed eyes.

He heard Dove's intake of breath. What was she thinking? He had to let thoughts of her go if he wished to speak clearly.

"Himiin, he was of my band. He married a maiden called Wren." Wewukiye swept a gaze around the men seated in a circle.

"Why have you come to our village? It is a long journey from your home." Chief Joseph stared at him.

"While visiting with Crazy One, I met Dove." He offered her what he hoped revealed a not too friendly smile. The relief in her eyes gazing at him for a brief moment stunned him. Had she thought he would tell the council of her attempt to end her life?

"What has meeting this maiden to do with you arriving as we are questioning her?" Thunder Traveling to Distant Mountains was known for his quick thinking.

"Crazy One told me of the drawing you found and that you questioned Dove. I found it and showed it to Dove. I could see it represents the earth that has been Lake Nimiipuu hunting grounds. It was my idea to have someone in the village find it." He crossed his arms, showing his firm stand. Untruths did not flow from his tongue. He found the drawing. Where and how—would not be so easy.

"Why did you or Dove not bring it to us?"

Thunder Traveling to Distant Mountains glanced at Dove then swung his dark accusing gaze back to Wewukiye.

"I know you have lost faith in Dove." He felt her gaze upon him. "Had she brought this to you, would you have believed her or treated her as you are now?" He kept his gaze level with Thunder Traveling to Distant Mountain before slowly including Chief Joseph in his question.

The chief and his two sons sighed.

"It is not a matter of faith lost." Chief Joseph tapped his finger into the palm of his other hand. "The White man's paper we did not sign gives them the right to live on our hunting grounds. If we live in peace with them we do not have to leave the bones of our fathers." Chief Joseph stared pointedly at Dove. "We cannot risk losing our earth by accusing one White man without proof."

Dove raised her head. The glare she shot Chief Joseph made Wewukiye grimace. He was helpless to stop the words he saw forming on her lips.

"When the child growing inside me appears, you will see Evil Eyes violated me. And then you will have to whip him as you would a Nimiipuu who took a woman without her consent." Dove pivoted and stalked out of the lodge.

Wewukiye watched the faces of the men. Their brows furrowed in disbelief, whether from her accusation or her disrespect, he did not know.

Chief Joseph held up the drawing. "Where did you find this?"

"In the valley two ridges toward the setting sun."

The chief motioned for him to sit. Wewukiye moved closer to the council and sat cross-legged with the council fire between himself and the others in the lodge.

"What took you there?" Chief Joseph asked.

"Hunting." They did not need to know it was not animals.

Thunder Traveling to Distant Mountains cleared his throat. Wewukiye watched the man his equal in size. If only they knew he'd watched each man, young and old, seated at this council come into the world or join this band. He had watched over this band since the time of their father's fathers and beyond.

"How is it you have been among our band and this is the first we've met?" Disapproval rang in Thunder Traveling to Distant Mountains's voice.

Wewukiye wanted to groan. He feared this most by showing himself. But Dove did not deserve to take punishment for a deed of his doing.

"I have camped on the mountain, only visiting with Crazy One who introduced me to Dove." He glanced at each man seated. "I am on a quest for the Creator."

The men murmured and shot glances to the Shaman sitting to the right of Chief Joseph.

The old man studied him with narrowed eyes before lifting his hands in the air and chanting. The words combined a mixture of the lower and upper dialect. Did the man come from the upper Nimiipuu or simply testing him?

Wewukiye nodded to the man, letting him know he understood. The Shaman stopped chanting and lowered his arms.

He stared at Wewukiye. "You are to remain with us through the *Heel-lul*."

Wewukiye shook his head. "I must remain alone." To move into the village he would live in the lodge of the unmarried men and older boys. He had to have time to be in elk form. It was how he moved about the area quickly and kept an eye on the inhabitants' activities.

The Shaman nodded his head. "You may camp

as you wish, but you must travel with us to the Imnaha. It is the wish of the Creator."

The Creator's wish? Did this Shaman really speak with the Creator? Only Sa-qan spoke with the Creator. Whether the Creator or the Shaman granted it, he would be with Dove until the child was born. He did not break promises. His chest squeezed with loneliness thinking of never seeing the woman or her child after her people realized she told the truth.

"Why did you bring us this drawing?" Thunder Traveling to Distant Mountains broke into his thoughts.

"I recognized the lines to be around the home of your people. From my travels these marks"—he stretched out to grasp the drawing and pointed to two lines crossing—"are dwellings of the White men."

"How do you know this?" Thunder Traveling to Distant Mountains peered at him.

"I have traveled this land many times." He shrugged. "I am a wanderer."

"But we have not seen you before." The chief's son crossed his arms. All eyes narrowed on him.

"Because I did not wish to be seen."

"Yet you show yourself now, when the maiden Dove is to be questioned." Thunder Traveling to Distant Mountains stared through narrowed suspicious eyes.

Wewukiye did not flinch or look away from the man's formidable stare. "I do not wish others to be unjustly punished for my deeds."

Chief Joseph cleared his throat drawing everyone's attention. "You speak of our valley with much knowledge. Was the drawing you found near a *so-yá-po*'s dwelling?"

"Yes." Wewukiye hoped the Creator understood the reason for his half-truths.

The chief glanced at Thunder Traveling to Distant Mountains and nodded to his younger son, Frog. Their silent communication revealed to Wewukiye they knew which White man lived two ridges from the lake.

"Did you see the *so-yá-po* who just left here?" Frog asked.

Wewukiye did not see the man, but he assumed they meant Evil Eyes. Every essence of him wanted to say yes, but he must tell the truth. "I did not see a *so-yá-po* leave the village."

"Have you seen the White man who lives in the dwelling?" Thunder Traveling to Distant Mountains joined the conversation.

"Yes. He has hair the color of dead grass and eyes of different colors." He stared straight at Thunder Traveling to Distant Mountains. "I watched him lift another *so-yá-po* by the neck, cutting off his air, and drop him on the ground like a stick." Wewukiye glanced at Chief Joseph, Thunder Traveling to Distant Mountains, and Frog, before he scanned the men ringing the fire. "That *so-yá-po* is full of rage and does not care that he hurts others."

Frog grunted and stood. He paced behind his father and brother. Chief Joseph's shoulders sagged a bit, and Thunder Traveling to Distant Mountains continued to watch him.

"You may go." The chief waved his arm toward the opening of the buffalo hide structure.

Wewukiye stood. He made eye contact with each man and left the lodge.

He stood in front of the lodge scanning the area in search of Dove or Crazy One. Men, women, and children stared back. His appearance would cause talk, but he would enter their village again to save Dove from being questioned. He was the one who took the drawing from the White man's dwelling, and he should be the one to suffer the consequences, not her.

The drawings on a hide covered dwelling revealed Crazy One's tipi. The shaman's comment still stunned him. He knew the man held powers, but did he actually talk to the Creator? He would ask Sa-qan. *If she spoke to him again.* Once she discovered he had revealed himself to the Lake Nimiipuu he knew he would get a stinging lecture.

He stopped in front of Crazy One's dwelling.

"May I enter?" he asked loud enough for the inhabitants to hear, but not the surrounding curious onlookers.

The flap moved and Crazy One smiled at him. He ducked into the small tipi. His heart stalled once his gaze lit on Dove's pale, worried face.

He knelt beside her, taking her cold hand in his. "All is well. I told them it was I who found the drawing, and my idea to leave it for them to find."

"They believed you?" Her voice shook with disbelief.

Her cold hand and trembling lips spun regret in his gut like a tidal pool. He pulled her into his arms and hugged her. The slight bulge of her belly pushed against him. "Yes they believed me. They now doubt Evil Eyes." He spoke into her hair. Her head tucked protectively under his chin. Her curves, a perfect fit in his arms, surpassed all his dreams.

She pushed against his chest, and he released her. Her cheeks grew darker, her eyes remained downcast. "Do they now believe me?"

The one thing he wished to give her he could not. Her proof would have to come with the child growing in her.

"They did not say. But they questioned my knowing you." He took her hand, encouraged by their recent embrace. "The Shaman said the Creator wishes me to stay with the band until *Heel-lul.*"

Her eyes widened and shone like stars in the

darkest night. A smile slowly tipped her small mouth. "You would travel with us, stay in the village, and be near when I give birth?"

"No."

Pú-timt wax mita-t
(13)

His one uttered word punctured Dove's body like a knife jab. Fear and hurt spun a hard knot in her chest. He'd promised to help her. She stared into his beautiful blue eyes, trying to understand his refusal.

She tugged on the hand he still held.

He didn't let go. His solemn eyes peered deep into her hers. "I will travel with the band and be with you until the coming of the child." He shook his head. "I cannot live in the lodge of the unmarried men."

Was that a glimmer of fear in his eyes? Why would he fear living with the other men?

"Where will you live? They will not allow you to stay with Crazy One and me." *Unless they married.* Her body heated at the thought. Was that his plan? He knew her fear and would not push his attentions. Having him always at her side she would never be fearful or alone.

"I will camp alone, outside the village."

"Who will cook for you or tend your fire?" She didn't like the idea of him being alone. Something could happen to him. Now that the others knew of him, what might the other warriors do knowing he didn't abide to the ways of their band?

He smiled and her concerns banished. "I will seek nourishment and company from your fire." He glanced at Crazy One. "And always when Crazy One is here. I will not come into this dwelling if you are alone."

She opened her mouth to tell him she wasn't

afraid of him anymore, but he placed a finger over her lips.

"I will not enter when you are alone to keep your honor."

Her face heated with embarrassment. Of course the others would keep an eye on their friendship. Did Thunder Traveling to Distant Mountains…

"Did they ask if you and I…" She couldn't say the rest. Her heart hammered in her chest shoving air from her.

"No." He took her hands. "As your child grows some may talk. It is best we don't feed their thoughts."

She nodded, staring at his hands holding hers. This kind of contact she never dreamed possible with a man after what had happened to her. Now, she could not touch him outside this tipi without others thinking wrong thoughts.

"I must go. I'll return in the morning and help pack for the journey to the Imnaha."

"It is not a man's job to take down the dwelling or pack." She turned to Crazy One for her support.

"Would you make them think she is not a good woman?" Crazy One stepped up and swatted Wewukiye's shoulder.

"She's growing a child." Wewukiye watched Crazy One then peered into Doves eyes. "You should not do things which could harm the baby."

"I must do my work as always. Crazy One can handle what I must not do." Dove savored his concern.

"Crazy One is not young." He ducked from the gnarled hand swinging at his head.

"Am I not your niece? Who else cares to help sweet Dove?"

She called herself his niece. That held more meaning than calling him her uncle. The woman was different but not crazy. Why did she not call him her nephew and she his aunt? Before she could dwell on the thought Wewukiye captured her attention.

"I will help. I can gather wood during the night, hiding it for you to find in the morning. I will do the same with water." He smiled at his cleverness.

Dove returned the good-natured smile, her heart opening wider to the man. Many times during the last three moons she thanked the Creator for sending Wewukiye to the lake that night and saving her. Today, she thanked the Creator for this man who showed her the *so-yá-po* did not take away her ability to want a husband. Not just any husband, but the man standing in front of her, grinning.

"But a warrior does not do woman's work. You will need to ready your weapons to hunt with the others." The moment the words left her mouth she realized, never had she seen him with any type of weapon. Not a knife or a bow and arrow.

"I will travel with you. I will provide meat for you. I will not join in as one with your band."

The firm set to his square jaw and the spark of dignity lighting his eyes made her wonder at the band and family he left behind. Surely, they would miss a warrior such as he.

"How is it your family will not worry you are gone so long?"

He glanced at Crazy One then settled his thoughtful gaze on Dove. "My family knows I am on a knowledge quest."

She stared into his eyes. Untold stories hid within them. She also witnessed a stubborn set to his jaw and knew he would not tell her what he hid.

"It is time I go." He stood, pulling her to her feet.

She'd forgotten her hands remained tucked into his warm large ones. His touch filled her with strength and security. His strong fingers squeezing hers sent waves of heat tingling up her arms and warmed her suffering heart.

"When will you return?" She cringed at the pleading tone in her words.

His lips curved into the captivating, mischievous grin she'd witnessed him bestow on Crazy One.

"I believe you are going to miss me."

The arrogant, playful tone should have angered her, but she smiled back. "I only wish to know if you will stumble into our camp when we are in the middle of tearing down the dwelling."

He frowned. "I do not stumble anywhere. I shall be here when the sun peeks over the ridge."

She nodded and cast her gaze to his moccasins. If her relief and excitement shone in her eyes she wished to keep those feelings hidden. She must remain aloof or fear becoming too attached.

Movement outside the dwelling shot her gaze to Wewukiye. Someone approached.

He released her hands and strode the three steps to the opening. He threw back the flap and stepped outside. Who would wish to speak with them? Had the council not believed Wewukiye?

Dove stepped toward the opening. Crazy One caught her arm. "Has my uncle not helped you?" She pulled on Dove's arm, tugging her away from the exit. "Has he not the knowledge and powers to keep you safe?"

Dove stared into the old woman's watery eyes. She again called him her uncle, and now she talked about powers. Her face heated remembering his gentle touch on her belly and how it settled her food.

Who was this warrior with sunshine hair?

****

Wewukiye crossed his arms and stared at Frog, the younger son of Chief Joseph.

"My father wishes you remain with the unmarried men." Frog took the same stance.

"Tell your father I am honored for his offer, but I will remain on my own." He was sure the chief had not offered, he'd ordered.

"I know not of your people. You will respect the ways of our band." Frog did not raise his voice, but his tone pulled people from their tasks to watch.

"I do not disrespect your ways or your people. I am on a quest and will remain apart from the band at night. I will help Crazy One and Dove on the journey to the Imnaha and back." He scanned the growing crowd. He knew not who might be Dove's family. If they had believed in her, he would not have had to show himself. Anger they could abandon her seethed in his gut.

He opened his mouth to say as much. A shrill eagle call pierced the gray sky. Sa-qan.

Wewukiye flinched. She had spotted him in the village. He would much rather face the whole Lake Nimiipuu band than his sister.

"I will return when the sun peeks over the ridge." He pointed to the ridge behind Frog. The warrior narrowed his eyes. Wewukiye had nothing more to say. He turned and walked from the village.

They would watch him, of this he was certain. Once in the cover of the woods, he shifted into an elk and loped up the mountain in search of Sa-qan.

She sat on a limb. The magnitude of her displeasure shone in her yellow eyes.

"How could you show yourself to the Lake Nimiipuu? What untruths did you tell?" She paced the length of the limb. "This is not good." Her head shook, and her tail feathers twitched.

"I could not let Dove take the blame for my hasty actions." He placed his antler on the branch to stop her pacing. "They are questioning the friendship of the White man." He smiled.

"That is the least of your concerns." She poked her pointed beak in his face. "How did you explain your hair and the fact they have not seen you before?"

"I told them I am of the upper Nimiipuu band, one whose ancestors had hair the color of sun and I am on a quest." He nodded. "I have not told untruths. We are of the band with hair the color of the sun. I am on a quest to help Dove."

She smacked him with her wing. "We are of that band from many, many seasons ago. What if they question you? Or ask others?"

"There will be no one from the Upper Nimiipuu venture this way now. Everyone is moving to lower ground for the coming of the snow."

"You are too confident. With the Lake Nimiipuu moving away from the mountain you do not have to protect the woman. There is no need for you to remain among them."

"I have promised Dove I will remain with her until the arrival of her child." He ducked his head and added. "I will travel with them to the Imnaha."

"That is not necessary. Our niece can take care of her. They will not abandon the two. It is not the way of our people." Sa-qan tapped his head with her wing. "You cannot be selfish and stay with them to make your own mind light."

"I promised the woman I would be with her through this. She draws strength from my presence." Was he being selfish? His dedication and attraction to Dove rivaled his dedication to the Lake Nimiipuu. The Creator placed him and his siblings here after his selfish father caused the death of many warriors on a hunt. He would not become his father.

"She is not slow if she has worked through the deceit of the *so-yá-po*. She will soon see through you and discover the truth. What will you do then?"

The concern in his sister's eyes surprised him. How had she circled from anger and reproach to concern?

"When she has questions, I will answer them honestly. It will be easier for her to know the truth after the baby is born and I return to my full duties." The thought of leaving her once they proved the White man's attack weighed like a boulder on his shoulders.

"It is the wish of the Creator that you help the Lake Nimiipuu see the White man's deceit." Sa-qan spoke so low he thought he'd heard wrong.

"What I am doing is not putting me in disfavor?" He wanted to shout his gratitude to the Creator. From the moment he raised the woman's lifeless body from the depths of his lake, he connected with her and had to keep her safe. His chest expanded with pride in the knowledge he'd been right.

Sa-qan flapped her wings, drawing his attention. "You must guard the woman. I have seen many *so-yá-po* gather at the cabin of Evil Eyes." She narrowed her eyes. "Anger floats from his chimney with the smoke of his fire."

Wewukiye knew this anger. He had witnessed it on two occasions. "I will travel with the band, remaining outside the camp at night. The council is not happy I do not wish to live in the unmarried warrior's lodge."

She nodded. "I will keep an eye on the *so-yá-po* and let you know if he is up to anything."

He had planned to slip into elk form at night and run back to the valley to check on Evil Eyes's actions. The knowledge his sister watched the man would allow him to remain near the band at night. "That would be helpful."

"When do you leave?" Sa-qan peered down the mountain in the sparse light of the moon filtering through clouds.

"They will dismantle the village tomorrow."

"I will contact you when you have arrived at Imnaha." Sa-qan spread her wings and bent her legs to launch.

"*Qe`ci`yew`yew*, thank you, sister."

Sa-qan leapt into the air and sailed into the dark night. Wewukiye stared at her glowing white head until he could no longer see it.

Sa-qan had remained adamant their brother Himiin leave the mortal Wren alone when they met many seasons ago. She had not come around to the likelihood of the two merging until after the Creator granted Himiin his human form to be with Wren. He'd noticed since then his sister had mellowed to the thought of merging spirits and mortals.

Could she be experiencing the loneliness he'd suffered before saving Dove? Was the Creator rewarding them for their season upon season of watching over the Nimiipuu?

The wind blew a cold breeze under his hair, and he stared up at the brightening moon. He shook his grand antlers and stomped his feet. Becoming mortal again did not appeal to him. He enjoyed his freedom and superiority being a spirit and continuing his vigil over the generations of Nimiipuu.

The vision of Dove, holding his hand and smiling when he said he would travel with them to Imnaha stalled his hooves in the decaying forest floor. His chest warmed. Now he knew and understood the strange mix of emotions Himiin faced.

Wewukiye raised his face to the sky and stared at the brightest star.

"Brother, how did you know when it was time to let a mortal in?"

Pú-timt wax pí-lept
(14)

Dove woke to the rustling sounds of Crazy One rolling up her blankets and tulle mat.

"Are you sleeping well? Will not my uncle be coming?" Crazy One stacked her bedding by the door and stirred the coals in the fire.

Dove slowly stood. The larger the baby grew the more her back ached each morning. She rolled up her blankets and mat, adding them to the pile by the door.

"Why do you call Wewukiye your uncle?" She took the dried *kouse* bread from the older woman and sat down to eat it by the crackling fire. The heat warmed her front. A spiral of smoke rose into the air, disappearing out the smoke hole at the top of their dwelling.

"Is he not my uncle?" The woman bit into her bread and chewed. Her eyes sparkled like stars in a black sky.

"He cannot be your uncle. You are older."

"Why is he not my uncle? Was not my father his brother?"

The woman stated her questions with such conviction Dove wanted to believe her, but someone of Wewukiye's age would be considered a brother or cousin.

"Then Wewukiye's brother had to be many seasons older to be your father. He would have been near death when Wewukiye was born. Which means your father's parents would have been dead or close to leaving this earth. How could either have brought

Wewukiye to this earth? It does not make sense." She chewed on the bread and thought about their vast ages.

The woman must either be fooling with her or she really did believe Wewukiye was her uncle. Was he really a relative, or had he come across the woman in the forest, and seeing her strange behavior, talked her into believing he was a relative?

This thought evoked fear and distrust. The food in her mouth stuck in her throat when she tried to swallow. Wewukiye had banished all her fear and distrust of him from nearly the moment they met. How was it his touch and gentle eyes made her believe he would bring her no harm? And his hand soothing her sickness...Did he hold powers?

The hoof beats of the Sun Herald's horse vibrated the ground and drummed in her head.

"Rise up! There is work to do. We leave the lake soon!" His shouts reverberated through the hide covering.

Dove listened to the movement outside their safe home. There would be much work today. Their belongings would be packed on horses and their dwelling taken down. They would leave for the Imnaha the moment their belongings sat atop the horses.

She shoved the remainder of the bread in her mouth, stood, and dipped a handful of water from the pouch hanging on the side of the tipi. The coolness washed down the last crumbs stuck in her throat.

Within minutes, she and Crazy One had all their belongings bundled into baskets, ready for the journey. Dove carried the first basket out of the dwelling. She placed it on the ground a few steps from the door. Straightening, her gaze fell upon Wewukiye walking through the village, leading four horses.

He smiled and her earlier thoughts disappeared. He had yet to break a promise.

Her gaze traveled beyond him to the people busy loading belongings on horses or beginning the task of taking down their homes. Many stopped to watch him walk by, his head held high, his stride long and confident.

She wanted to bask in his gaze and touch him, but to do so with the others watching would start false beliefs among them. She nodded to Wewukiye and ducked back into the dwelling. Her breathing accelerated replaying the way he moved through the village. Thumping in her ears mimicked the thud of her heart.

"When will my uncle arrive?" Crazy One's eyes shimmered with mirth.

Dove covered her burning cheeks with her hands. The old woman could see how the man flustered her mind and heated her body. To travel with him and not show her true feelings for Wewukiye would prove harder than when she stood up to the elders and told them of Evil Eyes attack.

Crazy One dragged a basket out the door. Dove shook off the new emotions tangling in her body and carried another basket outside.

"Will four horses be enough?" Wewukiye asked Crazy One. He took the basket from Dove. His hands remained over hers a moment. Their gazes locked.

Good morning. You slept well, for the dark circles no longer shadow your eyes. We must remain aloof while others look on. His words floated in her head, and his lips did not move.

He gently tugged the basket from her hands and turned to the horses. She stared at his back. She heard his voice, but his lips did not move. How could that be?

Crazy One grabbed her elbow, directing her back into the dwelling. Dove shook her head and rubbed her hands over her eyes. She had heard his deep lulling voice as clear as if he talked to her. Had she missed his lips moving because she stared into his eyes?

"Do you want to cause a spectacle? Did he not talk to you without talking?" Crazy One pinched her.

"Ouch!" Dove rubbed the pained spot. "Why did you do that?"

"Why did you not hear me? Do I have to remind you to speak only in your head to my uncle?" The woman thrust the bedding into her arms.

"How is it I can hear him in my head? Can he hear me, too?" Dove stepped to the door and stopped. She stared at the woman. Her heart raced with fear and exhilaration. "I don't understand what is happening."

"Do you not want to speak with my uncle? Is the village not watching?" Crazy One shoved another basket toward the entrance. "Can you not forget your fears?" She bumped Dove's legs with the basket, forcing her out into the gray cold morning.

Wewukiye grasped the bedding, staring deep into her eyes. *Do not be afraid. This is the way we must talk when others are watching.*

Dove released the bedding but held his gaze. *Can we only speak this way while staring at one another?*

No. I wanted to make sure you knew it was me. Wewukiye walked to the horse.

How is it we can talk this way? She glanced at the nearest people to see if they heard the conversation. They all continued their work unknowing of their discussion. Her belly quivered.

I will explain it all later. Wewukiye took the basket from Crazy One.

Dove walked to the opening of the tipi and pulled the sticks out that held the hide together. She stood on her toes and still could not reach the farthest ones.

"Let me help." Wewukiye stood so close his breath warmed the back of her neck.

She stepped away, and he removed all but the last four sticks. Even his height could not reach them. He knelt.

"Sit upon my shoulders."

She stared at him. The thought of sitting so intimately on his shoulders stirred like a covey of quail in her belly.

"It will be the quickest way to finish the task."

She stepped behind him and swung one leg over his shoulder. His large hand wrapped around her thigh. Heat rose from where his hand lay to the part of her body Evil Eyes defiled. Before she could extract her leg, Wewukiye stood. She swung her other leg over his other shoulder and clung to his head with her hands.

She leaned, her small bulge resting against the back of his head as her trembling fingers drew the last sticks from the lapped hides.

"I have finished." Her voice croaked like an old woman's. Her body pulsed where it touched his wide shoulders and strong neck.

He knelt and slowly released her legs. She hopped back as though a snake coiled on his sunshine hair.

Never fear me. I will always protect you. His words floated through her head like an inviting chant. Dove watched him as he folded the flaps back. How did they speak to one another without moving their mouths? Uneasiness at her acceptance of the fact weakened her legs.

She dropped to her knees at the edge of the structure and tugged on the stick holding the hide to the ground. Work would help her put things right. The stick clung to the earth. She wiggled and freed the wood as Crazy One knelt at the stake on the other side of the entrance. They met at the back of the tipi and piled their sticks together.

In unison, Crazy One and Dove grasped edges of the opening and began folding them back until they met again at the back of the structure. Wewukiye stepped between them and pulled the hide down the frame, folding until it formed a large bundle at his feet.

He picked up the bundle and carried it to the horses as though it weighed no more than a bundle of firewood. Dove watched his efficient movements.

"Does my uncle not walk strong?" Crazy One winked.

Dove huffed and set to work taking the poles down one-by-one as Crazy One walked around the edge of the structure unwinding the leather string anchoring each pole to the next at the top.

Dove placed the last poles in the indention of their lodge, and glanced around. Some families had left and others had their animals loaded and ready to start for the *Anihm*, winter, camp. She darted a glance at her father's lodge. Only the poles remained in the indention. Their belongings, people, and horses were gone.

A pang of regret sliced her heart. Since living with Crazy One not a single member of her family had tried to talk with her or even smile at her. Their leaving without making sure she and Crazy One would soon follow should not have ached. But it did.

Crazy One put an arm around her shoulder. "Are we family now?" She nodded and grinned her toothless grin.

A large warm hand squeezed her shoulder.

"We will take care of you and the baby." Wewukiye's gaze searched her face. "We are all you need."

He stepped away when she wanted to ask if that meant he would stay with her even after the baby arrived.

Wewukiye held a horse by the mane and motioned to Crazy One. The woman walked to his side, and he set her atop the horse with little effort. He moved to another horse and held out his hand.

Dove joined him. His gaze warmed and filled her with good thoughts. She took his hand. He squeezed her fingers and drew her next to the animal. Sensations tingled up her arm and landed in a warm radiance around her heart.

"If you become tired or uncomfortable tell me. We do not have to remain with the rest. I can get you to the *Anihm* camp."

She nodded.

His strong hands settled on her sides, and he placed her on the horse lightly like drifting snowflakes. Gentle hands remained as his gaze lingered, dipping from her eyes to her lips and back to her eyes. His long perusal filled her with elation and thoughts of touching her lips to his.

"Do you feel the fingers of cold?" Crazy One asked, breaking the spell.

"Yes." Wewukiye stepped away from Dove. Her nearness made him lose sense of time and place. Luckily, only a few Nimiipuu remained, and they hurried to catch up with the band.

He took his time digging in the pack he'd prepared. He pulled out a white wolf fur—one his brother wore as the spirit of the mountain—and wrapped it around Dove. The cold *Anihm* winds rolled down off the mountainside.

"This is beautiful." Dove smoothed a hand over the white fur.

He nodded and caught Crazy One's wink. His niece had given him the wrap worn by her mother.

He mounted the horse. Something he had not done other than in another's body since the Creator made him a spirit. Elation exploded in his chest sitting atop the animal's back. He urged the horse forward with a squeeze of his legs and relished the art of riding once again.

Dove maneuvered her horse in behind him. Crazy one, leading the pack horse, came behind her. All husbands and wives traveled this way. He shook his head. It could not be. He was a spirit and she a mortal. His thoughts should not shift from his duty—Keep Dove safe and help the child enter the world so Dove could prove the White man's disloyalty.

They traveled over small rolling hills and valleys covered with yellow grass waiting for the snow to blanket it until the warm winds and sun of *El-weht*. Topping the small hills, the other members of the band could be seen gradually bunching up.

Dove rode up alongside him. "Is it safe for us to remain this distance?"

He did not detect fear in her voice. Did she finally trust him?

"There are few White men in this area. And other tribes are also moving to their *Anihm* homes. We are safe and do not have to fear others watching and disapproving." Like now with her riding by his side rather than behind him. He preferred her at his side where they could speak to one another.

She nodded and smiled. "It is a freedom I cherish these days." She pulled the wrap closer around her shoulders.

"Do you wish to stop and rest?" If she caught cold or did something to harm the baby he would forever believe it his fault.

"I am fine. Do not worry over me. I will tell you if things are not right." She smiled. Her eyes glowed with health and determination.

"You are now the strong woman who will defeat the *so-yá-po*." His words faded her smile and eyes.

"Do you really think this baby"—her hand

massaged her belly—"will save my people?"

"I cannot tell beyond your life, but for what is to come through the next seasons, yes." He touched her cheek with the back of his hand. "It is why I was sent to save you."

Her eyes closed, and she leaned into his touch. Her cold cheek skipped happiness to his heart like a rock skimming across the water.

"I am glad you did. I see now that it would be an injustice to have allowed Evil Eyes to weaken me." She opened her eyes and gazed into his. "It is your strength that I cling to and hope to use to one day stand on my own."

She sighed deep and long. "I only wish when I do, you do not leave."

The whispered words struck his heart like a thousand arrows. He had to tell her he was a spirit soon, before she fastened the rest of her life to him.

As if conjured up with that thought Sa-qan screeched above them. His sister would not understand the need to show this woman his true self.

"Do I not see my aunt?" Crazy One said and stared into the gray clouds building into a dark mass.

Snow would soon fall. Wewukiye scanned the area for a place to settle for the night. Sa-qan circled a clump of trees ahead. *Thank you, sister.*

"We will spend the night over there." He pointed to the trees. "It feels like snow will cover us by morning."

Dove nodded and ducked her face into the fur of her wrap. The air blew cold, as a sprit he did not need the extra layers. The elements did not bother him. He, after all, lived in a lake when not roaming the Nimiipuu territory.

What would Dove think if she knew he was the monster of the lake all the grandparents warned the

Nimiipuu children to be wary of if they were not good? He chuckled.

The story started soon after the Creator made him a spirit of the lake to keep watch over the Nimiipuu and their supply of fish. With his spirit form coming from his name, bull elk, he did not think before emerging from the lake in his elk form. He scared the children playing at the lake's edge. They told the elders who used the children's fear to keep the children well-behaved.

They entered the cover of the trees. Yellow and orange leaves fluttered to the ground, building a cushioned floor. Dead limbs scattered around the area for easy firewood.

He stopped and dismounted. Dove's horse halted beside him. Wewukiye wrapped his hands around her waist and eased her to stand before him.

She wobbled a bit when he loosened his grip. "Was the ride today too much?"

"No. I have not ridden a horse since..." Her cheeks darkened. "The attack." She grasped his hands, pulling them away from her body.

He clutched her hands, holding her in front of him. The instinct to protect her overwhelmed him. "Promise, if you do feel things are not right you will tell me."

She nodded and he drew her against his body, wrapping his arms around her, and breathing in her essence. Her body relaxed, and her arms wrapped around him.

Her small hands pressing against his back ignited urges dormant for seasons upon seasons. Fire shot through his limbs and jolted his need to mate. The idea nearly sprang his arms wide open. It took all his concentration not to shove her from his hold.

He eased his arms away from her and turned to help Crazy One from her horse. The old woman's eyes sparkled. *Is she not the one for you?*

Her words rushed through his head, and he shot her a hard glare. *I cannot have these thoughts. She is mortal.*

Am I not mortal? Was not your brother mortal? She held out her arms, and he placed her on the ground.

Could he love Dove and the two of them remain in their own worlds? He watched her moving about the trees gathering sticks. Her body though covered in long moccasins, a long heavy blanket dress, colorful wool shawl, and the white fur still excited his senses. The image of her naked body, etched in his mind from saving her, further ignited him. Her cleverness and strength also fueled the urge to be more than her guardian. He wished her to be his. Forever.

Pú-timt wax pá-xat
(15)

Dove watched Crazy One start the fire while Wewukiye went in search of a small animal for their meal. He insisted she should eat more than kouse bread and dried salmon and berries. Crazy One waved him off and smiled at her.

He had left before she could ask him how it was she heard his voice in her head and he heard her thoughts. During their ride she had thought hard and could not determine if she had dreamed the exchange or if living with Crazy One had made her a little bit muddled herself.

"Will my uncle bring nourishment?" The old woman shook her head. "Is it not true the mate of a woman with child will not fare well when hunting?" She waved a chunk of bread at Dove. "Do you need to eat?"

Dove took the bread, easing the gnawing in her stomach. "What do you mean? Wewukiye is not my mate. He will be fine hunting." The thought of being his mate set well in her mind. But they were not husband and wife. Nor could they be until the council witnessed the proof of Evil Eyes's deceit. She stared forlornly into the fire. Nothing Wewukiye did indicated he planned to stay around after the birth.

Crazy One chanted under her breath and spun a piece of bread around and around in her hands. She could question Crazy One about the voices, but her pattern of speech would make it hard to understand the truth.

Dove chewed her bread, pulled the wolf fur

tighter around her shoulders, and dreaded the cold of the encroaching night.

****

Wewukiye shifted into his elk form and loped away from camp to speak with Sa-qan. He preferred man form for holding Dove and his elk form for moving about and carrying out his duties on the mountain.

He stopped beside a large boulder and watched the spiral of smoke from their camp seep from the grove of trees below. Dove would question him this night about the voices. Her sharpness and inquisitive nature would not let her wonderings go any longer.

A waft of air ruffled his hair and the click of nails on stone directed his attention to the boulder. Sa-qan balanced on the rock and carefully tucked her wings against her side.

"Why do you camp so far from the others?" She peered with such intensity, he shuffled his hooves.

"We do not travel as fast, and I prefer keeping my distance from the band. They distrust me. I do not wish to be watched."

She nodded and the breath he held slithered out between his teeth.

"It is wise to not raise their suspicions. Should they find out the truth, you will no longer be able to remain and help the woman."

The thought of abandoning Dove before the baby arrived hit him like the clash of antlers during rut. From his antlers downward, his whole body jarred.

He glanced at the spiral of smoke at their camp and then at his sister. "I have conversed with Dove without words."

Sa-qan stomped across the boulder, putting her beak to his nose. "That is not wise. To put thoughts into others is only for the survival of the Nimiipuu."

"I did not put thoughts. We spoke."

Her small eyes widened to twice their size. "She answered your thoughts with her own?"

Wewukiye nodded. Mortals took direction this way, but never had one communicated back. From their first meeting, her body and mind connected with him, making him wonder at her powers.

"Then she holds much power. Now I see why you have been compelled to help her. You have experienced her power." Sa-qan walked to the peak of the boulder and faced him. "Will you tell her you are a spirit?"

"I will have to. She has mentioned my staying with her after the child is born. I cannot walk away without her knowing why I must." He knew the next months would bring them even closer together, and he already did not want to leave her or the child, yet to come to this earth.

Sa-qan nodded. "With her power, she will understand."

Wewukiye spotted a dark shape crossing a knoll they'd traveled earlier. "Who is that? We are the last of the band. I made certain."

"It is Evil Eyes. I spotted him before the sun rested."

Hatred burned in his chest. Fear for Dove should the man stumble upon them shook his clenched muscles. "I must return to Dove and Crazy One. If he stops for the night let me know. Otherwise, I will keep a vigilant eye."

Sa-qan tipped her head and leapt into the dark night.

With a last glower at the White man, he ran through the dead matted grass toward the grove of trees. This man would not harm Dove again.

****

Dove ate the handful of dried salmon and berries Crazy One offered. How would Wewukiye kill an animal? She never saw him with a weapon or a

124

pouch to carry items to make a snare.

Her ears picked up the faint sound of running hooves. "Crazy One, someone on horseback approaches." Fear slithered through her body. Where was Wewukiye?

The old woman smiled and continued spreading her blankets on the ground near the fire. A small pile of wood to replenish the flames during the night sat at the end of her blanket.

"We should hide." Her gaze darted through the trees, searching for a log or boulder to hide behind until they knew who approached.

A figure stepped from behind a tree and she shrieked.

Wewukiye ran forward, dropping to his knees beside her. "Are you well? What has frightened you?"

She stared at his familiar, concerned face and sunshine hair. She swiped her hand down his golden locks, relief warming the icy fear that gripped her moments before. Dove slapped a hand against his hard chest.

"You scared me! I heard running hooves. I searched the darkness of the trees, and you stepped out scaring me." She glanced over his shoulder. "Did you hear the horse?"

His face paled, and he peered over her head. "I did not hear a horse."

She spun toward the direction he returned. The same direction she heard the sound. "How could you not when you came from the same area of the running animal?"

"Are you sure you heard a running horse? Perhaps it was some other animal. I did chase up an elk." His eyes gleamed willing her to believe his story.

She sighed. If he did not hear a horse, maybe she had heard something else and in her nervous state believed it to be a horse. She was hearing things again, only this time it was not his voice.

"Tell me how I heard your voice in my head this morning."

He stood, spreading blankets next to each other on the ground by the fire, opposite Crazy One's bedding.

He did not speak or glance her way. Did not ask if she wished to lie beside him. Though her heart thrummed at the prospect of spending the night beside him.

The cry of an eagle sliced the air. Wewukiye peered into the sky and smiled.

He held out a hand, helping her rise to her feet. They walked to the blankets, and with care, he helped her lie down. He reclined beside her, rolling her to her side and cupping his hard, warm body behind her. With him against her back and the fire tended by Crazy One at her front, she would remain warm all night.

"We can speak with thoughts because you hold great power." The whispered words warmed her neck or she would have believed they were in her head again. Her body nestled snug and warm against him while her mind raced. Powers? What powers?

"I do not understand." She tried to turn in his arms, to search his eyes for the truth.

"Shh..." He held her firmly against him with an arm protecting the bump in her belly. His lips grazed her neck.

Sparks erupted at the spot and journeyed down her neck and body, scorching her skin and scrambling her mind.

"I felt the essence of your powers the night I carried you from the lake. Your strength and the passion of your words, proved you were put upon this earth for the people. The Creator sent me to bring you back to your people to help them."

She again tried to turn, but he held her back tight against his chest. She wished to gaze into his eyes and seek if he spoke the truth. The Creator sent him? "How could the Creator send you?"

"My power is helping the Lake Nimiipuu. The Creator gave me that power."

Her heart raced. Images flashed through her head. Evil Eyes threats toward other maidens and her people, the freedom that embraced her when the water took her, the knowledge Wewukiye would not harm her, the satisfaction that burned inside of her standing up to Thunder Traveling to Distant Mountains and the council. Did she truly have power or did Wewukiye fill her head with this notion?

She struggled harder, and he released his hold. Dove spun to her other side and stared into his eyes. "Why would I have power now and not have known before?"

"Sometimes it takes being near another who has power to help nurture what you have." He touched her cheek with the tips of his fingers.

His light touch whispered elation through her.

"I have heard a woman with child has powers. Could this power we sense only be while the baby is within me?" She stared into his eyes watching, hoping his answer did not disappoint.

"Your power has been with you." He leaned in, closing his eyes, and placed his cheek against hers.

Her body trembled and warmed at the contact. Was this their powers connecting?

"How do you know I have always had power? How is it you can tell my powers? What are they?"

He clasped her head in his arms, kissed the top of her head, and chuckled. "I told my sister you would be full of questions."

The steady beat of his heart under her ear, lulled her. "You would not be so easy to trade thoughts with if your powers were weak or newly acquired. I could tell of your power by the heat and light when our bodies touch. What your powers are? That I do not know. We know our bodies ignite, we can share thoughts, and you feel the evil in others." He sighed and slid her up his body so their faces met. His eyes gazed into hers. "We shall wait and see what kinds of powers you possess."

He kissed her forehead. Their bodies trembled in harmony. From her toes to her forehead where his lips rested, vibrations rippled through her body, fueling her with warmth and unexplainable yearnings. Her hands roamed across his hard, wide chest and upward to loop around his neck. The movement pressed her tender breasts into his solid form.

He quivered, and air rushed from between his tightly clenched lips.

"I wish to feel your soft skin against mine, but we cannot act upon these thoughts. Only during our travels when we are not with the band can we sleep and touch as this." He cupped her face in his hands. The heat in his eyes made her blink. The color darkened to a deep blue edged with red.

She had witnessed his eyes changing color before and now knowing the powers he held she understood more of his unusual behaviors.

This closeness did not bring fears, only yearnings she did not understand. "Is the heat and unrest in my body from our powers?"

Wewukiye's gaze dropped to her lips. "No. It is the power of your body over mine." He brushed his lips across hers, gently, arousing her body even more.

Her arms tightened around his neck, and he deepened the kiss, covering her lips with his, and spinning her thoughts to warm carefree days. Three blonde haired children romped and played in a large green valley dotted with the purple *kouse* flower.

Her mind scrambled to make sense of the images. An elk rose out of the lake. She shuddered and her body warmed, ignited, and her thoughts embraced the image of the man wrapped around her body and her heart.

He slowly retreated from their kiss. "We belong together. I will find a way." He tucked her head against his shoulder.

The determination in his words and the safety of his arms gave her no doubt he would find a way.

A shiver of dread skittered across her skin, shattering her happiness. Wewukiye talked of her powers, yet helplessness overwhelmed her thinking of the life she spent with her family, the attack, and the attitude of the elders. If Wewukiye helped her prove Evil Eyes's deceit and remained with her, all the past sorrows in her life would be forgotten.

She snuggled into his arms chasing away the cold reality that nagged her heart. Judging from her past, she could not count on a happy future.

Pú-timt wax `oylá-qc
(16)

Wewukiye spent the night holding Dove and marveling in her easy acceptance of her power. On the journey to Imnaha he would see what other powers she held. The faint rustling of creatures and the sky beginning to glow with a new day meant they should rise and keep moving.

He had no doubt Evil Eyes would find them this day. Was he after Dove or trying to catch the whole band? And if so, why? With the man following the Nimiipuu trail to the *Anhim* camp, he would come upon them first. He planned to learn what Evil Eyes wanted and keep Dove safe.

Crazy One tossed a stick on the fire, sending small red embers skyward. "Does evil follow us? Should you not stop him before he finds us?"

Crazy One being the offspring of a spirit turned mortal, Wewukiye had given up wondering how she knew so much. "Yes." He reluctantly drew his arms from around Dove, rousing her.

"Is it time to leave?" She dug her palms into her eyes and sat up.

"Yes." He covered the fire with dirt, leaving traces for the man following them to stop and investigate.

Dove stood and rolled up their bed. Wewukiye watched her graceful motions, remembering the perfect fit of his arms around her soft body. If only he could hold her every night. His world would not be so lonely.

Crazy One slapped his hand. "Do we not need to

hurry?"

He tossed all thoughts other than stopping Evil Eyes from his mind. Their bedding secured on the horses, he helped Crazy One mount. Dove stood by her horse waiting, a brightness that rival the sun shone in her eyes.

He wrapped his hands around her waist and set her on the animal. "Follow Crazy One. I will catch up."

"I do not understand. Why are you staying behind?" Her hands gripped his arms, keeping his hold on her.

"Someone follows us. I plan to see who it is and join you."

Her body shuddered. She closed her eyes, and a frown marred her pretty face. "It is Evil Eyes. I feel his nearness." She opened her eyes and searched his face.

"Yes, it is Evil Eyes."

The fear and appeal in her eyes brought out his protective instincts.

"I will make sure he cannot catch us." He had a plan and hoped it would work.

"Be careful. I need you." She wrapped an arm around her middle. "We need you."

"I will be safe. Go. It is easier to deal with him if you are not here." He swatted her horse on the rump. The animal trotted after Crazy One who had already urged her horse into a walk.

He didn't need a horse to catch up with the women, but Dove would question his quick appearance if he pretended to catch up on foot. He rode his horse the same direction as the women before veering into a thick stand of trees. The horse would remain and not make a sound. He had bartered well, asking the warrior for a well-trained war pony.

Wewukiye made his way back toward the empty

camp. He transformed into his elk form and watched the opening.

The hair on his neck rose at the sight of Evil Eyes riding into the camp so close behind their departure.

The man scanned the surrounding area and dismounted, clutching his rifle in one hand. He knelt by the fire, holding a hand over the dirt and coals.

Evil Eyes stood. He bent, studying the tracks left by the women and the horses.

Wewukiye crashed out of the trees, straight for Evil Eyes's horse. The animal snorted and sprang forward, running through the grove. A blast rang out and a buzz whisked past his antlers. Wewukiye continued the chase making sure the animal ran well on its way toward home.

He pivoted and returned to Evil Eyes. Left on foot, it would be highly unlikely Evil Eyes would continue after the Nimiipuu.

Are you well? Dove's voice filled his head, her fear palpable. She'd heard the gunshot.

I am fine. Continue. I will catch up.

He snuck back to his horse, making certain Evil Eyes did not find the animal, and changed into man form. Creeping through the trees and leafless underbrush, he neared the campsite.

Evil Eyes cradled the rifle in his arms, staring in the direction his horse had run. Did he expect the animal to return? Wewukiye did not fear being shot. He could heal a wound, but he wanted to speak to the man.

He walked out into the open. Evil Eyes whipped around, his gun pointed at Wewukiye. His eyes widened as his gaze traveled from Wewukiye's hair to his moccasins.

"Who are you?" His harsh tone grated in Wewukiye's ears.

"I am Wewukiye."

The gun had dipped down, but he jerked it up. "You don't look like an Injun. You tryin' to fool me into shootin' you?"

"Why would I do that? I do not trick people." He walked closer to see the man's reactions.

Evil Eyes wiped a hand over his face and stared at him with his two colored eyes. "I ain't fallin' for no tricks by that Injun-lovin' agent."

Wewukiye wondered about the man's words. He would have to see if Dove knew what Evil Eyes meant.

"Why are you following the Nimiipuu?"

"I ain't tellin' you." He shoved the end of the gun at Wewukiye as if to poke him.

Wewukiye grabbed the long end of the weapon and yanked it out of the man's hands. Even in man form his physical strength exceeded that of a mortal. He tossed the rifle over the trees. The man's eyes widened.

"Go home. If I catch you following the Nimiipuu again, I will not be so tolerant." Wewukiye turned his back to the man proving he did not deem him a threat.

"You stinkin' sonabitch!" The man rammed into his back with his head.

Wewukiye spun, grabbed the man's head in an arm lock, and twisted Evil Eyes's arm behind his back. "You do not listen."

The man cried out in pain, but he did not care. The man had inflicted pain on a woman. *His woman.*

Sa-qan screeched. Wewukiye glanced in the sky at Sa-qan floating overhead. *Brother, do not harm him. It is not the way of the Creator.*

Every muscle screamed to inflict pain upon the *so-yá-po* as he did to others. His head warred to do the right thing.

Let the man go and hurry to Dove.

He shoved the man face first to the ground and

ran to his horse, mounted, and raced toward Dove. Anger bubbled and simmered in his chest. He had the chance to make sure this White man never harmed Dove again and had let him live.

You are to help prove his evil to the Nimiipuu not avenge Dove. His mind and emotions swirled like a whirlpool of water. He could not seek revenge. Not as a spirit. He must guide the mortals of the Lake Nimiipuu, not fight their battles. This knowledge did little to appease the anger within.

The small procession of Dove and Crazy One came into view. Wewukiye slowed his heart and shoved his rage out of his mind. He would not scare Dove by riding up in a ball of anger.

He reined in his horse and fell in beside Dove.

Her gaze covered him from head to toe. "All is well?"

"I do not believe we will be followed anymore." The man held a huge grudge, but he also should have enough intelligence to head back to his home rather than continue following them on foot.

"I heard a gunshot." Again her gaze traveled the length of him.

"The bullet did not come near me. I took his gun away." He chuckled at the startled expression on Evil Eyes face watching his gun fly over the tree tops. Would the man hunt for his weapon before heading back? Most likely. It would be his protection and help him gather food.

"And you are not harmed?"

"No." Her concern warmed his chest.

Dove's heart unclenched. At the ringing of the gunshot, her heart had squeezed into a lump of cold ice. Fear Wewukiye had been hurt, or worse, killed, had forced her to send her concern to him. She smiled. Communicating through thoughts offered a wonderful way to always keep the other close.

"Will he return?" The quick change of

expressions on his face told her things did not go as he had wished.

"Not today, but I fear he will not give up his plans."

She sucked in air at the notion Evil Eyes had been so close. "W-was he after me?"

Wewukiye shook his head. "I do not think so. I tried to find out what he wanted. He did not believe I was Nimiipuu. He asked if I were a trap by the Indian agent." He stared at her. "Do you know why he would say that?"

"Agent William has been a friend and family of the Lake Nimiipuu through a marriage. He does not easily find favor with men like Evil Eyes."

Wewukiye stopped his horse. She stopped, too, waiting for him to maneuver his horse beside her.

"Have you told this agent about Evil Eyes?"

She shook her head. "I have not seen him since…" She could not say any more and did not believe she could tell the agent what had happened. Her anger had covered her modesty when she told Chief Joseph and Thunder Traveling to Distant Mountains. Now, she did not think she could repeat it to a White man even if he did care.

"Where do we find him?"

The excitement in Wewukiye's eyes gave her hope they may have found another to believe her attack. But it also sunk her stomach like a heavy rock.

"I do not know where he stays." She had witnessed the man several times over the years. He always visited Chief Joseph and his family. She glanced at Crazy One's back. "I am sure Crazy One will know."

Wewukiye nodded and rode his horse up beside the old woman. A shiver crept up Dove's back and hunched her shoulders. Could she tell another White man the vile things Evil Eyes did?

Pú-timt wax `uyné-pt
(17)

On the third day, Wewukiye led Crazy One and Dove toward the erected tipis circling the edge of the flat area along the shore of the river. The tall ridges on either side of the river held off the cold wind.

Men and women worked in the middle of the encampment setting up the large meeting lodge, while elders worked on the sweat lodge near the river's edge.

Many turned from their tasks to watch he and the women arrive.

"Is not that the space for my dwelling?" Crazy One pointed to a larger gap between two tipis.

The relief in Dove's eyes gave rise to how she would endure the trip back to the Wallowa country when she would be close to having the child. He had kept their pace slow, allowing her many opportunities to get off the horse. He enjoyed their nights. Dove slept well in his arms. They could no longer have that bit of comfort now that they joined the band.

Wewukiye grabbed a pole from the stack in the indention waiting for the tipi.

"You must not help us. It is woman's work." Dove took the pole from him. Her lips curved in a slight smile, and her eyes held his gaze.

"I wish to help." He wanted to make her life easier. Do all the things he knew he should not.

"Did I not ask you to tend the horses?" Crazy One waved her hand between their locked gazes.

Wewukiye shook his head, smiled at the two,

and led the horses away from the encampment.

He escorted the animals in the direction of many horses grazing in a canyon. On the trip, he had learned Crazy One owned a considerable amount of good horse flesh. In their communications he never asked her about her wealth, only her well-being. When he asked the boys to help him gather four of Crazy One's horses for the trip, they did not tell him the war pony they offered him had been sired from the line of his brother's prized horses. Now, he wished to ride the horse more often.

The trip also brought other information to light about Crazy One. He had believed the band humored the woman thinking her crazy, he now knew they called upon her for her visions bestowed upon her by her spirit father. Although Chief Joseph and his sons requested Dove not cause problems, they looked to Crazy One to help them reveal the truth about the attack.

His new understanding of the elders respect for Crazy One would help him with his promise to Dove. They would reveal Evil Eyes's deceptions. He released the horses and headed higher up the cliff side until he found a stand of leafless sumac. He could not shift into an elk until dark. How was he to keep himself busy? He did not hunt or need to repair weapons and could not help the women without raising suspicions.

He sat in the bushes and called to Sa-qan. They hadn't talked since she followed Evil Eyes. He stared down at the activity below. Preoccupation had kept him from realizing Crazy One's importance to the band. He now saw her dwelling sat in order of importance one above the *tiw`et* and one below the shaman. With only the most honored elders between she and the chief's family.

Wewukiye closed his eyes and visualized the summer village at the lake. His eyes sprang open at the crackle of twigs beside him.

Sa-qan stood on the ground next to him. "You called brother?"

"Dove views living with Crazy One as a punishment, but it is the council's way of protecting her." His chest swelled with pride.

"Yes. I have known that all along. Even though you placed her with Crazy One, they still could have restricted her to the old women's lodge." Sa-qan peered into his eyes. "Why is it you are just now seeing this?"

Pride gushed out his lips on a disgusted whoosh of air. "I do not know why it took me so long. I still feel my presence is needed for Dove and for the truth to come out." He was through worrying about bringing disgrace to Dove or himself. "Did Evil Eyes return to his home?"

Sa-qan nodded. "I followed him all the way back. He was not happy to find his horse standing inside the animal dwelling."

Wewukiye cringed. "He did not hurt the animal did he?"

"Only scorched the animal's ears with his harsh words."

Relief ebbed. Spooking the animal had provided the easiest way to put the man at a disadvantage, but he did not want the innocent animal to come to harm.

"Agent William. Do you know where to find him? Crazy One says he lives in several places." After learning of the agent's familial affiliation with the Nimiipuu, he had to find the man and have Dove tell him of her attack. To have the attack written in the White man's word would be good. Crazy One had spoke of Agent William with high regard. Insisting he was an advocate for the Nimiipuu. This knowledge encouraged Wewukiye the White man would listen to Dove and believe her.

"If he is in the area he would be at Fort Lapwai." Her eyes narrowed. "You do not plan to travel there do you?"

"I wish Dove's attack be noted by a *so-yá-po*. She says he is one with her people."

"This is foolhardy. You cannot travel all over and be seen by many." She walked away and back. "It is wrong you have shown yourself to the Lake Nimiipuu, to walk into the mission…" She shook her feathers and stared at him. "I do not understand this need to help one, when the whole tribe is at risk to the *so-yá-po* and his greed."

"Dove is the key to helping the Nimiipuu." His gut rippled with anxiety. "I would not have risked so much had I believed otherwise."

She shook her head. "I will see if I can find the agent. But I do not think it is wise to go to the mission."

Wewukiye watched his sister soar into the air. If only he had her ability to fly he could collect the answers they needed.

****

Dove pressed her hands into her lower back. The days on the horse, and now the rigors of erecting the tipi intensified her aches. She stared longingly at the sweat lodge. Did she dare ask to use the structure? She was certain most would believe she would desecrate the spiritual nuances by setting foot in the lodge.

"Is it not a long day?" Crazy One nodded toward the sweat lodge. "Should we not loosen tight muscles?"

"I would like that very much." She glanced around to be certain no one lingered close by. "Will I be allowed? It is not usual for a woman with child to use one."

"Is not the sweat lodge used to make one stronger in body and spirit?" The anger in the old

139

woman's words rang strong and clear. She straightened from dragging a basket into the dwelling. "Should the old man not be awakened?" She exited the tipi.

Dove stepped out to watch the old woman stalk across the ground between their lodge and the sweat lodge. She giggled at the woman's flailing arms and motions as Crazy One spoke to the old man who tended the sweat lodge.

The woman stormed back across the grounds. "Does he not see you carry the future of the Nimiipuu?" She stormed into the dwelling. She chanted and tossed herbs from her pouch onto the small fire they had started as soon as the tipi stood erect.

"It is all right. I do not need to use the sweat lodge." She touched the woman's arm, stopping her chant.

"Does he think your condition will weaken the warriors? Is he so blind to not see you are more powerful?" Crazy One spit into the fire and flames leapt to life.

"Do not harm him. He only knows what he knows. It has been passed down that women with child bring bad luck to their warriors." Her stomach clenched with confusion. Why would her not being able to use the sweat lodge make the woman so angry? In all her years she had not seen a woman with child enter the sweat lodge also used by the men. The thought of moist heat on her back brought a smile to her lips.

"I seek the women of this lodge." Wewukiye's strong voice rang from outside the dwelling. His presence offered the help she needed.

Dove ducked out the opening and stared up into his wonderful face. The concern etched in his brow and confusion flickering in his eyes led her to wonder if he knew of Crazy One's anger.

"What happened? My ears burn from the old woman's chants." Wewukiye lowered his voice and motioned to a log he must have brought for sitting in front of the dwelling.

"She went to the old man of the sweat lodge to see about the two of us using it. He would not allow a woman of my condition to use the lodge." She glanced at the tipi and the low growl of Crazy One's voice. "She did not like his answer. I fear for him. I have never seen her so angry."

Wewukiye peered at the lodge and stood. "I will speak with her alone."

She nodded and stared at the opening Wewukiye disappeared through.

Wewukiye held out his hands as Crazy One focused her red glare on him. She had also inherited the changing colors of their eyes. "You know all through the ages it is believed to allow a woman with child into the men's sweat lodge will weaken the warrior's power."

"Does she not carry the future of our people?" Crazy One shoved gnarled fists on her hips.

"I can make a sweat lodge for the two of you to use. Would that make you happy? You can be the tender of the lodge and allow who you wish inside. I'm sure the elders would not interfere."

Anger wafted from her like tendrils of smoke from a fire. "Are you not a good uncle?" She patted his arm. "Do you not make Dove's life happy?"

He hoped he made her life happy. The young woman deserved much happiness. She had so little to this point in her life.

"I will speak with the old man of the lodge and Thunder Traveling to Distant Mountains." He ducked out of the tipi.

Dove walked quickly up to him. "Is she better?"

He nodded. "I have appeased her and will seek permission to set up another sweat lodge for the two

141

of you."

"Do you think they will allow this? Do you know how to build one?"

He noted the skepticism and awe in her voice.

"I will soon find out." He frowned at the growing clouds and cool air. "Go back in to wait."

Wewukiye watched her enter the dwelling and set off in search of the old man of the sweat lodge. He barely remembered using a sweat lodge as a youth before becoming a spirit. He would need the man's skills to learn how to build one. Crazy One's spiritual powers would be enough to make the place sacred.

****

Wewukiye spent the remainder of the day learning how to construct a sweat lodge. The entrance must point to the rising sun, the fire pit the right depth to hold coals and warm rocks. He found a spot beside the river he wished to use and strode to the dwelling of Thunder Traveling to Distant Mountains. The warrior's young wife, Springtime, stared a moment before casting her gaze downward as Wewukiye entered the tipi.

"I seek your permission to build a sweat lodge for Crazy One and Dove. The old man of the sweat lodge made an enemy of Crazy One." He sat crossed-legged on the opposite side of the fire pit from Thunder Traveling to Distant Mountains.

"Women with child do not use the sweat lodge." Thunder Traveling to Distant Mountains's gaze drifted to his wife. A slight smile tipped the corners of his mouth.

Wewukiye peered closer at the woman and realized she, too, was with child.

"Crazy One believes it would be good for Dove." He spread his hands open in appeal. "My aunt has a forceful presence that is hard to disobey."

Thunder Traveling to Distant Mountains

nodded his head. "This is true. She is much like her mother, tenacious as a badger, and filled with the essence of her father." His eyes narrowed, scanning Wewukiye's face. "My father sees much in you that matches her father."

Wewukiye held his body from squirming under the man's scrutiny. There would come a day when they would know the truth. To remain a mystery would be best until then.

"I am of her father's people. Do you give your permission for me to build another sweat lodge? All women who wish to use it are welcome." He didn't glance at Springtime but glimpsed her move closer to her husband.

Thunder Traveling to Distant Mountains stood. "Show me where you wish to build the women's sweat lodge."

Wewukiye stood also. Their gazes met at the same level. He moved to the opening, a scraping sound filled the silence when his shoulders pushed through the opening. The sound echoed as Thunder Traveling to Distant Mountains exited.

They strode side-by-side to the edge of the river. Wewukiye motioned to the marks he gouged in the dirt with a stick.

"The door will face the water and the rising sun." He motioned to the peaceful view of the river rolling by.

Thunder Traveling to Distant Mountains nodded. "I will tell my father I have granted permission." He glanced over his shoulder at his dwelling. "When will it be finished?"

Wewukiye smiled. His wife would no doubt be second after Dove to use the sweat lodge. "I wish to have it finished by tomorrow night."

Thunder Traveling to Distant Mountains nodded. "Do you wish help?"

"No. I have talked with the old man of the sweat

lodge."

"As it should be." Thunder Traveling to Distant Mountains stared across the water.

Wewukiye watched the water ripple, sensing the man's need to say something else.

"You have grown close to Dove. And you believe she was attacked by our friend—"

"I do not believe, I know."

"How? Did you see?" Thunder Traveling to Distant Mountains held his eyes on the river.

"I did not see, but I believe it happened." No woman would bring shame to her family by trying to end her life if such an outrage had not happened. He would not tell this man of her disgrace. He shifted, watching the man next to him. "The man is not a friend of the Lake Nimiipuu. Be ever watchful of him."

"You are not of our band. How do I know you are not making trouble with the *so-yá-po* to gain our home?" Thunder Traveling to Distant Mountains continued to stare at the fast moving water.

"I call no band my home. I am Nimiipuu and will always place my people before my own life." The conviction in his words came from his heart and his duty as spirit of the lake.

"This I believe and because of these words, I will trust you know what you are doing. But should my people come to harm through your need for revenge, I will take you before the council." Thunder Traveling to Distant Mountains pivoted, drilling him with his dark brown gaze.

Pú-timt wax `oymátat
(18)

Dove pulled her shawl tighter around her body and watched the gray blanket of dusk slip up the canyon walls as the sun set. Wewukiye spent last night and all of today working on the sweat lodge.

She and Crazy One walked with him to see the finished sweat lodge. The cold night air bit at her cheeks, but the smile curving her lips warmed her inside as she witnessed the newly erected structure. The dwelling resembled the old man's sweat lodge exactly.

"This is a special place," she whispered and stared into Wewukiye's eyes. The color deepened taking her breath away and reflecting his pride in his work.

Crazy One strolled around, smoothing her hands all over the outside and chanting through the inside.

Dove stood to the side, watching the woman chant and the man scoop water from the river in an animal skin pouch.

"This should be enough water." Wewukiye placed the large pouch beside the opening. "I've stacked wood inside to last several uses."

"Thank you for building this wonderful sweat lodge and stocking it with wood, stones, and water." In the growing darkness Dove moved closer. She missed being held in his arms and had trouble sleeping the night before knowing he slept alone somewhere beyond the village. Seeing the beginnings of the sweat lodge when she awoke led her to believe he spent most of the night working on the structure. She stared into his glowing eyes. His easy smile, solid stance, and twinkling eyes did not give the appearance of one who worked all night and day.

"Anything you wish, I will see it comes true."

His low husky voice sent shimmers of excitement skittering across her skin.

She took one more step closer and whispered. "I wish I could sleep in your arms."

He glanced around then took a step, their bodies barely touching. "Think of me while in the sweat lodge. I thought of you with each stick I shaped and each rock I placed. My spirit lives within the walls and will hold and keep you safe."

"Is it not time for you to leave?"

Crazy One's voice and gentle pull on Dove's arm drew her gaze from Wewukiye and her body from the magical hold he held on her.

Wewukiye captured her hand. *Think of me.*

His words clung to her mind. She savored them like being embraced in his arms. Crazy One led her to the opening.

"Is it not best to take off your clothes?" The old woman undressed and ducked into the structure.

Dove quickly shed her moccasins, wool shawl, and blanket dress. She quickly stepped inside the warm dark lodge. Heat from the blazing fire met her as solid as a wall of thick hides, taking her breath away. Crazy One's skinny fingers gripped Dove's arm, directing her to a rock with an indention perfectly shaped for her bottom.

Crazy One chanted and the flames grew lower with each stone she placed in the middle of the fire.

Dove studied the lowering flames and glowing rocks. Darkness descended like the gradual lowering of sleepy eyelids. The heat penetrated her body warming the aches and easing her tight muscles. The low flicker of red images waving on the squat wall drew her gaze to the reflections. Did she see a likeness to Wewukiye's warm smile in the visions?

Crazy One's chants lowered in pitch. Steam hissed and filled their enclosure as she slowly dripped water onto the rocks.

Dove closed her eyes, breathed in the moist warm air, and wrapped her arms around the leather belt securely holding the life growing in her.

A small flutter in her belly, under her arms, shot her eyes open. Her mind focused on the amazing ripple. The life inside her stirred again. Her heart melted to the sensation. There was one person she wished to share this with. *Wewukiye.*

Warmth wrapped around her as snug and safe as his arms. A whisper of heat, the slight stirring along her skin, the gentle weight of his hand when he soothed her belly replaced her hand cradling her swollen belly. She sucked in air, experiencing his presence as fully as if he held her.

Her head lolled back against the hardness of his chest, cradling her and bathing her neck in his hot, moist, enticing breath. Tremors of excitement tickled and cooled her skin. The weight and warmth of his hands sliding down her moisture slickened arms released a spark of fire in her center. Heat and pressure, so like his hands, moved across every inch of her skin, dallying here and there, rubbing out the aches of her back, and igniting her inner fire of desire.

His feather-like touch explored as cool puffs of air, sweet and intoxicating, covered her face and neck.

Her past experiences in a sweat bath never filled her body with desire or left her feeling sated and cared for.

Wewukiye enjoyed holding Dove in his spirit form of water. In the state of steam, he wrapped her with his love, dropping kisses upon her face and neck, easing away all her aches and marveling in the sensation of the life within her. Her firm, young body responded to his water form with equal acceptance.

When she said his name, he sensed her yearning to be with him. She now embraced the pleasure of the child growing in her. He could not have stayed away if the Creator himself had held him. This strong woman and her child meant everything to him. And he would do all he could to ensure their happiness.

She sighed and relaxed deeper into his body. His own urges had surfaced at his first touch of her skin. Now he wished only to please her.

He ran his palms over her buckskin belt, wishing he could touch her skin. Her hands covered his, holding them in place.

I wish this baby were ours.

His heart stuttered. She knew he was here. He glanced at the old woman's back. Did his niece also know of his presence? If so, she did not show it.

Do not go. Dove's hand pressed tighter over his.

He splayed his fingers, allowing hers to fall between, gathering her fingers inside his palm. He kissed her neck.

Never.

With their joined hands, he wrapped his arms around her under her breasts, reveling in their gentle weight upon his arm. Dove's easy acceptance of their intimacy swirled gratification in his chest. If she could feel him as a spirit, hope sprung in him that they could remain close after the birth of the baby.

"Is it not time to enter the water?" Crazy One pivoted on one foot.

Wewukiye kissed Dove quickly behind the ear and drifted out of the sweat lodge.

Outside the lodge, he returned to man form and

hurried away from the river before the two women exited to wash the sweat from their bodies.

****

Dove walked into the freezing water and quickly washed away her sweat and impurities. She hated rinsing away the heat of Wewukiye's hands loving her. His whispered word, *Never*, hung in her mind and her heart. He would not leave her and the baby, but who or what was he? After their shared experience she knew he could not be a man. No one, not even the strongest shaman, could move about such as Wewukiye.

Her skin shivered drawing her dress over her body. She wrapped the shawl around her shoulders, and quickly donned her moccasins.

She stared up the canyon wall. *Where are you?*

"Is it wise to go to my uncle?" Crazy One placed a hand on her arm.

"I know he is not like any other. I must talk with him." Dove peered into the darkness, making out darker clumps of bushes and rock on the canyon wall.

"Is he not watching you? Should you not walk carefully?" The old woman gave a gentle shove toward the canyon wall.

Dove understood and did not hesitate. Wewukiye would find her. She did not fear anyone seeing her leave the camp. This time of night, everyone remained in the central lodge telling stories. She strode past a tipi, away from the circle of dwellings. Her gaze probed the dark ground to avoid tripping as she traveled up the slope of the canyon wall.

"You will become cold up here."

Wewukiye's deep voice in the cold silent air spiraled warmth from her head to her toes. His arm wrapped around her shoulder, directing her toward a glowing fire inside a shallow cave.

"This is where you stay at night?" She peered into his face as he lowered her to sit on a blanket spread on the ground.

"It is where I will spend tonight." He sat beside her, drawing her body next to his. "This is not good you seek me. If the others learn you spend time alone with me it could hurt your plan."

She touched his solid angled cheek. "I seek answers and wish to seek the truth in your eyes. How is it you and I can talk without saying words? How is it you can hold and love me without being seen?" He started to open his mouth. She placed a finger on his soft, warm lips. Her body heated remembering the sweet warm puffs of air she knew were kisses. "Why does Crazy One insist you are her uncle when you are so much younger than she?"

Dove wanted to know everything about this man who she wished to share her life and hold close to her forever.

Wewukiye sighed, kissed the top of her head, and drew her closer. "You have felt things and understood far more than most mortals. My sister Sa-qan and the Creator would not like this, but I feel you should know the truth."

At the mention of the Creator her desires cooled, and her attention riveted to his words. "How is it you speak of the Creator as if you speak with him?"

"You have asked many questions. They will all be answered when I am finished with my story." He urged her head to lean against his chest, and he tightened his arms around her, pressing her body next to his.

She draped her shawl around his shoulders believing he held her so close to keep them both warm as the cold *Anihm* air swirled into the cave.

"Many seasons ago, long before the coming of the people with skin the color of antelope, my brother, Himiin, my sister, Sa-qan, and myself were of ages to go on our vision quests. Our father fell in with the trickster coyote. He listened to greed and hid behind cowardice, causing many deaths to the warriors of our band. Our people became mad with grief and his deception. Our band turned on us—his children—and the Creator took us from their midst."

Dove shifted to gaze into his eyes. Pain filled his usually content gaze. An ache started in her head and moved to her heart for the young men and woman.

"He made us spirits to watch over the Lake Nimiipuu, the people of our mother. Himiin traveled about the mountain as a wolf, keeping the people safe from evil spirits. He carried our father's betrayal the deepest. To keep him from returning to our birth land, the Creator did not allow him to leave the mountain. Himiin fell in love with the mortal, Wren. She was the daughter of the Lake Nimiipuu chief and given to a blackleg warrior to bring peace. This did not work out. Wren was killed by a Blackleg arrow. Himiin gave up his spirit to save her. In return, the Creator gave him a mortal body. They married and helped build the Lake Nimiipuu. Crazy One is the last of their children."

Dove pushed away from him to stare into his eyes. "Then you *are* her uncle?" She settled the words into her mind. The woman talked in questions which she had learned to decipher. Her adamant use of the word uncle had Dove believing the woman was a bit feeble. This strong young warrior *was* her uncle.

Her mind whirled with the information. All of it. He was a spirit. She ran her hands over the buckskin shirt stretched across Wewukiye's broad chest. The muscle underneath was hard, solid, and hot against her fingers.

Wewukiye captured her hands, holding them over his heart. "When my brother neared his death he asked me to watch over the Lake Nimiipuu. He saw the coming of the White man and knew they would not honor the Nimiipuu. When I heard your story, I had to help you. It was my brother's last wish." He raised her hands to his lips. "I did not realize you would come to mean so much to me."

The baby fluttered, and she drew his hand to the slight bulge of her belly. She wanted him to feel the life growing in her—a life she now believed would give their people strength.

The warmth of his hand heated her belly, moving throughout her body.

"This baby has also come to mean a great deal to me." He shook his head. "Sa-qan says I should not have revealed myself to you and your people. I believe it is the only way I can help. But they cannot know I am a spirit." His gaze shone bright blue scanning her face.

She nodded. "Many would not understand. I still do not understand it all, but I accept, since I have witnessed the wonders you perform." Her heart belonged to this spirit. How would they continue once they had their proof and all could see the child she carried?

"I understand you are not mortal, but how can we talk without saying words and how can you hold and love me without being seen?" These answers she wished more than any other. The two attributes brought them closer together.

"You possess *txiyak,* powers not as strong as a spirit but more than a shaman. Because of this you and I have connected and can speak between us with no one else hearing or seeing. You experienced my spirit form in the sweat lodge. It is water. As steam I can flow and wrap around you."

The knowledge she held txiyak strong enough to converse with a spirit stuttered her breathing and heart.

"H-how do you know it is txiẏak I possess?"

He shrugged. "That is the only way to explain your acceptance of me and all things that have happened since we met."

She nodded, agreeing. "What happens next?"

"I wish to visit with Agent William. To have him write down what Evil Eyes did to you. Do you think you can make the trip to Fort Lapwai if Sa-qan finds him there?" Concern glistened in his eyes.

"It will be a long hard trip and hard to talk with this man." She stared into his face. "If you will be by my side, I can do it."

"That is the hard part. I will be by your side in spirit only. I cannot show myself there. It is too close to the band of my people. It has been many lifetimes since the Creator made me a spirit but Sa-qan fears trouble should I be seen." He held her hand. "My essence will be with you, and you will feel my strength." He peered into her eyes. "Your txiẏak grows stronger each day. That is how you sense and hear me."

Dove sensed someone approaching. She stiffened, unsure if she should move from Wewukiye's embrace or hide her face. Fear curdled in her stomach to be found consorting with the man.

"It is Sa-qan." Wewukiye sighed deeply. "I had hoped to tell her you know all about me and your txiẏak before she discovered it."

A bald eagle stalked into the cave opening. The light of the fire gleamed off the shiny white feathers on its head. The pointed beak, small yellow eyes sparking with anger, and long talons digging into the cave floor as the large bird stalked forward sent chills down Dove's back.

Pú-timt wax kúyc
(19)

Wewukiye's throat clogged with fear. He had hoped to tell Sa-qan about Dove's growing spirit essence and their growing intimacy without Dove listening and before she found out like this.

Sa-qan stopped at his feet. Her piercing eyes focused on the woman and then him. *Why is she here?*

Her internal thought rang loud as a shout. He glanced at Dove. It was apparent she did not hear his sister for she stared at the eagle with curiosity.

"You may speak in front of Dove." This comment dealt him a glare as pointed as an arrow.

"You are a stunning creature." Dove's voice offered more strength than he could conjure at the anger of his sister.

"How is it you know of me and talk as if you are not surprised or afraid?" Sa-qan stared at Dove.

"Her powers grow each day. She sensed your approach." Wewukiye loosened his embrace, but did not allow Dove to pull away. He shrugged. "We have talked about my family."

"Finding you two together like this is not proper." His sister ruffled her feathers.

"I had questions I wished to ask Wewukiye face to face. Ones I could not ask in the presence of others." Dove held his sister's gaze.

"Why did you seek me?" He wanted the conversation away from him and Dove.

"Agent William is at Lapwai." She shifted her gaze from Dove to him. "A nephew of the Nimiipuu band is bringing his family to this area for the winter. I have suggested Crazy One talk to him about marrying Dove."

Dove straightened, drawing her shoulders back and thrusting out her chin. "I will not marry someone I do not know."

She stared straight into his eyes. Her panic forged with his. He would not allow her to become anyone's wife but his.

"Why do you suggest a marriage?" He narrowed his eyes on his sister.

"She cannot remain in Crazy One's care, not with a child coming. The old woman cannot provide for them. You will return to your duties. Lightning Wolf has two wives and four children. They could easily provide for Dove and the child. This would also bring back her honor."

"Her honor will be restored when the baby is born and the band sees Evil Eyes attacked her." Wewukiye could not hold the anger rising with each mention of Dove becoming another's wife. Not even knowing the offered husband was the offspring of this band and related to his brother. He could not allow her to marry anyone. She belonged to him.

Dove placed a hand on his arm. "What if the child does not prove my accusations?

"It will. The Creator would not have brought us together if it were not to prove the white man's evil ways to your people." His hand clenched. It had to be so. Why else would the Creator have brought them together if not for the reason of this helping the Lake Nimiipuu? As for her marrying anyone other than he... He raised his chin and narrowed a haughty glare at his sister. "Dove will not marry. I will provide for her and Crazy One."

Sa-qan paced to the opening and back. "You are becoming like our brother. Decisions are to be made with your head, not your heart. You are a spirit of the Lake Nimiipuu first. Your wishes do not matter."

"Why must it be that way?" Dove rose to her knees, leaning toward Sa-qan.

Wewukiye's chest expanded with pride. This woman, his woman, held much courage.

"I would think using your heart would help make the decision of your head stronger." She clutched Wewukiye's hand. "Together we are stronger. That will help the people more than our remaining apart."

Sa-qan shook her head. "When you use your heart decisions are not weighed fully. Emotion does not ask the questions which bring forth honest answers."

"What is more honest than what your heart says?" Dove stretched her hand toward Sa-qan as if to make contact.

Wewukiye watched in fascination as his sister peered into Dove's eyes. Their gazes held, and their eyes widened in disbelief then crinkled at the edges in humor. He had witnessed the moment the two connected on a level higher than mortals. Sa-qan blinked and Dove loosened her grip on his hand, her body relaxed, and a slight smile tipped the edges of her lips.

Sa-qan unfolded her wings then folded them back against her body. "It is true. Your spirit essence is strong, nearly as strong as mine." She shook. "But that does not make a difference in where she is to live. She must still marry our young nephew."

Wewukiye fought the anger rippling in his gut. "No. Once the baby arrives I will find a way to help provide." He swallowed the disappointment he felt for his sister's unyielding need to marry Dove to their nephew.

He stared her in the eyes. "Now we must figure out how to get Dove to Lapwai to talk with Agent William."

"This is foolishness. The trail between here and Lapwai is treacherous this time of year." Sa-qan pointed a wing at him.

"We must go now before it is harder for her to travel." He placed a hand on Dove's belly, ignoring his sister's frown. Dove and this child belonged to him and lived in his heart.

"I agree with Wewukiye. My words must be written in the *so-yá-po*'s hand before the truth is revealed to my people." Dove placed her hand over his. "If we journey slow and rest often, I will be fine traveling to Lapwai."

"How will you explain the trip to the elders?" Sa-qan narrowed her eyes.

She believed he had persuaded Dove to do whatever he wished. If she only knew how turned around her thinking was.

Wewukiye glanced at Dove and then back as his sister. "We are still working on that."

"Do not bring any more discredit to yourself." His sister stared at Dove. "My brother can rush into things without thinking. Be sure the reason is solid and the elders will have no doubts to your sincerity."

His sister's words stung even as he acknowledged they rang of truth. He had gotten himself in trouble over the years by rushing into things.

Dove nodded.

"It is late. Do not linger here, the sentries will soon discover this cave." Sa-qan walked to the entrance. "Keep me informed of your plans." She disappeared into the dark night.

Wewukiye drew Dove back into his arms. "Sa-qan is right. The glow of the fire will bring the sentries. Come. I will escort you back to the village."

"What if they come upon us? I should go alone."

The worry dulling her eyes, tugged at his heart.

"You will never walk alone. They will not see

me, but you will know I am there." He kissed the top of her head. "We will discuss the trip to Lapwai tomorrow with Crazy One."

He stood, gripping her hand and drawing her to her feet. "It pleases me you no longer fear my touch."

Dove placed a hand on his cheek. "It was not your touch I feared, but my reactions. You have never given me cause to fear you. Tonight...In the sweat lodge, your touch warmed me like a comforting fire and warm bed." Her lashes fluttered down to conceal her eyes. "Your touch promised strength, excitement, and"—her lids raised, and her dark brown eyes shone with her admiration—"love."

He lowered his head to kiss the palm of her hand. "It is how I wish you to always feel when I am near. I cannot tell you how our future will be, but know I will always be near and hold your heart."

"That is more than I could ask." Dove stood on her toes and brushed her lips to his.

Her actions, though brazen, gave her a sense of power. His hands roaming her body in the sweat lodge ignited a deep, powerful yearning. The need pulsed in her woman parts and burned under her skin. Even his sister's warning could not dampen her desire to touch and be touched by this man. She slipped her arms around his neck and pressed her body to his.

Wewukiye wrapped his arms around her, returning the kiss. His lips parted, his tongue slid across the seam of her lips, and she opened, allowing him access to her essence. Their kiss and intimacy sparked deeper desires and surged glowing light through her body, warming.

She sensed others at the same moment Wewukiye broke from the kiss. His firm body turned to smoke in her arms. She stood alone in the cave but felt his presence.

He Who Runs Fast and Many Scars stepped into

the entrance of the cave.

Dove pulled her shawl tighter around her shoulders, covering her small bulge of belly.

They both frowned, blinking their eyes in the bright glow of the fire. Their dark stares quickly found her across the fire.

"Why are you not with the others?" He Who Runs Fast asked.

She swallowed the lump of dread crawling up her throat and watched Many Scars studying the few possessions stacked against the wall of the cave.

"I wished to be alone, to think." She glanced out the entrance. "I did not realize it has become so dark."

Ask them to escort you back.

She walked toward the entrance. "Would you walk me back to the camp? I sought solitude when I left, but now I am fearful to walk in so black a night."

The two shared a quick glance. Many Scars shook his head.

One Who Runs Fast motioned to the cave. "Why did you come to the cave of the warrior with sunshine hair?"

A lump of regret clogged her throat. She did not realize they knew Wewukiye stayed here. If they knew this why did they come here? Did they watch him? Did they wish to talk to him?

"I was walking and saw a glow. I investigated and found embers. No one was here, so I tossed wood on the fire and sat to warm myself before heading back." She hated to spin such a tale.

I am here. Do not fear the untruths you tell. They are small compared to the bitter words of Evil Eyes.

Many Scars scowled and waved his hand toward the entrance. She scurried by him and He Who Runs Fast, stopping a minute when the black of the moonless night blinded her way. Wewukiye's reassuring hands on her shoulders moved her around bushes and rocks as she wandered down the cliff side listening to the movements of the men behind her.

At the edge of the encampment the men silently drifted into the darkness. A soft puff of air heated her neck.

Sleep well, I will see you tomorrow.

The sudden cold seeping through her clothing told her Wewukiye had gone. She pulled her shawl tighter and hurried to the dwelling she shared with Crazy One.

Inside the structure, the warmth of a well-banked fire filled her with the sense of home. Crazy One hunched over a form made of bent willow branches.

"Did not my aunt meet you?" She glanced up, a mischievous glint in her eyes.

"Did you tell Sa-qan where to find her brother and I?"

"Was it not time she saw the truth?" She wrapped a length of rawhide around the willow.

"What truth?"

"Is it not the Creator's wish you and Wewukiye be together?"

"How do you believe this when Sa-qan wishes to marry me to a nephew?" Betrayal burned in her chest. She had connected with Wewukiye's sister. And still she knew the spirit would remain her strongest obstacle in being with Wewukiye.

"Is it not best you have a family to help with the child?" Crazy One stared at her, her gnarled hands stilling.

"How could I even think of lying with another when Wewukiye has my heart?" The thought of even touching a man other than Wewukiye beaded sweat upon her brow and trembled her insides.

"Are all marriages of the heart? Are not many

made for convenience when the man is of an age he only feels a protector?" Crazy One showed the black gap in her teeth as she smiled a mischievous smile.

She thought of the married couples she knew. "That is true. There have been many warriors who marry the wives of their brothers... But you said the Creator wishes Wewukiye and I be together." She narrowed her eyes. "How do you know this?"

The idea warmed Dove more than the flames licking toward the smoke hole above. Did the Creator really wish them to be together? But how? She removed her shawl and sat cross-legged across from Crazy One.

"Is it not in the way your gazes meet and the power my uncle has given you?"

Dove smiled. Yes, Wewukiye had given her power. The power to love not only him and herself but the child growing in her. She lovingly ran a hand over her belly. They would be a family once she gave birth and the truth came out about Evil Eyes.

"We wish to go to Lapwai. Do you have an idea of how we can without the elders and Thunder Traveling to Distant Mountains stopping us?" She picked up the small piece of buckskin she'd worked and worked to make soft and supple to use for the baby's first tunic.

Crazy One set her project to the side and stood, staring into the fire. She stood so long, she began to sway. Dove started to rise to catch the old woman before she fell into the fire. Crazy One's eyes closed, and she began chanting. Her body swayed to the rhythm of her words.

Finally, the woman opened her eyes, and a smile revealed the gaps in her teeth. "Is it not your vision that shall set you free?" Crazy One patted her head. "Do you not sleep well and dream?"

"I don't understand.." Dove watched the woman drop herbs in a wooden bowl of water. She used a stick and picked up one small glowing rock and added that to the water and herbs.

The water stopped simmering, and Crazy One poured the liquid into a smaller bowl. "Is not tonight the night of dreams?" She held it to Dove's lips.

"I don't know what dreams has to do with going to Lapwai?"

The woman pressed the bowl to Dove's lips and tipped. She drank to keep the liquid from pouring down her front. The bitter drink nearly gagged her, but she drank and wiped the awful taste from her lips with the back of her hand.

Crazy One patted her head again. "Is it not time to sleep?"

Dove stared at Crazy One. The old woman's motions jerked and blurred. Dove raised her hand to pull the rawhide ties from her hair, but her arm could not lift the weight. Crazy One grasped her shoulders and settled her onto the tulle mat and blankets, covering her with a heavy, warm buffalo robe.

"What did you give me?"

"Was not your vision quest many seasons ago? Did you not come back forgetting you saw your *weyekin*? Will not this drink help you see things clearer?"

My weyekin? Dove's eyelids refused to remain open. Darkness descended.

White flashed bright and sunny. Heat warmed her face and the sun sparkled on the lake in the valley down below.

Le'éptit
(20)

Her dress barely covered her skinny adolescent knees as she scrambled through the summer bushes. Her mother, too sick to make her dresses, her grandmother too feeble, left Dove to wear garments others gave her. Her bare feet scuffed through the decaying foliage under the great pine trees. She sat on a large flat rock high above the lake and watched the sun shimmer and glisten off the blue surface.

Rumbling in her belly reminded her of her quest. When her father sent her into the forest four days before he had said, "You cannot eat or drink. Keep your mind open for your weyekin to speak to you."

She picked at the moss on the boulder and tossed it over the side. No one had ever spoken to her without giving orders. Her father had wanted a son. Her mother fell ill after her birth, and her grandmother no longer remembered the simplest tasks. The day she was born the sun had disappeared leaving the world black for a period of time. Many believed the sun's hiding during her birth brought hís ·qi, *bad luck upon her.*

As soon as she could handle the smallest of chores, her aunts showed her the things a grandmother would usually teach a young girl. After this quest, at ten summers old, she would be given all the adult tasks on her own. Why didn't her father marry another? Most warriors had several wives. Another wife would help with the chores.

The warm sun relaxed her body. Her eyelids drooped, and soon she no longer stared at the shimmering lake. Blackness surrounded her, wrapping her in a dark warm blanket, tossing her worries and fears away.

Something bumped her arm. Sleep held her heavy to the rock. The nudging continued. With much effort she pushed her body to a sitting position, rubbed her eyes, and blinked.

Big brown eyes and long lashes behind a black pointed nose stared at her. Fear did not squeeze her chest. She held her breath in admiration of this beautiful doe.

"You seek answers?" The soft words came from the animal, yet her mouth did not move.

"A-are you my weyekin?" *Dove reached out to touch the animal. The doe stepped back.*

"You must remain loyal to your people. One day you will sit with a White man and that talk will help your people and set you free."

"What do you mean? I do not—"

The doe pivoted and gracefully leaped away.

Dove snapped awake and stared at the smoke hole in the top of the dwelling. She placed her hands over her child. Why did she not recall her visit from her *weyekin* until Crazy One made her drink the nasty liquid?

She shook the sleep from her mind and thought about her dream and her vision quest. She now remembered running down the mountain to her village. She tripped, rolling and tumbling. Disoriented and confused panic and fear jumbled in her head. If something happened to her who would take care of her parents?

Her hysterical arrival at camp covered with twigs and dirt and bleeding in many places had brought shame to her family. They thought her appearance meant she could not take care of herself in the woods. They never asked her about her *weyekin,* and she had let the incident disappear from her mind.

Her arm cradling her child tightened. She would never mistreat her child. Understanding and love would be the nourishment this child would receive.

Tonight, during the nightly singing and storytelling in the great lodge, she would sing of her *weyekin*. The elders would have to see she must speak with the agent. Dove pulled the buffalo robe up under her chin and smiled, thinking of traveling with Wewukiye.

****

Wewukiye had wandered the river area all night as an elk trying to form a plan for a trip to the Indian agent. Everything he came up with would raise the elders' suspicions. He stepped out of the cave, focusing on the encampment below and Crazy One's dwelling. Dove stepped from the structure and stared directly at the cave entrance.

His heart raced. They could only be seen together in the presence of Crazy One after the sentries found her alone in his cave last night. He had little doubt the two had already informed Thunder Traveling to Distant Mountains what they discovered.

Dove's essence wrapped around him as if she stood next to him. *I remembered my gift to my people.*

That is good. I have not come up with a plan. He hurried down the side of the gorge toward the encampment eager to join her. Crystalline frost squeaked under his feet and glistened over the ground.

He arrived at Crazy One's tipi, his breath puffing in small clouds. Excitement fluttered in him like a quail taking flight. He wished to learn of her gift and to be near her.

Dove stood by the dwelling her shawl pulled tight around her shoulders, and her face glowing. A warm smile she bestowed only upon him lit her eyes. "There is no need to hurry. Crazy One is heating the *kouse*." She motioned to the log in front of the tipi. Frost glittered on the smooth surface.

"Bring a blanket to place upon the log." To treat Dove any differently because of the child would make others wonder about their relationship. Only the elderly whose bones did not deal well with cold would cover a log. He, however, could not allow her to take chances where the baby was concerned.

Dove tipped her head and ducked into the dwelling. He scanned the village, others mingled around their tipis, girls collected wood, men returned from their morning bath, placing their weapons at the ready by the entrances. In seasons past, this was done in preparation for warring tribes, now it was done in fear of the White man using their non-treaty status to take their home.

Dove joined him. A wool blanket draped over one arm, and she carried two steaming wooden cups. She handed the cups to him and folded the blanket on the log, dry seating for the two of them.

They sat. He held a cup to Dove. Their fingers touched, and he savored the spark of their meeting.

The brief touch ignited his desire for her. Just gazing upon her, he yearned to draw her into his arms. To touch her...his body sprang to life and wished to cling to her like the fluff of the cottonwood to rough surfaces. Within sight of the band, they had to keep a formal distance.

I wish to spend more time in your arms. Her eyes reflected her need to draw him close as well.

We must keep our feelings hidden around others or we will have to wait to meet away from prying eyes.

She sighed, her shoulders rising and falling in a deep sigh of resignation.

A woman sauntered by.

"Did you sleep well?" he asked, in a non-committal tone loud enough for the woman to hear.

"I had a dream I wish to sing about tonight." Dove glanced at the woman and took a drink. "I remembered the day I met my *weyekin*." She stared into the steaming cup of broth. "She was a doe. Her large brown eyes and slim muzzle stalled my breath at her beauty. The gift she bestowed on me will save my people." Dove's eyes shone with hope. "This is why I must see the agent William."

Wewukiye wanted to embrace her excitement, but he had to ask what he knew the elders would ask. "How is it you are now remembering this?"

She bit her bottom lip and raised eyes shimmering in tears. Her mouth twisted in a sullen smile. "Have you heard why my parents do not stand up for me?"

Heartache and pain flashed in her eyes before tears glistened in her brown gaze.

"No. I have wondered from things you have said, but I did not ask Crazy One. I wished to hear your feelings."

She swiped a fist across her eyes and stared at her feet. "The day I came upon this earth the sun hid, casting the day into night. My mother never regained her strength. My father said I brought *hi·sqi* to our family by being born during the dark day."

Wewukiye wished to pull her into his arms and show her he did not believe her to be bad luck. Being born during the eclipse of the sun gave her the power he recognized.

"The day you came to this earth, during the dark day, gave you the powers that now grow with each moment we touch. Your ability to speak with me without words and sense the evil in others is special, not a curse."

Dove started to place a hand on his arm and

quickly drew it back. If only they did not sit among the encampment. Anguish seared through his body for her. "What does this have to do with you forgetting your *weyekin*?"

"After my gift was revealed, I ran down the mountain to tell my family. I tripped and rolled, gathering sticks, dirt, and scratches. I feared for my parents should something bad happen to me. I entered the village my heart racing. My father accused me of panicking in the wild and further proving my *hi·sqi*." Dove stared into his eyes, her strength shining like a thunder storm. "I believed my father correct in my unsound qualities and did not remember my encounter until last night. Crazy One gave me a drink and suggested I would recall my gift."

Wewukiye shook his head at her strength and the disgust he harbored toward Dove's father and the holy man who had not discovered her true essence.

"Has your stomach not been rumbling since you woke?" Crazy One exited the dwelling carrying three wooden bowls of mush.

"*Qe`ci`yew`yew.*" Wewukiye took the offered food even though he did not require the nourishment.

"Did you sleep well and have good dreams?" Crazy One asked Dove, squeezing between she and Wewukiye on the log to sit upon the blanket.

"Yes. I remember my *weyekin* and gift. I will sing of this tonight." Dove scooped the mush with her fingers and ate.

Wewukiye smiled at her appetite. It was good to see food did not upset her stomach anymore. Her cheekbones no longer appeared sharp and her skin glowed a healthy bronze. Her shawl and large dress hid the growing child, but he had the privilege of feeling the slight bump and yearned for the day he held her child in his hands. The baby would be the future of the Lake Nimiipuu. He felt this as strong as he felt Dove's *txiy̓ak.*

"Will the elders not question your singing now?" Crazy One asked.

"They will. If my father is there he will learn the story of how his disfavor blinded my memory. His disfavor of me has been on my shoulders all these years, but tonight, I will toss it off."

The defiance sparkling in her eyes worried Wewukiye. "Do not mention me or your *txiy̓ak,* only the gift of your weyekin. While there are many who would understand, there are those who have taken in the word of the *so-yá-po*'s God. These people would not understand."

"Thunder Traveling to Distant Mountains is a dreamer. He once told me the day I was born was a sign of good not bad." She narrowed her eyes. "At the time I did not believe him. And with his actions since my attack"—she stared into his eyes, shook her head—"I believed he thought otherwise now."

Wewukiye glanced at Crazy One. The woman smiled and nodded. Her meaning was clear. Dove's time had come to show her people she cared for them.

"Will you come to the ceremony tonight?" Dove asked. *I wish your presence.*

Her plea flowed through him melting his resolve to stay distant from her people. He feared too much contact with anyone other than Dove and Crazy One would grow suspicion about his history. To enter the communal lodge would open him up to the band. He would be expected to sing of his gift. Panic, an emotion he experienced once as a child when the band found out about his father's bad judgment and crowded around his father and his siblings, twisted in his belly.

"Is it not time you stepped among the people completely?" Crazy One leveled an inquiring stare on him.

His gaze darted from the old woman beside him, to the village coming to life, and settled on Dove.

I need you to watch the people and give me strength.

"The ritual of singing of your gift is sacred. I cannot sing of my gift. It will bring too many questions." He stared at Dove, willing her to understand.

"You do not have to sing of everything. Is there not a gift you have that you could sing about?" Dove started to reach toward him. Crazy One grasped her hand, holding it in hers.

"Do you not have the gift of travel to bring people together?" Crazy One nodded. "Can you not sing of your travels?"

Wewukiye's heart lightened. He could be there for Dove. He could sing of his travels. Of the people he knew. The things they taught him.

"Yes. I have many stories of my travels." He peered into Dove's eyes. "This journey I take now with you will have a satisfying ending for all."

Elation bubbled within as her eyes signaled she wished for the same ending. He did not know how, but Dove and her child would be a part of his life from this day forward. Even if he had to become mortal. A shiver raced down his back. Never in his years as a spirit had he thought of becoming mortal again.

The qualities he favored as a spirit would make a great leader. Arrogance, decision making, authority figure. He stood. Being mortal would also make him vulnerable and temporary. A chunk of frozen lake landed in his gut; cold, hard, and jagged. He did not want to be mortal. He needed time away from the woman whose essence plagued him with desire and fuddled his mind.

"Where are you going?" The uncertainty in

Dove's voice led him to believe she read his mind.

"I must think about what I will say tonight." He focused on her face. "I will return for the ceremony."

He strode from the village and up the side of the canyon. Images swirled in his head, the passing of his seasons of being a spirit. The wonders he saw and helped perform. Sorrow clenched his chest and fear, an emotion he'd forgotten, pricked his memory at the vision of his brother's body and mind slowly decaying as a mortal.

Wewukiye glanced down the canyon to the cluster of teepees. His gaze sought Crazy One's dwelling. Dove stood beside the structure watching him. The fear lessened thinking of her, but the images of his aged brother lingered.

Could he do that for Dove? For her child and their people?

Le'éptit wax ná-qt
(21)

Dove stood outside the communal lodge. Her heart thudded in her chest. To sing of her vision now after all these years would throw suspicion on her. But it was the way of her people, and her gift would forge her path to the agent.

Each person who entered the lodge stared as they passed. She had avoided such events since Evil Eyes's attack and living with Crazy One. The old woman had entered already, but she could not. She waited for Wewukiye. The stricken expression on his face that morning plagued her all day. What had twisted his features and put fear in his eyes?

A slip of moon gave little light. She stared into the darkness. *Where are you? Am I to do this alone?*

I am coming. We should not enter together.

His words brought a smile to her lips. He would never let her down. He was the only person she could count on.

Her father approached the lodge. He stopped and ushered those behind him to enter. "Why are you here, daughter?"

"To sing of my *weyekin*." She pointed her chin up and peered down her nose at him. She would not let her father take away her assurance.

"You did not see your *weyekin*. How can you sing of your gift?" He stared at her with the same uncaring expression she endured as a child.

"I did. You were so upset over my appearance at my return you flung my vision from my mind." She drew her body straighter, taller, sensing Wewukiye's presence. "I have remembered and will sing of it tonight."

Her father narrowed his eyes. In the past, his expression would have sliced her heart with fear. Tonight, she smiled and entered the packed lodge seeking Crazy One. The old woman sat in the singing circle.

She sat cross-legged in the spot Crazy One indicted. The old woman patted her shoulder and stepped back into the crowd of people who would listen and not sing this night.

Is not my uncle here?

I know. Her *txiyak* grew. This was the first time she could also speak with Crazy One. That revelation and her skin tingling and warming the moment Wewukiye stepped into the lodge increased her confidence. His essence seeped into her, calming her nerves. The other occupants watched expressionless as he sat in the singing circle directly across from her.

Three fires blazed down the middle of the long structure. The middle fire glowed in between them, but it felt as though he sat beside her.

"My father has asked me to begin the ceremony," Thunder Traveling to Distant Mountains announced. He chanted and passed the singing stick to the man on his left. The man stood, singing of his *weyekin* and the gift given him, and how he used his gift on a hunting trip.

The stick worked its way person by person toward Dove. The closer it came, the more her stomach knotted. The young girl beside her sang of her gift and how she fulfilled it each day by helping with family chores. She handed the singing stick to Dove and sat.

The smoke in the lodge from the fires drifted across the heavy silence. Panic squeezed her chest, realizing she must sing for the first time in all her seasons. Many faces watched, their expressions curious to see what brought her here this night.

You are strong and true. Sing of your gift.

She stood, drew in a breath, and smiled at the flutter in her belly. The child wished a song.

"I was but a child of ten seasons when a beautiful doe spoke to me. She told me to remain loyal to my people. One day I would sit with a White man and set my people free.

My gift is to visit with the agent to help my people avoid prosecution from the White man. Of this I have dreamed and now I sing."

Dove peered through the smoke at Wewukiye. He nodded.

You have done well.

She handed the stick to the next person.

Her father stepped into the ceremonial circle. "How is it my daughter is just now singing of her *weyekin* when it was many seasons ago that she went on her vision quest?"

Dove glanced at Thunder Traveling to Distant Mountains.

"I would like to hear as well."

Her heart raced. Her hands shook. She knew they would question. All knew the winter after your quest you sang of your gift. She had believed her father, who refrained from engaging in matters, would not confront her publicly.

Tell them the truth. You are strong.

She inhaled deeply and peered at her father. "The day my gift was bestowed on me, I fell down the mountain. I returned bloody, covered in dirt and sticks. You did not ask me how it happened or if I were hurt. You said I had once again been a disappointment." She glanced around the lodge, making eye contact with those of her immediate family. "I had learned through my seasons to not stick up for myself. Instead of rejoicing in my gift, I thrust it from my mind to wallow in how much I disappointed you."

Crazy One stepped forward, placing her hands on Dove's shoulders. "Did my care not help her to remember?"

Mumbling broke the silence that had filled the lodge from her first word.

Thunder Traveling to Distant Mountains raised his arms. "Dove you will visit my father tomorrow." He motioned to the woman next to her. "Sing of your gift."

Relief drained Dove's legs of strength. She sank to a sitting position and tried to concentrate on the woman's song.

You did well. I am proud.

Wewukiye's words sent a wave of pride washing through her weakened body.

Many sung their songs before the stick passed to Wewukiye. Again, the lodge held an unnatural silence as all waited to hear his song.

The pureness and huskiness of his voice captured Dove's heart and held her attention.

"I travel the lands of Nimiipuu as was told in my gift. Mother Earth is my home, my heart. My gift is to learn from all Nimiipuu and help them grow in strength and become one united force to save their mother earth and prosper with her always."

He handed the stick to the next person and slowly sat back down. Dove watched the faces of the people. His words weighed on each man, woman, and child. She witnessed their deep inner reflections and a springing of hope shine in their eyes. He held an aura they all respected.

You have a beautiful voice and an honest heart, she told him.

He inclined his head slightly. *Meet me at the cave when all is still in the camp.*

Her face heated, and her heart quivered. She

had hoped for time alone with Wewukiye. But did they dare meet at the cave? The night before played in her mind.

What about the sentries?

Walk that direction. I will find you.

She nodded slightly.

The final person sang of his gift. She waited for several to tell stories and silently slipped from the lodge. Crazy One caught up to her.

"Did you not tell them the truth? Will they not be fools to ignore the strength of your words?" The old woman motioned for her to enter their dwelling.

Dove placed wood on the glowing embers. Smoke rose from the flames lapping at the wood. The acrid scent burned her nostrils. She wished to inhale the earthy scent of Wewukiye.

"Does not my uncle wait for you?" The old woman sat beside the fire, drawing the willow frame she worked on every night onto her lap.

How did she always know what had been spoken between she and Wewukiye? Heat rose up her neck, infusing her cheeks. Did the woman hear every word they exchanged? She shook her head. She did not hear words spoken between the old woman and Wewukiye. The woman was wise and realized they would meet after the opening of their souls tonight at the gathering.

"Where are the sentries?" She raised her head from her work. "Do you follow your heart?"

"Is it safe for me to find Wewukiye?" Dove wanted more than anything to spend time in his embrace, but if it would damage what she established this night, she would remain in the tipi.

"Does he not look after you? Does he not wait?" The old woman waved her hand toward the opening.

Dove smiled, pulled her shawl tighter around her, and ducked out the entrance. The darkness of the night stalled her feet. She walked a straight line up the canyon wall directly behind their dwelling.

Her heart pounded in her head, and her breathing rasped. In her exuberance to see Wewukiye she forgot to take her time.

"You should rest." Wewukiye stood by her side. Earth, wind, and grass scents wafted around her. His arm settled upon her shoulders, tucking her against his strong body.

"You are all I need." Her words spoke true. She could handle anything with him by her side.

"We cannot go to the cave this night. The sentries have already walked by twice. They wish to catch us together." He faced her.

His eyes glowed in the dark night. "Do you trust me?"

"With my life and that of my child."

He blinked. His eyes appeared brighter and bolder blue. "Your words fill me with gladness."

Before she could respond, he scooped her into his arms, and started at a run along the canyon wall. The ease of his strides and unlabored breathing did not surprise her knowing he was a spirit. His show of stamina marveled and excited her.

Far from the encampment, he stopped. She remained snuggled against him, her arms draped around his neck, the child cozy between them.

"What is your wish this night?" he whispered in her ear.

"To remain in your arms, feel the beat of your heart, and strength of your body." She pressed her lips to his neck.

"It is so." He carried her into an area padded with dry grass and surrounded on three sides and the top with rock.

Her feet slid to the ground, his hands came to rest on her hips. She raised her face to peer into his eyes. He drew her closer, lowering his head, and brushing his lips tantalizingly across hers.

Eager to experience everything he had to offer she pressed her body to his. Sensations of desire, honesty, and acceptance undulated through her body. To be one with this man would fulfill her every need.

She kissed him open-mouthed, running her hands under his tunic, stroking the hardness of his muscles.

Wewukiye wished to treat Dove with tenderness. He also wished to fulfill her needs. He returned her kiss, ardor for ardor, slipping her shawl to the grassy floor and gently placing her upon it. His body and her clothing would keep the cold night air from her.

The bulge of her belly reminded him they could go no farther than kisses. There could be no doubts to who planted the seeds that brought this child to grow in Dove's belly.

He deepened the kiss, feeling protective and jealous. His heart ached for her to have gone through the attack. Rage simmered in him over the brutal White man being the one to take her innocence. He wished to show her the gentleness she deserved.

Dove's small hands continued their exploration under his tunic, searing a path up his back.

He pulled out of the kiss and hissed, rolling to his side and drawing her tight against him. He wanted to stroke her skin but dare not, for fear he would not be able to stop.

He kissed her forehead. "Your hands must not touch me—"

Pleasure shook his body and blinded his thoughts at the soft touch of her hands ignoring his request and skimming up his belly and exploring his nipples. Wewukiye wrapped his arms around her, hugging tight, holding her hands still between their bodies.

"Do not touch my skin with your skin. I cannot control—" He growled at the playful movement of her fingers. The sensation of her touch aroused him physically and spiked lightning in his mind.

Her lips brushed along the underside of his jaw. The brief touch flared fire that jerked his manhood to a bulging, throbbing need.

He pushed away from Dove and stood, pacing the small area like a starving mountain lion. He wanted her. All of her.

"Did I do something wrong?" Dove knelt on the blanket, her hands raised in a plea. Her eyes shimmered with confusion.

"You have done nothing wrong." He paced trying to defuse the fire of need pulsing through him.

"Why do you pace and run from my kisses?" She stood, walking toward him.

He backed up, slamming his back against a cold, hard boulder. "I want you as a man wants a woman."

The corners of her mouth tipped into a seductive smile, and her eyes sparkled. "That is my wish. You have filled my empty life in every way. Now I wish you to be one with me."

"To become one is my desire as well."

She stepped close, her breasts and belly touching him. Her head tipped back, and she peered into his face. "You will not harm me or the baby. I have talked of this with Crazy One."

He wasn't sure he liked the idea of his niece discussing the mating of a man and woman knowing it involved him.

"If someone were to learn of us, they could question your accusation that Evil Eyes fathered this child." He placed a hand on the side of her belly.

He put his other arm around her shoulders, drawing her firmly against him. A tremor rippled through her body.

"Is it that or because Evil Eyes has tainted me

and you do not wish to be one with me?"

The sadness and disappointment in her voice pierced his heart.

He grasped her head in his hands and kissed her with all the pent up emotions he held for her. She sagged and he scooped her into his arms, carrying her to her shawl, and placing her upon it.

"I wish to be one with you but believe it is best to wait until after the birth." He kissed her closed eyelids, her nose, her chin. "We will be one the minute you have healed. I promise I will not let anyone come between us."

He kissed her neck, and she snuggled close, wrapping her arms around his neck.

"I will count each day together as a blessing and dream of the day we become one."

Wewukiye held her sleeping body, wishing he could bring them both the ecstasy they wanted. But he could not harm her chance at proving the *so-yá-po*'s deceit. Even as his body ached to make her his.

He watched the moonless night begin to fade and roused Dove. "You must return to the camp before the sentries change or the sun herald wakens everyone."

Le'éptit wax lepít
(22)

Dove emerged from the tipi after the Sun Herald welcomed the new day. Wewukiye had escorted her to the dwelling without anyone seeing them. She had spent the time between returning and emerging into the cold gray morning thinking about her actions and his reactions. Evil Eyes attack had convinced her she would never want a man to touch her. Now, she craved Wewukiye's touch and the mating she understood would be nothing like the attack. But his honor as a spirit and his dedication to help her fulfill her gift had him restraining his own desires.

That was why she would give her whole being to him. He would never take more than she was willing to give.

Thunder Traveling to Distant Mountains walked up from the area the men bathed. She quickly picked up the rawhide bucket of water Wewukiye left each night by their dwelling and entered the warm isolation of the tipi. Did the others realize Wewukiye performed her chores?

"Is not my uncle a good provider?" Crazy One held out a bowl of mush.

"He takes very good care of us. I wish we could live as a family." Dove sighed.

Crazy One chuckled. "Is he not honorable? Does not my uncle suffer for your sake?"

She stared at the old woman. "How is it you know everything we do?" She sat down, her stomach uneasy with the knowledge. "I do not like that you seem to know our every move."

"Do I not know my uncle? Do I not watch your love, your sorrow?" She patted her shoulder. "Do you know some needs are stronger than a spirit?" She winked and dug into her bowl.

Dove pondered the woman's words. Did that mean even Wewukiye would eventually not be able to fight his need for her? The idea lightened her mood. If they continued to spend time alone together, she could show him how much he meant to her.

"Crazy One. It is One Who Flies."

The voice outside the dwelling jolted Dove from her reveries. Was he here to summon her to Chief Joseph again?

Crazy One smiled and patted her shoulder as she stood and walked to the opening.

"Why do you come to my dwelling so early?" she asked without opening the blanket.

"Chief Joseph and Thunder Traveling to Distant Mountains wish to speak with Dove." He coughed. "I am to escort her."

Crazy One winked at Dove. "Do they not listen now? Should you not finish your hair?"

The old woman stepped out of the dwelling, and Dove hastily braided her hair, checked to make sure her clothes befitted one of her status, and ducked out the tipi.

Her racing heart stopped when Wewukiye walked into the circle of dwellings. She wanted to run to him, but Crazy One captured Dove's arm and shook her head. Dove peered at the woman.

Do not let them know how much I mean to you. Wewukiye's plea filled her head. *I will be by your side, but you must be strong. Do not express your feelings toward me.*

I will try. She nodded to Crazy One, and the woman released her arm. One Who Flies watched her with a critical eye.

Dove nodded to One Who Flies and fell in step by his side. She felt the weight of disapproving eyes. A peek over her shoulder revealed her scowling father. She straightened her shoulders and held her head high crossing the distance from her dwelling to the chief's lodge.

One Who Flies held the blanket back, and she stepped into the largest dwelling other than the communal lodge. Wewukiye sat cross-legged near the fire, his back to the entrance. Thankful she would not meet his gaze, knowing the strength it held over her, she downcast her eyes and approached the three men seated across from him.

Chief Joseph motioned for her to sit beside Wewukiye. She crossed her ankles and sank to the floor as best she could with her added weight, making sure she kept ample distance between her and Wewukiye.

"Most Nimiipuu receive their gifts from their *weyekins* at a young age and sing of this soon after." Chief Joseph watched her with watery eyes. "How is it you have been told your gift now?"

"My chief, my gift was given to me at ten summers. Things happened afterward that hid my *weyekin's* visit until the kindness of Crazy One helped to set it free."

He nodded. Thunder Traveling to Distant Mountains and Frog exchanged a look across their father.

"This gift, tell it to me." Chief Joseph leaned forward.

Dove licked her lips and glanced from the chief to his sons and back to the chief.

"My *weyekin* told me one day I would sit with a White man and set my people free. I believe this means I must travel to the Agent William and tell him of my attack by the *so-yá-po* with two different eyes, Two Eyes as you call him." She stared unflinching at the chief. "I wish his evil to be written in the White man's scribbles for others to see."

Chief Joseph studied her, the pop and crackle of the fire sounded like an explosion in the weighted silence. Thunder Traveling to Distant Mountains and Frog both remained solid as rocks on either side of their father.

Chief Joseph nodded. "Your steadfast conviction about this attack makes me think you wish revenge."

"I do seek revenge."

The chief's eyebrows rose, and he started to speak.

Dove interrupted out of fear he would not listen otherwise.

"I seek revenge so you can see he has evil plans for our people. You did not suffer his violence or his vicious words." She closed her eyes and gulped. Images of the attack swirled in her mind.

Stay strong.

I'm trying. She sucked in air and opened her eyes. "I only wish to help my people. Please allow me, Crazy One, and Wewukiye to travel to Lapwai and speak with Agent William."

Chief Joseph peered first to his oldest son and then his youngest. "We will discuss this." He dismissed her with a wave of his hand.

She stood and started for the door.

"Wewukiye," the chief said.

Dove swung back around. Fear for him radiated to her toes.

Go. I am fine.

She pivoted to the entrance and stumbled out into the cold winter air. They had to let him travel with her. He would help her keep her conviction to speak with the agent.

Wewukiye sat tall and proud waiting for Chief Joseph to continue.

"Why is it you do not stay in the lodge of the unmarried men?"

"Since I am not one of this band, I prefer to be alone."

The three men's curiosity charged the air.

"But you are not alone. The sentries have found Dove near your cave." Thunder Traveling to Distant Mountains crossed his arms and glared at him.

"She feels a stranger to her own people and seeks solitude as well. I have given her permission to use my cave when she wishes." He had hoped this conversation would not include Dove.

Thunder Traveling to Distant Mountains raised one eyebrow. "And this is why you do women's chores?"

Wewukiye held his head high and stared at the man. "Crazy One is old, Dove carries a child who will prove to you the *so-yá-po* you call friend is not who he says. I do not wish anything to happen to her or the child."

Frog leaned forward. "Why is it we never see you fixing your weapons or hunting?" He sneered. "Do you help the women because you are not a warrior?"

Wewukiye stared at the insolent mortal. "I do these things for the good of the Lake Nimiipuu. I do not need to prove I am a warrior." His body surged with anger, bulging his muscles and piercing Frog with a fierce glare. The warrior was the first to look away.

"How does tending the old woman and Dove's chores and working all through the night to erect a sweat lodge help the Lake Nimiipuu?" Thunder Traveling to Distant Mountains drew Wewukiye's attention from Frog.

"Your own wife has used the sweat lodge. I have made the sweat lodge for all women who wish to relieve the aches in their bodies." Wewukiye did not wish to verbally spar with the man.

But he had to convey how important the trip was for the whole band. "I was born to Mother Earth to help the Nimiipuu. Dove's health and the health of the child within her will prove the *so-yá-po*'s deceit." He studied the faces of the men. "Whether you help us or not does not matter. We will prove the truth."

Wewukiye stood. "That is all I will say. She will travel to the Agent William, with or without your permission. It is Dove's gift."

Wewukiye walked away from the men and out of the dwelling. Let them think about his words and actions. He could not reveal any more without them learning his true identity.

He strode across the open area between the circle of dwellings following Dove's trail in the ankle deep snow and stopped at Crazy One's tipi.

"It is Wewukiye."

Crazy One's head popped from behind the blanket opening. She winked and smiled. "Are you not making them think hard?"

He smiled at his niece. "I have given up wondering about your knowledge."

"Is Dove inside?" He believed she would rush out to see him. Her hesitant steps exiting the lodge reflected her reluctance to leave him alone.

Crazy One nodded, scanned the area and shoved the blanket away. "Am I not a good sentry?"

He quickly entered the small tipi. Dove sprang to her feet and into his arms.

"You were so strong. My heart pounded with pride." He whispered, holding her tight. This was how he wished to start every morning, embracing this woman to his heart.

"When they sent me away I feared... They have to let us travel together to the mission. I cannot tell the agent what happened if you are not there to keep me strong."

He held her head in his hands, seeking her eyes. "If they do not give us permission, we will go anyway. It is your gift to fulfill."

She placed her hands over his and nodded. "Of this I am also certain. I must tell the agent."

"We will give them until the end of the day. If they forbid our trip, we will leave the following night." Wewukiye hated to put Dove in the middle of more dissension, but since singing of her *weyekin*, he knew he must honor his duty to help her fulfill her gift.

She nodded and whispered. "Kiss me."

He smiled. "You become stronger and bolder each day." He brushed his lips across hers.

"Is that bad?" Her dark eyes simmered with ardor.

"No, it is a trait I like very much." He wrapped his arms around her, drawing her closer, snuggling against the bump of the child, and sealing their lips with a deep, open-mouthed kiss. Her essence seeped into him, filling him with hope, security, and love.

"Do you not wish Dove to come to you?" Crazy One's voice reverberated strong through the hide of the dwelling.

Dove pulled from Wewukiye's kiss and whispered, "Someone wishes to enter?" Her heart pounded with fear. They could not be caught. She wished they did not have to hide their feelings but until the child proved her truths, she could not taint her reputation.

He placed a finger on her lips and shifted to smoke before her eyes. She reached out where he had stood. Her hands filled with nothing. Her heart stopped, and her mind swirled. She knew he was a spirit. They talked to each other without moving their lips, she felt his presence in the sweat lodge, but this... She collapsed to a sitting position. His transformation in front of her proved not only his true state, but he also trusted her.

I am here.

Crazy One entered followed by Thunder Traveling to Distant Mountains.

Dove's heart pounded in her head. Did their quick decision mean they would forbid her traveling to Lapwai?

Thunder Traveling to Distant Mountains stood as tall and wide as Wewukiye, taking up much room in the small structure. Unlike the warmth and security Wewukiye wrapped around her with his presence, this man brought trepidation.

Be strong.

She nodded her head and stood. "You wish to speak with me?"

"My father, my brother, and I have discussed your gift." He watched her. "While it appears purposeful this came to you now, we do not discount Crazy One's abilities to help."

He held up a hand the moment she narrowed her eyes and opened her mouth to speak. She would not make something up to get what she wanted.

"We do think if your accusations are correct about Two Eyes it would be good to have your story known to the agent William."

"I do not tell untruths." Why did they not believe her? She would not tell them these things to start trouble if they were not true.

He nodded but made no comment. "We will send four warriors with you and Crazy One to Lapwai."

"What about Wewukiye?" She would not go without him.

Do not push. I will be with you.

"He is not of our band. If he chooses to ride along we will not stop him." Thunder Rolling to Distant Mountains crossed his arms. "The warriors will watch your conduct and report to my father."

"There will be nothing to report." She stared back at him. She needed Wewukiye to help her be strong, but she would not jeopardize her story or her people by poor actions.

"That is good." He walked to the opening and stopped. "We do not honor traitors—White men or our own kind." He disappeared.

What did he mean by that? Did he call her or Wewukiye traitors?

The acrid scent of smoke tickled her nostrils, and she swung around. Wewukiye stood on the other side of the fire.

"You heard?" She stepped around the small flames stretching toward the smoke hole.

"It is good they send warriors. That means they believe you and wish to protect you." Wewukiye captured her hand.

"You will ride with us?" Her breath hitched waiting for his response.

He shook his head. "I will not ride along as an escort. I will be with you as my spirit. This will keep any doubts from entering the White men or the Nimiipuu."

Dove pressed against him. "I understand. As long as you will be there, in whatever form, you will help."

His gaze traveled across her face, lingered on her lips, and he peered into her eyes. "I will never be far from you. But the trip will not be easy in the snow."

"Do we not need to pack?" Crazy One moved about the small confines picking things up and putting them down.

"I think she means you should leave." Dove giggled at the woman's antics.

Wewukiye slid his arms around her, pulling her close. "I will always be near."

His lips claimed hers, filling her with delicious

sensations, and heady thoughts.

The pressure released and smoke swirled around her.

She opened her eyes, and he was gone.

Le'éptit wax mita't
(23)

Dove and Crazy One rode side by side with Frog and Many Scars ahead of them. Too Short and Red Bird rode behind. Dove wiggled on her horse. They did not allow her to stop as Wewukiye had on the way to Imnaha. Even after crossing the cold wide river they only stopped long enough for the women to wrap blankets around their wet legs. They kept a steady, grueling pace through the day. Not even stopping to take a drink of water.

"Frog knows I am with child. Why does he not allow me a rest?" she asked Crazy One, trying to find a position that did not irritate.

The old woman peered at her. "Does not a warrior find fault with a woman who slows him down?" She lowered her voice. "Was that not the reason Chief Joseph sent his son?"

Dove stared at the woman. "You mean he hopes this trip will damage my character more?" An ache grew in her chest, throbbing and expanding until she could hardly breathe. She thought they finally believed her, and now she saw they only hoped to still her voice.

Crazy One reached over picking at nothing on her shawl. "Do they not know the power you have? Did not my uncle say he will keep you safe?" The old woman smiled.

Wewukiye. Are you here? Dove had to know the night would not be as unpleasant as the day.

I am with you always.
When will I see you?

When they stop for the night, I will find you.

Dove found solace in his words. She endured the jostling of the horse until they stopped at dark. The warriors vaulted off their horses, moving about in silence preparing the animals for the night. Dove positioned her mount beside a large rock and slid from the animal's back onto the boulder. Careful to not slip on the snow-covered roundness, she shuffled off the rock. Many Scars dropped their bundle of belongings on the ground and grasped the reins of their horses, leading them to the others.

Crazy One opened the bundle, setting out hard bread, pemmican, and dried berries for the warriors. Dove walked stiffly to the bushes and relieved herself. She hurried back to help Crazy One erect a hide for them to sleep under.

"Should we not make all sides covered?" the old woman whispered, winking.

"Why?" Dove tugged on the heavy hide, draping it over four poles shoved in the ground and rising no taller than her waist.

"Do you want others to see my uncle with you?" The old woman carried their bedding into the small area.

You will be with me through the night? To sleep in Wewukiye's arms would soothe her aches.

I will be there.

Elation added a new bounce to her steps. She even smiled at the grumpiest of the four warriors. None had tried to talk to her or Crazy One. The morning had started with Frog ordering their supplies loaded on Crazy One's horse. The warriors sat atop their horses, never saying a word, watching as she and Crazy One prepared their mounts.

Frog knew the reason for the trip, but did the others? Would it make a difference in how they treated her? She glanced at Frog studying her. His dark narrowed stare filled her with apprehension.

His gaze flickered to her belly as though he tried to see if she really were with child.

She turned her back on him and finished spreading her bedding. Crazy One handed her food, and they sat on a rock far from the men.

"I feel like a prisoner," she said to the old woman.

"Do they only follow orders?" Crazy One nodded toward the three men wrapping themselves in blankets and settling in for the night. The fourth stood at alert, watching the darkness drawing around them.

Dove shivered as the cold from the boulder seeped into her legs and bottom. "I am going to sleep."

She entered the enclosure and found Wewukiye reclining on her blankets. Her heart hummed at his presence. He held a finger to his lips. She smiled and quickly lowered to the blanket, facing him.

"You are a wondrous sight to behold," she whispered, touching his face.

He smoothed his thumb under her eye. "You are tired. Was today too much?" he whispered warm against her ear.

"I ached when we arrived, but now I feel only happiness." His presence swept away her fatigue and aches.

Wewukiye gathered her into his arms. She willingly sagged against his warm front, his hands massaged and relieved the tension in her back, legs, and bottom. His touch warmed her muscles, soothed her aches, and eased her doubts. She kissed his throat and breathed in his scent. Her mind wanted to continue enjoying his touch, but her body relaxed. He turned her, drawing her bottom against his waist. His arms folded around her, and she drifted to sleep.

Her body fit so well with his, Wewukiye

wondered they did not slip into one. He kissed her hair and placed a hand over the small bulge of her belly. This woman and this child had come to mean everything to him.

He had simmered watching the warriors continue at a relentless pace all day, never giving her a break from the horse. If they continued the same tomorrow he would enter Frog's body and manipulate him to give the women a rest several times during the day.

"Did I not tell her you would be here?" Crazy One entered the enclosure and sat on her bedding. Her watery faded gaze lingered on Dove's face. "Does she not carry the strength of our ancestors? Did she not once complain or cause Frog trouble?"

Wewukiye's heart banged in his chest. Dove was strong. Her strength grew each day. "She will prove Evil Eyes's deceit, and she will help The People," he whispered.

"When are you and she to become one?" The creases in the old woman's face deepened with her concern.

"I know we are meant to be together. The Creator will let us know when and how." His stomach quivered. He wasn't sure the Creator would be that generous, but he had to hold onto the hope. Without Dove sharing his life carrying on as a spirit would be meaningless. The Creator had to find a way for them to be together.

"Is there not much love between you?" She sported a toothless grin. "Did not my mother and father find a way?" She tossed a blanket over Dove, and he arranged it better.

His niece lay down, pulled her blanket up to her chin, and closed her eyes.

Wewukiye breathed in the herbal scent of Dove and held her in his arms, keeping her safe and warm through the night until he heard the warriors stirring. He repositioned Dove in his arms, kissed her lips, and dissolved into smoke, rising out of the women's enclosure.

He slipped into a small brown chickadee and watched the men moving about readying the horses and belongings for the day. Frog walked forcefully toward the enclosure. He called out once and tossed the flap back.

Crazy One stuck her head out. "Are you my man or the man of this woman?" The old woman stabbed her boney finger in the warrior's chest, moving him backward, freeing Dove to exit their enclosure and hurry into the bushes.

Wewukiye flew circles above her, watching that no other bothered her. *Did you sleep well?*

Yes. Why did you not stay so I could start my morning with a kiss?

Ah, but I did kiss you before I left. You are most delicious.

She giggled. He landed on the branch beside where she stood. He bobbed up and down. Her eyes lit with delight.

"Ah, little bird you do think highly of yourself. Your chest is all puffed up."

"Who do you talk with?" Frog's voice came from not far behind them.

Wewukiye flew off, and Dove faced the warrior.

"I was speaking with a bird. Do you not talk with the creatures that live on this earth with us?" She walked around the warrior and headed back to camp.

Can you become any creature you wish? Wewukiye's talents amazed her.

I do not become the creature. I enter them.

She stopped and Frog ran into her back, toppling her forward until he reached out grabbing her arm.

Would Wewukiye enter her? The idea did not

settle well.

"Why did you stop? Do you see trouble?" Frog stepped in front of her as though protecting her.

"No. I just..." She scurried around him and helped Crazy One finish storing their belongings in the hide they used for their enclosure.

C-can you enter me?

No. You would have to be very ill for me to slip past your txiẏak.

Dove breathed easier. Though she could deny this man who held her heart nothing, she did not like the idea of him slipping into her body when he wished.

How is it my txiẏak *would keep you from entering me?*

Your txiẏak *makes you aware I would enter you—other mortals without such power do not realize they are being entered. There are different* txiẏak *as there are different gifts. The creator bestowed upon me the ability to enter creatures to travel about and to keep peace. I am a spirit. You are a mortal with* txiẏak *to help you see evil and communicate with others who have* txiẏak.

With the horses loaded, the warriors and Crazy One sat atop their mounts. Dove led her mare to the boulder, climbed up, and settled on the horse's back. She did not like being at the mercy of the warriors escorting her. She also did not relish two more days of this fast paced riding.

I will give you breaks today.

Dove smiled. *Thank you.*

Frog stopped them several times during the day, allowing her to get off her horse and walk about stretching her legs and relieving the pressure of the child. She noticed the other warriors' irritation growing each time they stopped.

"We will be four days travel if you keep stopping. The women do not need to walk around. A true Nimiipuu woman would ride all day and into the night without stopping." Many Scars stood close to Frog, but Dove heard his words. He pitched his tone and volume to carry to her ears.

"My father told me to get this woman to Lapwai and back. I will not have her collapse when we return to the band." Frog walked away from the others.

Dove watched him closely. He fought with himself. She hastily dismounted and helped Crazy One set up the camp.

"Is not my uncle clever?" the old woman said, snickering and nodding toward Frog.

"Is he in Frog?" Dove whispered and stared in awe.

The warrior shook his head fiercely and stalked away from the camp.

"Does he like to be used?" The old woman shook her head sadly. "Will not my uncle be tired tonight from battling Frog all day?"

Sorrow for Wewukiye and all he endured to help her washed away her happiness. There had to be something she could do for him.

Their enclosure stood ready for the night, and the warriors fed. Dove glanced around, noting the sentry and the others relaxing on their blankets.

She crawled into her enclosure expecting to find Wewukiye. Their blankets and belongings met her gaze. No Wewukiye. She backed out. *Where are you?*

Resting.

I will help you rest. She walked into the trees, instinct directing her.

Her heart hammered at the sight of a large bull elk resting in a small grove of bushes. She approached cautiously, noting his sturdy legs folded under him, and his large head hosting massive antlers curled to his side.

His eyes opened, and his head came up. *How did*

you find me?

Dove stalled her steps and gawked at the magnificent creature. Her heart beat erratically now from the wonder of her discovery. This was why Wewukiye, Bull Elk, carried himself so regally and held such high esteem of his person.

"You are magnificent as a man and as an elk." She knelt in the snow beside him. "Do not spend your energy fighting with Frog tomorrow. I will be fine one more day of riding." His soft, thick hair cushioned her hand when she placed it on his shoulder.

His dull eyes brightened at her touch. "Do not give your *txiẏak* to me. You need it all."

"I am only touching you." She poured out nothing but concern for him, but she could not deny his body became more virile. His eyes took on a glow, the dull gray brightening to blue.

"Do not touch me. Save your *txiẏak*." He scrambled to his feet, breaking her contact with his body.

"Do you have enough energy to return to a man? I wish to know you are close." Dove reached out to him. If he did not lie by her side, she would not sleep well. His security allowed her to relax.

He shook his great head. "Go back to the camp. You will be fine. I will come to you when I have rested and gathered strength."

"I will stay with you until we can return together." She reached out to him, and he backed away.

"I am to protect you, not take your power. Each time you touch me, because I am drained, my body draws from your *txiẏak*. Leave me. I will soon be rested." The high arch of his neck and muzzle tipped up haughtily proved her finding him weak wounded his dignity.

"If you will not come back to camp with me, I

will stay with you. Here. In the trees." Her body shivered from the cold seeping through the darkness, but she refused to allow him to remain alone when she could help.

"You are cold." He walked to her side. "Come I will walk you back and remain." He knelt on his front knees. "Climb on my back."

She peered into his eyes. "You are strong enough to carry me?"

"When we touch our power combines, making the weaker stronger. Since you refuse to return without me, I have no choice but to draw from you and to keep you safe." He motioned with his head. "Climb on."

Dove sat upon his wide, warm back. His slow even gait lulled her worries. She yawned, leaning forward wrapping her arms around his powerful warm cushioned neck. No matter his appearance, her body joined his in harmony.

Wewukiye's heart stuttered at the easy acceptance Dove made of his many forms. She looked beyond all and saw straight into his essence. Her *txiẏak* grew with each day, giving her strength. When her child came to this earth, Dove would be strong enough to exist without his help.

His hoof caught on a rock and he stumbled. Her weight shifted forward, and he quickly righted himself to keep her from toppling to the ground.

"Wewukiye are you well?" Her sleepy voice heated his body.

"Yes, I was distracted." The camp came into view. He knelt and she slid from his back. "Go to your bed, I will come soon."

She peered into his eyes and stroked his muzzle. "Hurry."

He nodded and she slowly walked toward her makeshift dwelling, peering over her shoulder every other step.

"Why are you out wandering?" Frog's deep, suspicious voice carried to Wewukiye.

Fear speared his chest. The warrior already held distrust for Dove.

"I am of a condition that requires frequent trips to the bushes."

Her regal attitude lightened Wewukiye's mood. He quickly whisked out of the elk form and traveled to the woman's blankets in the makeshift dwelling. Crazy One slept on the other side of the structure.

The hide parted and Dove stepped in. She jolted at the sight of him. Her lips tipped into a seductive smile. *You must be growing stronger to move so fast.*

Your power and beauty revive all things.

She knelt beside him, cupped his face in her hands, and peered into his eyes. Passion, love, and acceptance shone upon him. *I wish you to always be by my side.*

Finding him in the forest and giving her power to him were unselfish acts that reflected her true nature. To have such a warm, compassionate woman care for him...His heart banged in his chest, growing larger and experiencing more with each touch from this woman.

That is my wish as well. He leaned, pressing his mouth to hers, taking what she offered. A flash of light and scorching heat joined their hearts.

"What are you doing in there?"

Le'éptit wax pí-lept
(24)

Dove jerked out of their kiss. Wewukiye stared into her shocked eyes. The flash of their kiss reached outside their bodies, lighting the inside of the structure. Crazy One rubbed her eyes with her fists.

"What was that light?"

Frog's insistent tone angered Wewukiye. No doubt the warrior would barge in.

Tell him all is well.

"All is well." Dove's gaze held his. Uncertainty swirled in her dark eyes.

"What was that light?" The hide at the entrance moved.

Wewukiye shifted to smoke and drifted to the top of the enclosure.

Frog stuck his head through the opening. His searching glare traveled slowly around the small area.

Crazy One sat up. "Why do you wake us?"

"A light flashed in here and there is smoke." He sniffed and scanned the narrow length of ground between the women's blankets.

Wewukiye wished he had the strength to slip into the warrior and give him fits all night.

"Are we not leaving early in the morning and riding a long day?" Crazy One leaned forward, shushing the man with her hands. "Do you not know when to leave?"

Frog's glare landed on Dove. Wewukiye's smoke undulated in frustration. His urge to protect the woman overruled all other thoughts. Restraint, not to show himself and stand between the warrior and his woman, hung as precarious as the last leaf of *sekh-nihm* on a windy day.

"Do you have nothing to say?" Frog tipped his head toward Dove.

"I am tired." Dove reclined on her bedding and drew a blanket around her.

The warrior snorted and shook the structure, pulling his head out and jerking the hide closed.

Wewukiye seeped through the hide and watched the warrior. Frog glanced at the structure many times as he walked to his blanket. He settled down, but riveted his gaze to the hide-covered structure. The warrior's head finally relaxed, and Wewukiye returned to Dove.

He shifted into man form and wrapped his arms around her. Her power would blend with his during the night and come morning he would hold his full essence. Earlier he had fought against her need to help him not wishing to draw away her energy. Their kiss proved their combined *txiyak* made them both stronger. He kissed her head, and she squirmed tighter against him.

Hold me always.

I promise.

How had this woman existed among the common mortals so long without he or Sa-qan noticing her *txiyak*? True it was his presence that fed her power. Still, the root of her power had to be within her when she came upon this earth. Did the Creator pick her for a specific reason? So many questions for him to ponder through until the warriors stirred in the morning.

****

Dove woke with renewed energy. Wewukiye's arms did not hold her, but his presence remained wrapped around her like a warm blanket. She opened her eyes dreaming of the morning she would wake to peer into Wewukiye's handsome face.

"Is it not late?" Crazy One had her bedding rolled and ready to load.

"How is it I did not hear you moving earlier?" Dove sat up, stretched, and began rolling her bedding as well.

"Did I not nudge you two times? Did you only smile and murmur my uncle's name?" The old woman grinned and packed her bedding outside.

Dove quickly finished her packing. Together she and Crazy One dismantled the makeshift dwelling and ate a chunk of smoked *o`ppah* bread watching the warriors load the horses.

Fresh snow coated the ground.

She stiffened as Frog stalked from the direction she and Wewukiye returned during the night. The warrior stared intently in her direction. Did he find something?

The new snow covered our tracks.

Relief washed through her at Wewukiye's words. They all mounted their horses and continued.

****

Two more days passed. Wewukiye only entered Frog at Dove's request for a break. He could no longer follow them as an elk. The open rolling hills provided little coverage. He now followed in the body of a coyote. The small animal allowed him to run swift and keep up with the horse, darting through the dying grass and bushes unseen.

The coyote's keen nose caught the scent of many people and animals. They would soon emerge on the hill above the fort. Wewukiye puzzled how he would join Dove while she spoke to the agent. His problem grew watching the group enter the populated area. He could no longer follow. He slunk along the outer edge of the buildings, frustration quivering his tail at the disappearance of Dove among the White men's dwellings.

A large shaggy dog lunged from behind a barrel and barked. Wewukiye jumped and prepared for battle. His head cleared when the pounding of his heart lessened. He swirled out of the coyote, entering the dog. Now he had means of remaining near Dove.

He trotted through the people and buildings, seeking the procession of Dove, Crazy One, and the warriors. He found the group sitting atop their horses in front of a large building. Frog signed "speak to agent" to the soldier standing at the entry of the tall building. Why would Frog sign? Frog had schooled at the mission along with his brother.

Wewukiye studied Frog's face. Ahhh, he felt the soldier too lowly to benefit from his words.

The soldier's hands flailed like an injured bird, signing poorly. Frog shook his head and the man gave up, stomping across the planks and into the building.

Wewukiye took this moment to trot up to Dove's horse. *I am here. Walk with me into the building.* He glanced up the side of the horse to where Dove sat. Her smiling face peered down at him. Her eyes twinkled with mischief. The sight spun warmth and camaraderie in his chest.

Sa-qan continually reprimanded him for not taking his commitments seriously. To see this fun-loving spark in Dove during a moment of seriousness exposed another of her surprising facets.

He winked and the soldier's heavy steps approached.

Frog told the other warriors and Crazy One to wait with the horses. He dismounted and held Dove's horse, offering no help as she slid to the ground. Wewukiye gave thanks for the large dog frame that housed him. He sidled next to Dove giving her support should she need it from sitting upon the horse so long.

She grasped the hair on his neck. Her contact

enabled him to draw her fatigue and aches from her body.

Frog entered the building, Dove followed with Wewukiye by her side.

"Hey! That mutt can't go in there!" The soldier kicked at him.

Dove crouched by Wewukiye's side, wrapping her arms around his neck. She couldn't talk about the attack to the agent without Wewukiye present.

"I wish the dog to be present." She buried her cheek against the scruffy, dirty hair of the dog, staring at the soldier, daring him to take another swipe at the animal.

Frog strode back to the door. "What have you done?" He asked her in Nimiipuu.

"I wish the dog to be present." Dove would defy any who kept Wewukiye from entering with her.

Frog shook his head. "Living with Crazy One has made you just as feeble. This is not even your dog. Chase him away."

Dove shot to her feet. "Crazy One is not feeble and neither am I. I wish to have this creature with me. He likes me for who I am."

"You ain't bringing that dog in this building." The soldier raised his rifle, pointing it at the dog.

"Sergeant Kennedy, why are you pointing your rifle at a dog?" An average-size White man, with a face nearly as aged as Chief Joseph's, bearing fuzzy cheeks and snowy-white hair, stood on the other side of Wewukiye.

The soldier tipped his rifle down. He opened his mouth to speak and snapped it shut watching the newcomer sign hello.

"Frog, I am pleased to see you," the newcomer said in Nimiipuu.

"William, I have brought Dove to speak with you."

The man faced Dove. His warm smile melted her

fears.

"Welcome to Fort Lapwai, Dove." He placed a hand on the dog's head. "Sergeant Kennedy, step aside. If Dove wants to bring in her pet, so be it," William said in the White man's words.

Dove liked the man already. He had a calm demeanor and showed true happiness upon seeing Frog. She followed William and Frog into the building, down a long room, and into a room with furnishings more elaborate than the ones she witnessed at the mission many years ago.

William motioned for them to sit. She stared at the chairs, plump and covered in cloth. They promised more comfort than the wooden mission chairs.

William sat and so did Frog. The warrior didn't hesitate, proving his acceptance of White men's furnishings.

She sat and bounced once, liking the softness under her bottom. Wewukiye sat beside her legs. She placed a hand on his head. *I like this man.*

He nodded.

Frog and William discussed the weather and Chief Joseph's family. Enthralled with all the items in the room, she gazed about as the conversation between the men barely drifted into her ears. The Nimiipuu's spare belongings could fit on the piece of furniture William sat upon. She could not believe all the things in this room were necessary to live.

William cleared his throat, and Dove glanced his way. His thoughtful gaze rested on her. She tried not to squirm.

"Frog says you have important words to tell me."

She held his gaze and nodded. "I wish to have you put on paper what happened to me five moons ago. I wish it to be known to punish the *so-yá-po* who..." She swallowed the lump of dread creeping up her throat.

You can do this.

She gripped a handful of the dog's hair to avoid sliding into a deep, bottomless cavern—one she knew as fear.

Dove straightened her back, squared her shoulders, and stared into the man's concerned eyes. "A *so-yá-po* who claims to be a friend of the Nimiipuu came upon me in the woods one day. I had wandered farther than the others gathering berries." Her body shook remembering the sunny day and how it had become so cold and bleak within a few beats of her heart.

I am here. Fear nothing.

"When I tried to run, he threw his coat over my head and knocked me to the ground. I fought and struggled. He struck me several times until I stopped. I could not see, only feel and smell." She gagged remembering the stench of his clothing. "He pinched my legs and shoved my clothing." Her face heated remembering the sound of the crude language he had used during the attack.

"I understand what you are saying. He took you against your will." William reached out to her.

She shifted away from him unable to stop the reflex action. She knew he was a kind man, but he was a man and he was white.

"I'm sorry there are men who behave like animals."

The hair on the dog's neck ruffed up.

"I don't understand why you are telling me this." William glanced at Frog.

"She wishes us to punish the man, but we feel it would only make matters worse for our people." Frog shrugged. "Not many would believe a Nimiipuu woman over a *so-yá-po*."

"I agree. I'm not sure what you wish me to do." William studied her.

"I have the proof he took me." Dove stood, tossed

her shawl on the chair, and smoothed her blanket dress over her growing bulge. "When this child is born he will have one blue eye and one brown eye, just like the evil man who harmed me."

William sat back in his chair. "You're saying Jasper O'Rourke did this to you?" A rush of air rippled his lips, and he steepled his fingers. "Now I see why you want someone to know about this."

Dove watched the man. Did he believe her? Was he going to do anything?

"O'Rourke thinks highly of himself. And I've seen his mean streak, but to accuse him of this—" William shook his head. "He could rally the government to push you onto the reservation."

"That is why we have asked Dove to not cause trouble." Frog glared at her.

"But do you want this man to hurt more maidens? How can you fear him so much that you do not protect your people?" Dove held the fear gurgling in her stomach. Of Chief Joseph's sons, all knew Frog held the strongest temper. The glare he bestowed upon her shivered her skin.

Wewukiye pressed against her legs. His confidence and strength flowed into her.

"No, it is wrong to look the other way if someone is hurting your people. But we have to go about this the legal way." William stood and crossed to a small desk. He pulled out paper and a writing stick. He sat in a chair by the desk and smiled at her. "You coming to me is the right way. I will take down your statement. When the baby is born, have someone come get me. I'll be the witness of his likeness to O'Rourke."

Happiness swirled and warmed her chest. The White man believed her. She placed her hand on Wewukiye's head. *Thank you for telling me to come here.*

She told her story again slowly, allowing

William time to scratch his writing stick across the paper.

"Come sign your name." He held the writing stick out to her.

Dove's hand shook as she grasped the writing stick. She had not written her name since her two seasons at the mission school. She printed the letters M-A-R-Y.

William scratched his head and stared at her. "I thought your name is Dove?"

"At the mission they called me this and taught me to scribble this." Resentment at the teachers' refusal to call her by her given name came back. Her reluctance to accept their ways forced her decision not to return after two seasons.

"Damn missionaries." The man mumbled in the White man's language.

He crossed out her marks and on another piece of paper drew letters.

"Copy these letters onto the paper here."

She copied the letters. D-O-V-E.

"That's your name." He smiled and took the writing stick from her.

She liked the roundness and softness of the letters.

William glanced at Frog. "Camp in the area behind the stables. And come by in the morning before you leave. I have something for your father."

Frog nodded and walked to the door.

Dove stood. She nodded to William and followed Frog through the building. Hope spun inside like a leaf swirling on a sparkling stream. Not only did Wewukiye believe in her, she also had the faith of the White agent William. Her leaders must also believe in her or they would not have allowed her to speak with him.

Her light steps carried her across the wood floor like bird wings, floating and gliding. She stepped out of the building and met a whirlwind of snow and breath-stopping cold air.

Frog motioned to the others to follow him. She grasped the rope on her horse and followed. Wewukiye stayed by her side as they walked through the village and stopped behind a large structure with fences holding many horses.

A shiver of apprehension tickled the back of Dove's neck. Someone watched them. *Do you feel them?*

Yes. Wewukiye moved closer to her side.

Le'éptit wax pá-xat
(25)

Dove couldn't shake the feeling someone watched, and watched with menace in mind. She held Crazy One's horse as the old woman dismounted with the help of Many Scars. The woman had sat too long in the cold. Her body moved in jerks and starts.

Dove scanned the area for firewood. "Crazy One needs warmth. Where can I find wood?"

"Too Short, find wood. The women cannot move about alone here." Frog waved toward the large building. He strode to the horse carrying their hide and poles. "I will help you set up the structure."

To know Frog would help with women's work showed his favor for Crazy One. Dove draped a blanket around Crazy One and helped Frog.

They soon had a tipi large enough for them all to sleep under this stormy night. She did not like sharing with the men, but she understood they all needed to be out of the weather. Too Short unloaded an armful of wood. She started a fire in the middle of the tipi and settled Crazy One on a folded blanket near the growing heat.

The warriors forbid Wewukiye's dog form shelter in the structure. *Are you well?*

I am fine. I would be better by your side.

She smiled. His presence filled her with security the vigilance of the warriors did not offer.

Dove dug through their pouches and handed the men and Crazy One bread and dried fish. She wished for water to boil and put warmth inside of

Crazy One.

"Can we get some water? I would like to make a warming tea for Crazy One."

Frog nodded to Many Scars. The warrior picked up a rawhide bucket and left the structure.

Do not leave. I will be back. Wewukiye instructed Dove and fell in behind the warrior trudging through the white world of heavy snowfall.

He circled the warrior and the well, watching the warrior struggle turning the handle that wound a rope around a stick. Relief flashed across the warrior's face when a bucket emerged. He filled his rawhide bucket.

Wewukiye sensed another person drawing closer. He focused on the man raising his arm. Wewukiye leaped. His teeth clasped the man's arm and Wewukiye growled. The warrior swung around, saw the confrontation, and grappled with the man. Wewukiye stepped back, giving the two men room to fight. He saw the glint of a knife clasped in the *so-yá-po*'s hand at the same time the two fell to the ground.

The two struggled and flipped across the ground too quickly for him to sink his teeth into the attacker's leg. He barked and ran in circles around the two. *Dove, send Frog to seek Many Scars.*

The pounding of feet and shouts exploded from the fort and the tipi. He stopped barking as a soldier and Frog each grabbed their own.

"What's going on here?" the soldier asked, taking the knife from the White man.

Many Scars sucked in air and pointed at his opponent. "This man jumped me as I filled the bucket."

The *so-yá-po* glared at the Nimiipuu. Wewukiye wondered at his hostility. Nimiipuu visited this fort often. Why would he single out Many Scars to harm?

Frog interpreted Many Scars's accusation to the

soldier.

"Why are you causing trouble?" The soldier shook the White man. He firmly held his lips together, his narrow eyes shooting hatred at the Nimiipuu.

"I'll lock him up until you leave tomorrow." The soldier dragged the reluctant man away.

Is all well? Dove's worry penetrated Wewukiye's thoughts.

For now. He watched the warriors discuss the event again. Many Scars pointed to him and the two studied him. Frog shook his head and picked up the water bucket. They headed back to the tipi. Wewukiye walked behind them, listening to their conversation travel from suspicion to anger and back to suspicion.

"William would not allow harm to us." Frog stated flatly.

"Someone does not want us here. I saw other Nimiipuu. Why did the man pick me to attack?" Many Scars stopped. His eyes burned with suspicion and disquiet.

"I do not know. When I visit with William tomorrow, I will tell him of this man." Frog stopped at the tipi. He glanced at Wewukiye, then nodded, holding the flap open. He had won over the warriors.

Wewukiye sauntered into the small structure. His gaze fell upon Dove kneeling beside Crazy One. She glanced over at their entry. Her eyes lit with happiness and a small smile tipped the corners of her lips. Her welcome warmed him more than the fire.

He walked past the women and lie down behind them, licking the snow from his paws.

I am pleased Frog allows you to join us.

It shows on your face.

Frog placed the water next to Dove. "Do not leave this dwelling without a warrior."

Dove's eyes narrowed slightly. Her annoyance bristled in the air.

Do not argue. He is only thinking of your safety. A so-yá-po jumped Many Scars. It is not safe here for us. Do as Frog asks.

Dove accepted Wewukiye's caution and cast her eyes down. Worry accelerated her heart. Had her truth brought this on them?

The tension in the two warriors rippled through the small structure. They huddled on the other side of the fire whispering with the two who had remained in the tipi.

She dipped a cup of water from the bucket and dropped in a small rock—red from the fire.

The water rippled and moved as the hot rock heated the water. She dropped in calming herbs from her pouch. When the water stilled, she handed the cup to Crazy One.

"Are you not a sweet child?" The essence of life that usually surrounded the woman slowly grew and glowed as she sipped the warm drink.

Dove spread the blankets for their beds then started for the opening. Wewukiye joined her by the time she put a hand on the blanket entry. "I wish a moment outside." She said to Frog.

He nodded and stood. She ducked out into the thick white world of falling snow. She clutched the scruff of Wewukiye's neck and allowed him to lead her a short distance from the tipi. Frog's presence offered security, not anger or embarrassment, after the events of the evening.

Dove grasped the dog's fur and scurried to the warmth of the small structure. She quickly curled onto her blanket. Wewukiye snuggled against her back, and she fell asleep, wishing she could feel his arms around her.

****

The following morning, Frog stormed back to

their camp. Dove overheard him tell Many Scars the man who attacked him had been set free. Frog confronted William and learned the man had an accomplice in the soldiers. The agent would find out who the man was, but he could do little about the incident.

"William suggested we stay here until he finds answers." Frog stormed to the already loaded animals. "Our business here is done. We will return to the band." He mounted and waited for Many Scars to help Crazy One.

He made no move to help Dove. She stared pointedly at Frog. She needed a boost to mount her horse. The area offered nothing to stand on to raise her closer to the horse's back.

He leaped off his horse and bent his leg to make a step for her to stand on to mount the animal. Anger and frustration seeped from him like a storm slithering down the side of the mountain in summer.

Dove scrambled to mount her horse and put distance between herself and the warrior. Wewukiye had disappeared before the warrior returned from meeting with William. Wewukiye's essence lingered, reassuring her he remained near.

Frog mounted his horse with a flourish. The growing morning sun cast glittering stars across the white expanse of snow. The hooves of their horses squeaked with each step they took. The cold air bit at her cheeks. She drew her shawl up to cover all but her eyes. The trip back to their *Anihm* home would take longer and be more brutal than their trip to Lapwai.

The long cold day froze her toes and fingers. Her breath came in puffs when she dismounted that evening. They had stopped often without her asking Wewukiye to intervene. Frog realized their cold limbs needed frequent exercise to circulate their blood.

She worked as quickly as her stiff body allowed, setting up the cover for she and Crazy One. The old woman had become quiet the last part of the day. The cold seeped into her, drawing away her energy.

Too Short scrounged for wood and started a fire. The warriors and Crazy One huddled around the growing flames.

Dove spread the blankets and hides in their structure and straightened, closing her eyes. *I welcome your company tonight.*

As do I. Strong warm arms wrapped around her.

She opened her eyes and looked down at the male arms holding her back against his solid front. *I have missed you.*

He spun her, and his lips rested upon hers. The sealing of their spirits heated her to her toes. She pulled back fearful they would emit light and cause Frog to burst into the enclosure.

"Do not fear. The light of the other night joined our spirits, we are now one."

His breathy whisper beamed radiance as bright and warming as their kiss the night she discovered him as an elk.

She pressed back into his arms, lifting her lips to his. "I have felt one with you since our first embrace."

He kissed her deep and long.

The enclosure shook and Crazy One stuck her head in the opening. "Do you not want to feed yourself and the child?" She offered *o'ppah* bread and dried berries.

"Eat." Wewukiye released her.

Dove took the bread and drew the woman into the enclosure. "Wrap in your blankets and rest." She did not like the weakness she witnessed in the woman brought on by the snow and cold air. She needed the woman to help bring her child into this earth and the woman had become the family she lost.

Wewukiye helped ease Crazy One to the hide. He sensed his niece's weakness. Touching her he cringed inside. This trip proved hard on her. Her years upon this earth were coming to a close. Her strength and belief in Dove would give her the will to remain to help her with the birth. Beyond that, he now saw why Sa-qan thought Dove should marry their nephew. Lightning Wolf's family would provide companionship and shelter.

In his head, it would solve many problems. In his heart, he could not accept her living with any but him. "Now that Lightning Wolf has joined the Lake Nimiipuu for the winter you have met him. Do you feel he would make a good husband?"

Dove looked up from tending Crazy One. Her eyes narrowed. "I like his wife, Silent Doe. But I would not take him for a husband." She shook her head. "I will not be in another family where I am useful and not loved."

Her statement caused elation and sorrow. He was glad she would not marry his nephew, but he ached for the child who felt unwanted.

Dove carefully wrapped the old woman in many blankets, leaving few for herself.

"You must not become weak. It is not good." He picked a blanket off Crazy One to place on Dove's bed.

"I will have your arms to keep me warm. What I have is enough." Dove tucked the blanket around the woman's feet.

He noticed Dove's food sat untouched upon a blanket. "You must also eat. I cannot give you nourishment."

Dove smiled. "Your love nourishes me."

He shook his head, but acknowledged he, too, was nourished by her love and acceptance. Wewukiye sat, drawing her against him to sit in the vee of his legs. "Eat." He handed the bread to her.

"The man who attacked Many Scars, I have seen before." He whispered in her ear.

She chewed her bread. Her jaw muscle moved against his cheek. The rhythm and motion instilled the sensation they were one. He placed his hand under her shawl and over the bulge of her belly. The slight rippling motions and gentle push against his hand heightened the sensation of oneness.

Dove finished eating and reached for the water pouch hanging from the crook on one of the poles. He grasped the bag and watched her swallow. A droplet of water trickled from the corner of her mouth.

He leaned down licking the moisture from her skin. The combination of cold water and her warm skin against his tongue sliced his body with need so deep and primitive he wondered at his sanity.

Dove shifted and their lips met. He slid them to recline on the buffalo hide and wrapped his leg around hers. His desire roared through him like a blast of fire—hot, burning, insistent.

Her arms wrapped around his neck. She pressed her body tight against his, moving in slow rhythmic motions, further awakening his instincts to mate.

The shrill cry of Sa-qan screamed through his head freezing him in place and reminding him he could not cause Dove any harm.

He drew out of her embrace, kissed her again, and whispered so close his lips caressed hers, "Sa-qan calls."

"I heard."

He sighed and smiled. "I will return to keep you warm."

She nodded and he wrapped her in the remaining blankets. He kissed her forehead and shifted into smoke, exiting the enclosure and drifting into his elk form a good distance from the sleeping warriors and their horses.

He had contacted Sa-qan that morning to linger at the fort and learn about the man who attacked Many Scars. Her news would either lessen his guard or make him more vigilant. The gnawing inside, drew him to fear the later.

Le'éptit wax `oylá-qc
(26)

Wewukiye skidded to a stop on all four hooves in the knee-high snow at the sight of his sister huddled on a boulder.

"What have you discovered?" he asked, peering through the falling snow.

"The snow is your friend. It hides your tracks."

Her words rippled fear along his rib cage. "The man from the fort follows?"

"He and two others left the fort half a day behind you. They know you are the Lake Nimiipuu at *Anihm* camp and will head that direction." She ruffled her feathers, sending the snow that gathered on her flying.

"Who are they?"

"I could not hear well. He comes from the valley of the Lake Nimiipuu."

Wewukiye stomped his hoof. "I know his face but cannot remember where I came across him."

"Be watchful and keep all who travel with you safe." Conviction in Sa-qan's tone enforced his mission.

"They are all good of heart. All will be watched over."

Sa-qan nodded. "I will watch the men. If they are close I will let you know."

"*Qe`ci`yew`yew*, sister."

Sa-qan leaped into the air and silently disappeared among the falling snow.

Wewukiye charged through the snow in the direction of the fort. He wanted to watch the men himself. He found them two ridges over from where Dove slept. Their hobbled horses shuffled in the snow scrounging for feed. They had a tarp set up, open to the front and angling to the ground in the back. All the men slept rolled up in blankets under the tarp.

He could learn little here this night. He loped back to the camp of the Nimiipuu, shifted to smoke, and seeped into the women's structure. Dove snuggled close, pressing her body into his open arms.

"What did Sa-qan want?" she whispered.

He did not want to keep secrets, but he also did not want her worrying. "White men left the fort headed this direction." She stiffened in his arms. "Do not worry, they will not find us."

She relaxed in his arms, and he kissed her head as her breathing evened.

He would leave early and follow the men. If the wind showed favor with him, he could hide in the trees and their words would drift to him.

****

Dove woke with a start. The piercing cry of an eagle rang in her ears. Her body shook as she sat up. Noise outside the enclosure did not sound like other mornings. Horses snorted and stomped their hooves. Men's raised voices added to the unsettling sounds. She woke Crazy One and immediately began gathering their belongings.

She peeked through the opening.

Three White men scuffled with the warriors.

Visions of White men, soldiers, and Nimiipuu clashing on horses with women and children running for cover flashed in her mind. She squeezed her eyes closed. They had to stop this.

Where are you? No reply from Wewukiye riveted her to alert. She yanked her head back inside.

"Wewukiye is not answering me. There are *so-yá-po* challenging our warriors." She stared into

Crazy One's weary eyes. Fear for Wewukiye and those she traveled with surged cold though her body.

"Will he not come? Is he not here to protect all of us?"

"I hope you know what you are saying and he is fine."

A horse squealed and a man howled. She could not sit inside like a cowering mouse. She was the reason for the trip. Her action could not harm others.

Dove left the safe confines of the enclosure. Crazy One's gnarled hands grasped her ankle, but her strength easily shook the old woman free.

Too Short lay bleeding in the snow. A *so-yá-po* with injuries crawled toward the trees. Frog wrestled a man with a rifle. Many Scars and Red Bird struggled with a large man.

What should I do? Why didn't Wewukiye come? How could she help the warriors?

Thunk! The man with the rifle knocked Frog in the head. The warrior sunk to his knees and fell face first in the snow. The man glared at her, stalked forward, grabbed her arm, and dragged her to one of the saddled horses.

She struggled and fell to her knees, dragging her body through the cold snow, leaving marks and hindering his retreat. He knocked her alongside the head, shooting pain behind her eyes and churning her stomach. She slouched to the ground. He grabbed her roughly, tossing her over the horse like a dead animal. The pressure on her belly and her throbbing head spun her into darkness.

****

Wewukiye staggered to his feet. He rubbed a hand over his face and stared around him. Recollection came slow.

Three White men had galloped over the rise, surprising him. The next thing he knew explosions in his elk form ripped through him. He woke up and shifted to his man form.

He stared down at the elk. The violation of the body he'd occupied for so many years, roiled his stomach and surged anger—hot and vile. They took the hindquarters and the tender meat along the backbone. Leaving the carcass mutilated and wasted. *So wasteful.* So like a *so-yá-po.* A Nimiipuu took all of an animal they killed.

Rage pound in his head and accelerated his heart. He was left in man form until he found another animal to occupy.

Traveling as a man would take him longer to return to the group than as an elk. He glanced at the desecrated form. He would have to find another fine specimen to use as his conveyance in elk form. Over the seasons he had been hosted in many fine bull elk. They had all gone to the earth at an old age. This was his first loss at the hands of others—White men who did not revere their kill and use the whole animal. Anger rose in bitter bile in his throat.

He used the sun to determine the direction to find Dove and the rest. He set his path and trudged through the snow.

Urgency pushed him through the knee-high snow. He thanked the Creator for his endurance as a spirit and kept a steady pace.

Brother, there is trouble. Sa-qan's words struck him in the chest as mightily as the bullets which took his elk.

Dove? Dread sunk in his gut heavy as a granite boulder.

The so-yá-po took her. The Nimiipuu warriors split up. Two are taking our niece back to their winter home, two are following the so-yá-po.

He dropped to his knees. Why had he left her side? Pain, raw and searing ripped through his chest. He failed to be there when she needed him.

Brother. She needs you. Sa-qan's words burned in his head as a reprimand.

I've lost my elk vessel. He had to find a way to catch up to them.

Sa-qan's cry echoed in the clear morning air. Her form circled above him, highlighted by the bright blue sky.

Her call lured a hawk. The bird dived his way. He dissolved into smoke and entered the creature. *Thank you, sister.* Side by side they flew to help Dove.

****

Dove wiggled and her belly churned. Unbearable pressure in her head throbbed. She opened her eyes. Her body ached from cold and her position folded over the horse. She moved her hands, amazed they were free. She moved her feet, they also were free.

Through the pain shooting behind her eyes, she glanced at the man riding ahead of her, leading her horse. She twisted her head, glanced back, and spied a large man hunched over his horse. She could not slide off unseen.

She clutched the saddled, pulled her body up, and straddled the animal. The pounding in her head angered her stomach. She leaned to the side and retched.

Where was Wewukiye? Crazy One? And the warriors?

I need you. Sending the thought increased the throbbing. She closed her eyes and tried to concentrate on the sway of her horse. Moving her body with the jostling of the animal lessened the jolt on her pulsing head.

Her hands and feet tingled and ached from the cold. They kept up a relentless pace. The earthy scent of horse sweat normally relaxed her, but today it meant the horses were being pushed, and she was being drawn farther from the ones who could help her.

An eagle's cry pierced the air.

We are here.

Wewukiye's words brought tears to her eyes. She swallowed the lump of relief in her throat. *We need you.*

Warmth radiated through her body. She felt the presence of another. Her head ceased hurting, and her fingers and toes warmed and wiggled. *You said you could not enter me.*

It is I.

Sa-qan's voice soothed the last of her worries. The presence of another lessened.

You have left my body?

Yes. We will now enter the horses of the men. Hold this one steady. We will return.

Dove grasped the handle on her saddle and watched as both horses carrying the White men surged forward, catching the men off guard. The man in front of her dropped the lead rope to her horse, jerking to calm his horse and cling to the saddle. The man behind her shot past. Their horses raced through the snow.

Turn your horse around. Frog is headed this way.

She leaned down, caught the rope in her hand, and turned the horse to follow the tracks back to Frog. The essence Sa-qan infused in her body kept her warm. Her horse crested a hill, and she spotted two warriors on horseback loping her direction. She waved. Then remembered she would have to find a way to explain how she got away.

Frog rode up alongside her, his eyes scanning all around them. "Is this a trick?"

"No. Their horses gave them fits and took off. Where is Crazy One?" She hoped to focus him on something other than how she became free of the White men.

He narrowed his eyes and stared at her. "Their horses ran away? Why did yours not?"

She shrugged and nudged her horse forward. "It is trained better. Where is Crazy One?"

"The old woman is with Too Short and Red Bird. They are headed back to the *Anihm* camp." Frog rode on one side of her and Many Scars claimed the space on her other side.

"Why did they take me?" Dove asked already knowing he would not have an answer.

The warrior stared at her a long time. "I do not know. Have you seen these White men before?"

She shook her head. A slight ache started in her head, reminding her of the blow. "He did not treat me like he planned to let me live." The idea of what could have happened to her had Sa-qan and Wewukiye not arrived, radiated cold and numbing shivers up her back.

"You will live and so will the child you say will set our people free." Frog nudged his horse into a quicker pace, trotting ahead of Dove and off the trail the two processions of horses made. Many Scars dropped behind her. Single file they rode through the day and half the night, coming upon the other three as the moon started descending toward the mountains.

Her body ached from relentless hours on the horse and the cold seeping through her few layers. Crazy One placed a steaming drink in her hands and wrapped a blanket around her shoulders as she sat by the fire in the tipi they erected to house more than she and Crazy One. The injured warrior lay on a blanket. Crazy One tended his wounds.

All is well.

Dove smiled. She tried a couple times during the day to speak with Wewukiye. *They will not be back?*

They would need horses first. Their horses tossed them in a pile of snow.

She heard the smile in his words.

Why did they take me? All day she wondered about this. Did they hear what she told Agent William? Were they friends of Evil Eyes?

Sa-qan will keep watch over them. We believe they will visit Evil Eyes.

Even though she also believed that was the connection, a tremor of fear wracked her body knowing he and Sa-qan believed the same.

Crazy One returned to the fire and winked. "Is he not sleeping well?" She nodded to the wounded warrior and eyed the cup in her hand. "Is not my uncle what you need?"

"What about the other warriors? They aren't staying out in the cold all night?" She wanted Wewukiye's arms around her, but they dare not have the others questioning how he came to be here.

"Do they not take turns watching? Is their fire not warm?" She nodded to the bedding she spread far away from the wounded man. "Will you not be in darkness?"

Dove hugged the old woman. "Thank you."

She lay on the buffalo hide and drew the blankets over her. Soon warmth ran the length of her back and the back of her legs. Strong arms wrapped around her and air puffed against her cheek.

"Sleep well," whispered in her ear.

"Now that you are here, I will."

Wewukiye breathed in her herbal scent and relaxed for the first time since escaping the dead elk. Failure had ripped through him realizing the White men had taken her, and he had feared a repeat of her attack by Evil Eyes, or worse, her death. He held her safe in his arms and vowed to never leave her alone. Her powers exceeded those of mortals, but she was still a mortal.

Mortals and spirits could not exist together,

even though she had welcomed his differences with an open mind and heart. His heart squeezed with the knowledge they could not continue to exist like this. One day Crazy One's body would give out, and they would no longer have someone to help them be together.

. He loved this mortal, but how could they remain together without his identity being revealed?

Le'éptit wax `uyné-pt
(27)

Dove welcomed the melting snow and warmer days and nights. Soon they would move to the camas meadows and begin gathering the *kouse* bulbs. After the trip to see Agent William, the elders and Chief Joseph treated her with more respect. Her family still kept their distance, but others had begun to nod or talk with her as she moved about the encampment.

The trip proved hard on Crazy One. She did not move as spry as before and drank more herbs for her aching bones. Dove did most of the chores required for the two of them. Wewukiye always had wood piled by their dwelling and water in buckets by the wood. It tickled her no one questioned the appearance of the wood and water, and they now treated Wewukiye as one of the band.

She glanced up as the spirit of her thoughts walked across the open area. His stride, the width of his shoulders, and the carriage of his head posed a regal view. An outsider would think him one of Chief Joseph's sons.

A smiled pulled at the corners of her mouth. Her heart always expanded at the sight of him.

"You appear happy today. Is it the fine weather?" He stood back much too far, but correct for their status.

"The sun and the warm weather make me yearn to dig roots."

He laughed. "That is still a moon away." His gaze lit on the now obvious bulge of child. "You should be caring for a child by then."

She wrapped an arm around her belly. Happiness swirled. "I am anxious to meet this child."

"Do not be too anxious. To have the baby early would not be good." The mischief lighting his eyes made her laugh.

"Crazy one would not allow the child to come early."

Wewukiye nodded his head. "This is true. How is my aunt today?"

Dove's elation wavered. "She gets better as the weather warms. I fear she will not be of this earth much longer." Sadness washed over her saying out loud the words haunting her thoughts and fears.

"She will not let you or the child down." Wewukiye took a step toward her.

She longed to lean into his strong embrace. Instead, she stood tall. "This I know."

"Are you and Silent Doe meeting today?"

She nodded. The third wife of Lightning Wolf, a relative of Crazy One, had asked Dove to help her pound herbs into powder for Crazy One.

"We are working in front of her dwelling." She knew Wewukiye and Crazy One wished her to become friendly with the family. She enjoyed all three wives, Lightning Wolf, and the four children, but she did not like the idea of Lightning Wolf marrying her once the child came.

She stared into Wewukiye's eyes. She would only give her body to the man before her.

"Crazy One will not always be around. You need support of family. They will be your new family." Wewukiye again took a step toward her.

I wish to visit with you in the cave. She yearned to wrap her arms around him and ply him with kisses. He no longer slept with her, and their time together happened only in the open where watchful eyes took note.

After you help Silent Doe, come to the cave, but make sure no one sees.

The baby pushed on her belly and fluttered. She placed her hand over the spot and marveled at the size and shape of the foot. Soft, sweet, rich elation flowed through her.

The love and awe reflecting in Dove's eyes, struck Wewukiye like a club knocking his legs out from under him. His hand reached toward hers. An inner voice warned against it, and he jerked back. He clenched his fist to keep from reaching toward her again.

"Do you need to sit?" he asked, motioning to the log they used to visit.

"No. The child is strong. I can feel his foot as he grows and pushes for more room." She gazed into his eyes. Her love for the child shone like the brightest of stars.

Crazy One exited the tipi. "Is this not what you need to help Silent Doe?" She handed a hide bag to Dove. The heavy stone bowl and pedestal in the bag stretched the bottom.

Dove took the pouch. "You will be fine while I help?"

Crazy One nodded. "Is not my uncle going to take me on a walk?"

Wewukiye smiled and agreed, this being the first he had heard of their walk.

Dove glanced from one to the other. "Do not take her too far. Her body is still healing."

He smiled. "My niece does not want to walk; she wishes to warm my ears." A gnarled hand smacked his arm and he laughed.

Dove laughed and waved to them. He watched her cross to the far end of the dwellings. Her small body waddled slightly from the weight of the child.

"Do your eyes follow her? Do your actions make her yours?" Crazy One drew him behind their tipi

231

and up the side of the cliff, away from the activity.

"She is mine. I just cannot do anything about it yet." He pondered their predicament night and day. She would not marry anyone other than he. They were meant to be together. He just could not figure out how.

"Are your actions not seen by many?" Crazy One sat on a boulder in the sun. She patted the flat part next to her.

Wewukiye sat, staring down onto the encampment. His gaze quickly sought Dove kneeling next to Silent Doe as the two used long rocks to pound dried herbs to powder. His anger simmered noticing Lightning Wolf watching the two. He knew Crazy One had asked the warrior to marry Dove.

"Do not push Lightning Wolf to marry Dove. She will refuse, and I will not allow it."

"How do you know she will not see it the best for her child?" Crazy One picked at invisible things on his buckskin shirt.

He thought of the expression on her face as she experienced the movement of the child. Her eyes had lit with such love and contentment. Would she pick Lightning Wolf over him to give the child a safe home?

He shook his head. She would do what was right for the child, but would she do what was right for her? He could see her sacrificing her needs to give the child what he needed. Did his selfish wish to want her for himself override what was best for them both? This thought tugged on his mind and heart.

"Do you not make her feel like a woman?" Crazy One's eyes twinkled. "Does she not say your name in her sleep and moan?"

The thought of the woman dreaming of him, sent his blood racing and heating.

"This is why she belongs with me and not

Lightning Wolf." He stared into the old woman's eyes. "She would not give herself to him and would remain unfulfilled."

Crazy One nodded. "Do you speak the truth? Does not giving your child a family also bring fulfillment?"

Wewukiye stared at the woman in the village below. She had sacrificed so much already. An unloving family, the attack of Evil Eyes. Would she also sacrifice being fulfilled as a woman to give her child happiness? If she did—would he be able to abide by her choice?

****

Dove carried the powders and the tools she used back to Crazy One's dwelling. The old woman was not in their tipi. She put the items where they belonged and ducked out of the structure. She stepped behind the tipi and peered around. No one roamed in the area. She headed to the bushes she used to relieve herself.

Past the bushes, she continued up the cliff, stopping often to rest. Finally, she spotted Wewukiye's cave. She entered the dark interior.

Her eyes gradually recognized the walls and sparse supplies. She picked up two blankets and spread them one on top of the other and rolled a third blanket.

I am here.

She waited. Worry snuck into her thoughts sitting on the blankets waiting.

The light dimmed. Her heart thrummed in her chest. Did he approach or did someone follow her?

He stepped into her sight and security wrapped around her. Her breath caught. His masculine build, sunshine hair, and aura of strength, melted every muscle in her body.

He knelt on the blanket and opened his arms. She flowed against him, reveling in his warmth and security.

Her arms locked around his neck, her lips sought his. Their kisses no longer held innocence and exploration. His tongue delved into her mouth. She treasured the taste of him and the intimacy. Her body ignited proving the needs this man of her heart brought to her were right. She dreamed of the day they could take their desires all the way.

He leaned back, holding her at arm's length. His eyes glowed a deep, dark blue much like the summer lake.

"I wish to feel you in every way." She pressed her palm to his cheek.

"You know that is not possible until you have the child." His voice sounded rough.

"I know, but I want you to know this is my wish." She stared into his eyes. He had to understand. "You are the only man I wish to touch me in all ways a man touches a woman."

He drew her back against his body. "I wish the same." His hand roamed across her back, the other cupped her heavy breast.

She leaned into his touch. The sensation of water skimming across her skin followed his touch. The softness and refreshed pleasure elicited a throaty sigh.

He growled and captured her mouth with his once again. This time the kiss scorched her to her toes and left her dizzy. He reclined her onto the blankets, his body leaving no air between them. His hands continued to roam. As did hers—under his tunic and across the smooth hard muscles of his chest.

The sensation of his skin to hers spun all thoughts out of her head other than touching him intimately. She shoved his tunic up his body.

He grasped her arms. "No. If we take off clothes I will not be able to control—"

She kissed his toned belly.

"Aaaugh!" He pressed her tight against him breathing fast and hard against her ear.

"If you continue to torment me, I will not meet you alone anymore."

She pressed her lips to his. He countered, moving away from her.

"If you marry Lightning Wolf you will be sorry for your actions this day."

His words froze her inside and out like jumping into an ice covered lake.

"I do not plan to become a wife to Lightning Wolf. I do not plan to become a wife to anyone other than you." She shoved away from him. "Do you feel we are not mates?"

The anguish in her dark eyes ripped at Wewukiye's chest. He never wanted to cause her pain.

"I feel you are my mate." He kissed her lips tenderly, bestowing all the wonder he experienced at their connection. "I do not know how we can be mates and raise a child when I am of the spirit world and you the mortal world."

"We do well together now."

The wistfulness of her voice sucked the resolve from him. Reality would not allow him to forget the differences as much as he wanted to.

"I would need to leave you when my duties call me. Sometimes these duties take me far. I also cannot stay in man form constantly."

Her arms wrapped tighter around him. "I have witnessed you in other forms."

He kissed her cheek. "I cannot remain in the village while in other forms. I do not think Thunder Traveling to Distant Mountains would understand a bull elk roaming among the dwellings."

"What will we do?" she whispered.

"I do not know. But I will never give my heart to

another."

"My heart is only held by you and my body will only be touched by you."

He held her in his arms until the sun faded in the sky.

"Come, you must go back." He stood and drew her up beside him. She slid up against his body like a warm mist of steam, and he trembled in anticipation at the image.

"You excite my body in every move you make." He clasped her to his chest and heart, kissing her hard, thorough, and intimately. He released her lips and nibbled on her neck waiting for the ache in his loins to lessen.

Waiting to mate with her would be the closest thing to torture he had ever experienced.

Le'éptit wax `oymátat
(28)

Dove ignored the pain shooting through her lower back. The Nimiipuu band traveled a day's ride from the lake and their summer home. The women had spent ten suns in the meadow digging roots and drying them. She wasn't allowed to work beside them. She and Springtime held company in a makeshift birthing hut. Both due to have their babies soon, they talked of birthing and raising their children.

If not for being able to speak with Wewukiye in her head, Dove would have found the days of isolation hard to take. Crazy One and the other woman's mother came twice a day to the hut bringing staples.

Pain pierced again. She winced. Wewukiye peered back at her before she could hide her discomfort. Concern wrinkled his brow, and he stopped his horse, waiting for her to ride up beside him.

"Why are you in pain?"

They traveled as usual at the end of the band. Even though men were not to touch or see her now, he did not hold to the custom. He placed a hand on her leg. His touch eased some of her discomfort.

"Pain shoots across my back. It hurts to sit on the horse." She hated complaining. A wave hit, and she sucked in air.

Crazy One rode up on her other side. "Is she not having the child?" She pointed a gnarled finger at Wewukiye. "Should you not go get Silent Doe? Does she not want to help?"

Wewukiye swung off the horse and lifted Dove down. "I'll set up the tipi first. You stay here with Dove."

Another pain spiraled through her belly. "Does this pain hurt the child?" she asked Crazy One, fearing the time too soon and something would happen to the baby.

"Do you still feel the child moving?" Crazy One walked her in small circles.

"Yes."

Crazy One smiled. "Does not your child tell you all is well?"

Relief raced through her, relaxing her muscles and easing some of the pain. She watched Wewukiye struggle with the tipi.

"Just drape it over the limbs of trees. It is all I require."

He twirled around, his eyes wide and fringed with red, showing his frustration and uncertainty.

"Go get Silent Doe. Crazy One and I will fix the covering." She clutched his hand and led him to his horse. "Your concern means everything to me, but right now, you would better serve me by getting more help."

He kissed her lips, stared into her eyes, and mounted the horse. "I will be back soon."

"I know."

He nudged his horse, and they set out at a lope toward the disappearing line of Nimiipuu.

She turned to the task of spreading the tipi hide over branches. Lightning Wolf and his family decided to remain with the Lake Nimiipuu through the coming warm season. She knew it had to do with Silent Doe wanting to be with her during this time. She had formed a kinship with the woman. One she wished many times she shared with her own mother.

Crazy One no longer mentioned a marriage

between Dove and Lightning Wolf. That did not mean the old woman would not pursue it again. Dove had grown fond of all of Lightning Wolf's family, but she would not marry the man just to make things easier. She would not live with a man she did not care for as a woman should care for her mate.

Crazy One tugged on the hide. They stretched it between the trees and placed poles and rolled rocks onto the overhang to hold it down.

A pain originating at her back rippled through Dove's belly. She stopped to breathe, focusing on a tree farther away.

Dove caught glimpses of the old woman scurrying between their horses and the makeshift cover while she focused on the tree and not her pain.

Crazy One grasped her arm and led her to the covering. Blankets hung from each end forming two more walls. One flipped up making a doorway to cast light inside.

The woman lowered Dove onto a blanket spread upon the ground. "Is it not better to rest?" Her fading eyes searched the area beyond the opening. "Would it not be better to have stopped near a river?"

Nimiipuu women usually delivered their children in water. She too wished they sat near the lake. For those who had experienced the water birthing called it wonderful.

"I wish we were near water as well." Another pain rippled through her belly.

Crazy One patted her hand where she clutched her belly. "Will I be back with a drink and more blankets?"

Dove lay on the blanket, staring up at the hide covering. She hugged the roundness that rippled and contracted. Her child would soon rest in her arms and suckle from her breasts. A wondrous ache spread in her chest and filled her mind with happy sensations. She would bring a child to the band.

Crazy One dropped a pile of blankets on the ground and placed the rawhide pouch of water beside her. "Are you not about to experience what every woman dreams of?" The gleam and knowing in the woman's eyes reflected the joy warming Dove.

"Have you been a mother—a wife?" She knew little of the woman's life.

Sadness drew the woman's features down, adding years to her face. "Did I not love a brave warrior and did he not spill his seed?" The woman peered up at the covering. A tear slid down her cheek. "Are they not together watching over me?"

"I am sorry. I did not mean to bring you sorrow." Dove took the woman's cold, fragile hand in hers. "It must be hard to lose the man and child you love."

Crazy One glanced down at her. "Is now not a time of gladness not sorrow?"

Sharp arrows sliced through her belly. She clutched the bony hand she held. The sensation eased, and Crazy One withdrew her hand, replacing it with a small buckskin cloth.

"Is this not good to squeeze?"

"Thank you." Dove sipped the water and watched the woman bustle around the enclosure.

Silent Doe arrived bearing a wide smile and gentle hands that rubbed her back and eased her fears. "If this baby could have waited, the birthing would have been easier on you." She nodded toward the opening. "One more day and you would have birthed him in the lake of your people."

"I think he did not want a large gathering on his first day." Dove smiled and grimaced at the pain trailing from her back to belly and down.

She called to Wewukiye in her mind as each pain became stronger and the child pushed to see the world. His calm replies eased her pain and worry.

Crazy One and Silent Doe stayed by her side through the day and into the dark night. Her child finally emerged.

"You have a strong daughter," Silent Doe announced.

Crazy One cut the umbilical cord and put it in the pouch hanging from the cradleboard she so lovingly worked on during the cold winter nights. The cord would remain in the pouch and with the child for her lifetime unless she became ill. Then the shaman would use the cord to heal her.

Dove reached for her squirming daughter. Dark hair swirled on her round head. Her eyes scrunched closed as she squalled. Dove blew in her face. She hiccupped and opened her eyes. Two brown eyes, one lighter than the other, stared at Dove in surprise.

Her heart lurched, and her arms became weak. Silent Doe grasped the child as Dove's arms fell to her sides. The child looked just like her.

No one would believe her accusations against Evil Eyes.

Her body shook and numbness slid into her body.

Dove? Dove? What is wrong?

Wewukiye charged into the structure. Dove's power had surged and then faded.

She lay on the blankets, lifeless. Her eyes staring at nothing.

"You should not—"

Silent Doe's attempt to push him back out the structure went unheeded as he dropped to his knees beside Dove.

He drew her up into his arms and peered at Crazy One. "Did the birth not go well? Is she—" He could not say the word or even think it. They had come too far for her to leave him now.

A wail rang out as Crazy One splashed water on

the child. "Is not the child strong and the mother in shock?"

"Shock? Of what?" He shook Dove. "Look at me. What is wrong?"

Her eyelids flickered, and she murmured something.

He leaned closer to her lips. Moments before he planned to walk in and kiss her lips to show her how much he thought of her strength. Now all he could think of was kissing her and filling her with his strength.

"Eyes," she said on a soft wisp of air.

"You are too strong to allow Evil Eyes to take away your strength."

"Brown. Both." She turned her head into his chest and wept.

Wewukiye stared at the child wailing and squirming in Crazy One's hands. It could not be. This child would set Dove free.

He watched the old hands clean the child.

How could the eyes not be different? The White man's evil ways must be exposed. He knew Dove did not lie, but how could they prove her truth to the elders?

Wewukiye studied the child. A daughter. He smiled. She would be brave and strong like her mother.

"We will find a way to prove the truth. She is just born. We cannot ask so much of one so young. Your daughter is strong and will have her mother's *txiyak*."

Tears trickled down Dove's face. She gathered her daughter into her arms, and she kissed the child's head. "Together we will be strong, little one."

Wewukiye studied the mother and child. The love emanating from Dove wrapped the two in a golden halo. His heart cracked, and he grieved for the mother he could not remember. She had died before their father shamed the family. Had she loved him and his siblings with as strong an attachment as this woman did this child? He shook off the sad thoughts.

Dove smiled and pushed the tears from her face. "Meet the child of our people."

He kissed her cheek and stared at the child. The baby's hands curled in tight fists, yet she suckled noisily at her mother's breast under a blanket Silent Doe tossed across Dove's shoulder.

In his worry over Dove he forgot to keep his emotions in check. He glanced at the woman and read acceptance in her eyes. Had Dove told her of their love?

Silent Doe left the structure, and Crazy One stood guard at the entrance, giving them a moment alone.

Wewukiye placed a kiss on Dove's shiny forehead. "Congratulations on a healthy girl."

"Would you like to see her beauty?" Dove deftly drew the child out from under the blanket. The child's small lips continued sucking, her eyes scrunched closed. But he could already see her mother in her.

"She is a beautiful daughter. She glows with the goodness of her mother."

Dove's breath whooshed out on an audible sigh of relief.

"Is it wrong to have wished this child be a girl? I feared if she were a boy and had the eyes of her father I would not be able to love him. Because she is a sweet girl, with soft eyes I do not fear her. She will not grow up to be domineering and hurt others." The forgiveness she asked of him was not his to give.

"You are the only one who can judge yourself. I, too, am pleased you had a girl, but it is my own selfish reasons of wishing for more wonderful women like you among the Nimiipuu."

He reclined on the blanket next to her, looping an arm around her shoulders and drawing the two females next to his heart. "I am still uncertain how to make you my family, but I am sure the Creator will help guide us to the way."

"That is our wish. To be your family." Dove raised her lips to his, and he could not have refused her a kiss had the Creator himself grabbed him by the scruff of the neck.

He had missed the touch of her lips and the gentleness of her hands over the last two moons during her restriction to the menstrual hut. Had she been alone with just Crazy One, he could have continued his nightly visits. For he was a spirit and the belief a male would have bad luck being around a woman during her confinement did not pertain to him. No mortal could take away his power. Even a pregnant one with powers of her own.

He drew out of their kiss and she sighed.

"I have missed you. Had it not been for our internal conversations, I would have run from that hut and sought you—tradition or not."

He chuckled. "If Springtime had not been in the hut with you, I would have visited you every night."

Dove put a hand on his cheek as he stared down at the sleeping child in her arm. "Can you promise to never leave"—she glanced down at the child—"us."

His chest squeezed so hard he thought his ribs would crack. "I can only promise I will do everything I can to remain a part of your lives. I am not sure how we are to be together, but it is my desire to make it happen."

She kissed his lips. "That you wish to be with me is enough."

He stared into her eyes. The honesty, desire, and love he witnessed gladdened his heart. "I wish to be with you in every way a man wants a woman by his side. I will discuss the possibilities again with

Sa-qan. We just have to be patient that a solution will come."

"I will wait through eternity to be with you."

The child jerked, and her eyes shot open. Wewukiye glimpsed her soft brown eyes for the first time. A smug smile crept upon his lips. While the eyes may not be Evil Eyes downfall, they would find a way to prove his evil.

Le'éptit wax kúyc
(29)

Dove stood beside her horse waiting for Wewukiye to help her and the baby mount. Uneasiness tickled her spine at the prospect of rejoining the band at the lake. Lightning Wolf had arrived five days after the birth and escorted Silent Doe back to the lake. She, Crazy One, and Wewukiye had decided to remain to give time for the other two to explain to Chief Joseph they would have to rely on something else to prove Evil Eyes's attack and to send a messenger for Agent William.

The weeks by themselves allowed her and Wewukiye time to enjoy the child together before they returned to the band. When they were with the others they would once again have to hide their feelings until they caught Evil Eyes in his lies.

The day had come for them to return. The child was strong and growing stronger every day. Wewukiye wished the elders to behold the child and decide how to snare Evil Eyes.

"Do not look so worried. Soon all will be put right, and we may plan a future." Wewukiye kissed her cheek.

"I have felt eyes watching us all morning." She couldn't shake the feeling of intrusion.

"Sa-qan has been watching."

He wrapped his hands around her waist. Thoughts of someone watching disappeared, and her body leaned into his. She had healed from the birth, and her body desired to mate with Wewukiye. The urgency became so intense at times she could not keep her hands from touching him.

"I wish to be with you before we return to the others," she said it soft and low for his ears only.

His hands squeezed her sides; red ringed the edges of his blue eyes. "It is my desire as well."

"Crazy One." Dove did not take her gaze from his.

The old woman shuffled up to her. Dove placed the child tucked in the cradleboard into the old woman's hands. "We will be back."

Dove laced her fingers with Wewukiye's, and they strode into the trees. Her heart pounded in her chest and her ears. Finally, she would become this man's woman completely.

Wewukiye continued walking when she would have stopped. Farther into the trees, in a secluded area, he stopped and wrapped his arms around her, dropping light kisses over her face. His tenderness melted her legs. She would have slithered to the ground had he not held her so tight.

She had dreamed of this moment since the day she realized he would never hurt her and she would never love another. He slipped her shawl from her shoulders and spread it on the young summer grass. She slipped her hands under his tunic, sliding her hands up his body removing the garment. With his arms raised, she could no longer help remove the shirt, but she could splay her fingers across his taut muscles and feel the heat slice through the pads, down her arms, and burst flames of desire at the juncture of her legs.

She inhaled at the spear of need that struck.

Wewukiye clasp her head in his hands. His teeth scraped her lips and his tongue entered, sucking and demanding. The fervor of his kiss echoed the turbulence heating her body and making her skin sensitive to his touch, breath, and nearness.

She did not realize his hands no longer held her

until her dress raised and his lips left hers. The cool morning air tightened her nipples and swirled around her heated body, banking the fires.

Dove stepped back admiring his long, muscled body as he spread her dress near the shawl making a larger bed. She sat upon the garment and watched him remove her moccasins; his hands drifting up her leg and back down, again igniting a blaze she feared would consume her before he made love to her.

He stood and slowly untied the rawhide string keeping his leggings on his hips. His gaze never left hers as he removed his leggings and moccasins, kicking the clothing to the side.

The sight of his body with the early morning sun lighting it from behind, stopped her heart and stole her senses.

Glorious.

He knelt beside her. "I have dreamed of this moment since the night I met you." He skimmed a hand down her side, over her hips, and back up the inside of her leg.

The pulse of drumming, rhythmic and insistent, vibrated her insides where the child had grown.

"Your breasts are fuller, perfect for suckling a child." He kissed her nipples and down the heavy swell of her milk-laden breasts, nuzzling the valley between them. His hand continued the slow trail up and down her sides and thighs.

Her body throbbed and moved toward his touch. The drumming built—louder, stronger, until she thought the steady rhythm would drive her crazy.

"Please. My body craves yours."

The color of his eyes deepened and glowed. He spread her legs with his and staring into her eyes, he entered.

Thunder shattered the drumming in her head. All went still and lightning skittered through her body, scorching, tingling, exciting. She wrapped her arms around Wewukiye's neck to hold on as he moved inside her, becoming one with her.

He growled her name, kissed her fervently, and went still, his manhood pulsing within her and setting off more waves of mind numbing sensations.

She closed her eyes and floated as if swimming on a summer day in the lake, carefree, weightless, and content.

Wewukiye gathered Dove in his arms. Her love and acceptance of him made him whole. Until this moment, he thought his life was perfect. Now he knew the only way he would be content would be to have Dove with him always.

Brother, I now realize what you tried to tell me so many seasons ago.

He breathed her scent of milk, herbs, and Dove. His heart ached with happiness.

"I could remain this way with you for all eternity." He kissed her face. Her adorable face he saw even when his eyes remained closed.

"Hmmm... It would be my wish as well."

She snuggled closer, moving her hips, taking him deeper inside. His sight blurred from the awareness of her body quivering around him.

He thrust slow and pulled out slow.

"Oh!" Dove sucked in air and pressed her hips closer.

Smugness tightened his chest. He continued his slow ministrations, absorbing the quakes and quivers of her body, and swallowing her gasps and moans.

On the edge of his own sanity, she jerked, clasped his bottom, and thrust her hips hard against him as her body shuddered and he released.

His muscles weakened. He tried to hold his body above Dove's and not squish her, but his arms shook and his strength left him.

How could this be? A spirit never became weak

unless his power was drained. He stared into Dove's glowing face. Had making love to her depleted his power?

She ran a finger down his cheek. Sparks lit along his skin, giving him new energy. Her emotions mixed with his gave them both unequaled power.

"Why are you so thoughtful?" The pleasure lighting her face dulled to apprehension.

"You drain my power when we mate, then with a touch you restore it. Your power is stronger than mine when we join." He kissed her palm. "But I do not complain."

"Your loving me gives me power."

The cry of the baby traveled to his ears. "I believe your daughter is hungry." His gaze traveled to her breasts. A small bead of milk formed at the tip of each nipple.

"It appears my body also knows the sound of my child." Her cheeks deepened in color.

"It is no shame in loving your child." He kissed her lips. "Or loving the one of your heart. When Evil Eyes's deceit is discovered, I will find a way to be with you."

She ran a hand down his face. "It would make my life complete."

Wewukiye sat up and drew her with him. "Come, we must get you back to your daughter and then to the village of the Lake Nimiipuu."

He helped her dress and donned his clothing as she watched. The gleam in her eyes stalled his hands more than once. He could see they would require many moments like this in the coming season to quench their desire for one another.

Hand in hand they walked sedately back to their horses. Crazy One carried the baby on her back.

"Is she not hungry? Does she not have a strong voice?" The old woman shrugged out of the cradleboard. Dove took her child from the board. She loosened the tie at the neck of her dress and nursed her child draped in a shawl.

Wewukiye scanned the area. He now sensed someone watching. *Where are you sister?*

I am watching the approach of White men to the Lake Nimiipuu.

Anxiety rippled his shoulders. *Who are they?*

Agent William, two soldiers, and a skinny man.

He calmed. *Good. We will be there today.*

Dove stood, patting her baby on the back. "Is all well?"

"Yes. I have talked with my sister. Agent William is on his way to the Lake Nimiipuu. He will help us get the truth from Evil Eyes."

She laced the baby into the cradleboard and threaded her arms through the straps.

Wewukiye grasp her waist, lifting her onto her horse. His hand lingered on her thigh. "All will be well soon, and we can look to a future together."

A wide smile lit Dove's face. "It is all I have wished for."

He kissed her hand and lifted Crazy One on her horse. Wewukiye started to mount his horse and stopped short. The sensation of someone watching feathered across his neck. He handed the packhorse rope to Crazy One and the rope of his horse to Dove.

"You two continue. I am going to take a look around."

Dove started to protest.

"Go. I will be right behind you." He motioned them onward. The unease in the air flashed memories through his mind of the evil wolf who walked the mountain of his brother.

He could not go to the village without first seeking the source of his agitation.

Mita áptit
(30)

Dove stared across the light green rolling hills. The fear someone watched them still lingered. Twisting, she peered behind her. Nothing moved.

They topped a rise. The lake shimmered in the spring sun. Wewukiye still did not return.

Are you coming? She again twisted to see behind her.

I follow a man who follows you.

Her instincts proved correct. She shuddered and continued behind Crazy One into a copse of trees along the lake's edge.

The baby fussed and her breasts leaked. They had not stopped for some time.

"Crazy One, the baby needs to eat and be cleaned."

The older woman stopped her horse beside a log and climbed stiffly down.

Dove handed the cradleboard down to Crazy One and slipped from her horse's back. Her legs wobbled. This first trip on a horse since the birth of her daughter weakened her legs. She smiled. The pleasure Wewukiye shared with her could also account for her shaky legs.

Crazy One handed her the child and led the horses to the edge of the lake for a drink. Dove knelt on the ground beside the cradleboard and unlaced her daughter. She unwrapped the rabbit skin on the lower half of her baby and tossed the soiled grass to the side. Carrying the baby at arm's length, Dove walked to the edge of the lake and dipped the baby's bottom in the water.

Her daughter cried at the cold, but Dove dunked her bottom again. Children bathed in cold water were stronger. Her child would need much strength. Her small face scrunched and reddened. The mark of the man who fathered her would never be seen. But once they proved his evil ways, her daughter would be known to carry his blood. She would need to be strong to prove she was a Nimiipuu.

Dove stood, clasping her dripping child to her chest.

"No! No! No!" Crazy One's shouts startled Dove.

A force against Dove's back shoved her face first into the water.

The cold demanded she suck in air, only it wasn't air. Water quickly filled her mouth and lungs.

My baby!

She opened her arms, enabling her child to bob to the surface. The weighted pressure on her back drove her deeper under the water. The fight for her baby and the man she loved ignited a desire to live. She flailed her arms, clawing her way to the top of the water, to the sun glinting on the water's surface.

Wewukiye. The baby.

Wewukiye charged into the lake the moment he saw the man he had followed charge out of the trees and shove Dove.

His hooves nearly stalled at the thought of losing both of them. The water covered his massive elk form lunging toward the baby floating on the water. The man joined his race toward the child.

Wewukiye glanced Dove's direction. Her arms flailed weakly. Dove! Fear crackled down his spine and pound in his head. He couldn't lose her. He cast a glance at the baby. She was more vulnerable. He ducked under water and came up with the child on his head, cradled between his antlers.

The child is fine. He glanced once more at Dove,

still working to remain afloat. He hurried to swim under her, folding her body over his. He wished to lunge for the shore but realized that would dislodge Dove. With precise steps, to not jostle, he walked to the shore.

Wewukiye kept an eye on the man who sputtered and flounder in the water.

At the shore, he handed the baby to Crazy One and gently slid Dove from his back.

He charged the man, knocking him to the ground and holding him down with his thick antlers. One strike to the man's head with his large hoof knocked the man out.

"Dove?" Crazy One gazed at the limp woman on the ground near her feet.

Wewukiye changed into man form and knelt beside Dove.

"Dove? My strong woman, come back to me." Wewukiye leaned down placing his cheek near her nose. Her sweet breath did not whisper across his skin. He leaned down, listening for her heart.

Pain, searing and sharp, speared his chest. He picked up her limp body holding it tight to his chest. Tears burned a path down his cheeks. No, he could not lose her now. They had become one—she was his beacon of light and love.

Crazy One picked at his shoulder as he sat on the ground and cradled Dove in his lap.

"This is wrong. She has given so much to help her people. Why would she be taken now?" He stared at Crazy One through the tears in his eyes. Misery, an emotion he'd never experienced, shredded his body.

"Should you not get this man and this baby to the others?" Crazy One pointed her knobby finger at the man sprawled on the ground.

"But Dove..." He choked. He would never see her smile again or hear her beautiful laugh.

"Do you not owe her to finish her journey?" Crazy One smacked his head with her hand. "Do you want to keep her from her gift to her people?"

He had promised Dove he would help her prove Evil Eyes's deceit. He swallowed the sorrow balling in his chest and placed Dove on the ground.

Wewukiye stalked over to the man, slung him over his shoulder, and flung him across the back of Dove's horse. Crazy One had the child bundled in the cradleboard. He tied the cradleboard to his horse and placed Crazy One on her horse, handing her the ropes for both the packhorse and Dove's.

Kneeling beside Dove, he gently scooped her into his arms and led his horse toward the Lake Nimiipuu Village.

Each step he stamped in the ground stirred his anger further. If the elders would have only listened to her and stood beside her this would not have happened. She would still be alive, able to raise her daughter and fulfill her gift.

His anger could not reverse nor halt time. He stalked into the village. The people cleared a wide path. Each step vibrated up his leg, jarring his teeth and intensifying his sorrow.

Chief Joseph, Thunder Traveling to Distant Mountains, and Frog all stepped forward the moment he stopped in front of the chief's lodge.

Silent Doe ran forward, sobbing and touching Dove's face.

"I have brought proof the woman in my arms told the truth about the *so-yá-po* who attacked her. And I have brought the man who killed her."

Voices rumbled around him. Lightning Wolf stepped forward to take Dove from his arms.

"No!" Wewukiye held her tight against his chest and heart. "No one is to touch her but those that believed."

Crazy One touched his arm, moving him to the

side and taking the cradleboard off of his horse.

She walked up to Chief Joseph. "Does she not have the strength of her mother?"

She shook the cradleboard, and Wewukiye heard a pitiful mew from the child. His heart ached for the child who would not know her mother. The woman he loved. The woman who fought so bravely to help her people.

Chief Joseph unlaced the child and held her up, studying her. He blew in her face and frowned. "She does not have the eyes of Two Eyes."

"Do you have to tell Two Eyes? Can you not see what his reaction is when you say different?" Crazy One stared into the eyes of Chief Joseph and his sons.

Wewukiye nodded when the chief glanced his way.

Chief Joseph peered at the child, then his sons.

"Come here," he ordered Wewukiye.

Carrying Dove in his arms, he approached the old man.

Chief Joseph nodded his head to Thunder Traveling to Distant Mountains. He stepped forward, checking Dove's breathing, skimming his gaze over their wet clothing.

The baby cried and Springtime walked forward, taking the child from her father-in-law's hands. "I will nurse the baby."

Wewukiye could see she too had given birth. She took the child and retreated.

Thunder Traveling to Distant Mountains stepped forward. The sorrow in his eyes spoke of his regret. The warrior opened his mouth to speak and Sa-qan screeched.

The men she followed rode into the village.

My brother. Are you well? Sa-qan's words held the same misery pounding in his head and squeezing his heart.

I will never be well again.

Agent William and three other men rode up to the cluster of people. William's gaze landed on Dove still limp in Wewukiye's arms. "What happened? The child?" He dismounted as quickly as his aged body allowed. He stared at Wewukiye then peered at Chief Joseph.

"Joseph, your messenger requested my arrival." He pointed to Dove. "This woman spoke with me during the winter months. I made the trip to see if her allegations were true. What has happened?"

Wewukiye held his head high. He would keep holding Dove's body for all to see, until someone did something about the man who started it all.

"The woman gave birth to a child. There is no proof it is Two Eyes's child." Chief Joseph peered at Wewukiye. "We have only the words of this man and the claims the woman made. No proof."

"And the woman? What has happened to her?" William stepped up to Wewukiye.

"That *so-yá-po*"—he nodded to the still unconscious man on the horse—"shoved her and the baby in the water. She thrust the baby away from her, and I saved the child, but could not get to her—before—"

William scanned the area. "Who else witnessed this?"

Crazy One stepped forward.

"Is that all?"

"Is that not enough?" Crazy One's voice rang hard and challenging.

William faced Joseph. "Let me see this child."

Thunder Traveling to Distant Mountains led him inside the lodge.

Chief Joseph turned troubled eyes on Wewukiye. "My brother, set her down so the women can take care of her." He stepped forward, his hands motioning to the lodge next to his.

Take her there but only allow Crazy One to remain with her. Sa-qan's firm tone helped renew his composure.

Wewukiye nodded and walked to the lodge. "Come, my niece." He no longer cared if the band learned who he was. He only wanted Dove to fulfill her gift. Then he would walk into the lake and never set foot among mortals again.

Crazy One entered the lodge and held the blanket back. He knelt, placing Dove on a bed and kissed her cold forehead. A tear slipped from his eye and slid down into the corner of hers.

"You will forever hold my heart."

"Do you not want to help them find the man who caused this?" Crazy One pulled him to his feet.

He nodded, gazed once more at the serene face of Dove, and ducked out of the dwelling.

Thunder Traveling to Distant Mountains met him outside. "My wife will feed the child. Lightning Wolf will remain with our band and Silent Doe will raise the child as hers."

Wewukiye nodded. It was best.

William walked to his side. "When the man wakes, I want to talk to him. Then we'll find O'Rourke and question him."

Wewukiye grabbed a bucket, walked to the lake, filled it, walked up to the *so-yá-po*, and threw the water in the man's face.

The man sputtered to life and skidded back.

"Where's the elk?" the man said hysterically in the White man's words.

"What elk?" William asked.

"The elk that tried to kill me!" The *so-yá-po* stared wild-eyed at all the Nimiipuu gathered around him.

"Why did you kill the woman?" Wewukiye asked in Nimiipuu looming over the man, opening and closing his fists in an attempt to not grab the man and squeeze the life out of him.

A hand clasped his shoulder, drawing him away from the *so-yá-po*. He shook it off and found himself held back by Frog and Thunder Traveling to Distant Mountains. He could easily shake them off, but restrained himself as William stepped between him and the man cowering on the ground.

"Why did you kill the woman?" William asked in the language the White man understood.

If any more color could drain from the man's face it did. "W-woman?"

"The one kneeling by the lake." Wewukiye said in Nimiipuu, and William repeated for the sorry lump of man.

"I-I didn—"

Wewukiye shook off the brothers and stepped forward, menace drawing his lips back from his teeth.

The man scrambled backward until his back hit the legs of two warriors standing behind him. He glanced up at their stern faces then at Wewukiye. He gulped visibly and stared at Agent William. "Don't let them have me. Jasper said to get rid of the troublesome squaw and the kid and I could have all the land I wanted down by the river."

Wewukiye leaned down. The man pushed against the warrior's legs. Wewukiye grabbed him by the shirtfront.

"The land is not his to give. It belongs to Mother Earth." He shook the man and dropped him to the ground. Pivoting, he started into the trees.

"Where are you going?" William called after him.

"To bring back the man responsible for Dove's death." He didn't miss a stride. He would disappear among the trees, change to elk form, and scour the valley for the man.

"You must not go alone. We have to do this right or risk consequences on the Nimiipuu." William's words stopped him.

He wanted the man dead, but he could not bring trouble to the Nimiipuu. He sighed.

"Revenge is an evil partner, my brother," Thunder Traveling to Distant Mountains said, leading a horse over to him.

Wewukiye nodded, but he only saw Dove's sweet smile. He needed to make sure the man who stole her life paid.

Mita áptit ná ·qc
(31)

Cold flowed through Dove but did not chill her. The same floating sensation she experienced when Wewukiye made love to her seeped into her arms and legs.

Wewukiye? Where are you? Where is my child?

"He is with the others. Your child is well cared for." Sa-qan's voice startled her.

Dove moved her head and spotted a light-haired woman and Crazy One. She sat but her body remained on the blanket. Fear and uncertainty froze her movements. "What is happening?"

"You drowned in the lake." The beautiful woman brushed her moonlight hair from her shoulder and smiled. "I am Sa-qan."

Dove gazed at Crazy One who smiled and nodded.

"No, Wewukiye saved me. I had a child. My child, where is she?" Panic ripped through her spearing her heart. She had to save her child, save her people.

Sa-qan placed a hand on her arm.

Calm swirled over her like steam from the sweat lodge.

"Your child is fed by Springtime. She had a son three suns after you had your daughter. Silent Doe will raise your daughter as her own." Sa-qan smiled. "The elders and Agent William are with Wewukiye searching for Evil Eyes."

"But if I am dead why do you see and talk to me and I talk to you?" She needed Wewukiye, she did not understand.

"You are now a spirit. Your mating with and capturing the heart of Wewukiye added great strength to your power. You never wavered from your duty to your people. This impressed the Creator. He wishes you to continue your duty alongside Wewukiye." Sa-qan winked. "I agree you would fulfill your gift to your people as a spirit." She smiled and shot a glance at Crazy One. "I could use a female to talk to now and again. All these seasons upon seasons with only my brothers has become tiring."

Dove stood and walked around her body. "I do not understand. Wewukiye and you have bodies, why do I not have one?"

"You will once the Nimiipuu have mourned and your body is free from this earth." Sa-qan narrowed her gaze. "But you must not return to your village or people in this human body." She glanced at the form peacefully reclining on the blanket.

"How will I know my child?" Her heart weighed heavy knowing she would not hold or care for her daughter.

"We will teach you ways of being around without being seen. You will miss little of your child's years." Sa-qan tipped her head. "The men return. Crazy One take Wewukiye to the log by the lake. We will meet you there."

"Do you not want him to see the body again?" Crazy One gazed at the lifeless body on the bedding.

"If he wishes. We will not be here." Sa-qan grasped Dove's hand. "Think smoke."

Dove stared at the women. Both smiled and nodded. How had she become a spirit so easily? Wewukiye had spoken of her powers, but she had thought he spoke of this to make her strong and carry out her gift.

Think smoke. Sa-qan's words swirled in her

head.

Dove peered into the fire, watched the smoke drift to the smoke hole. She closed her eyes, breathed in the acrid scent, thought of the undulating gray wisps drifting toward the smoke hole. She warmed, relaxed, and floated out the top of the dwelling.

****

Wewukiye leaned over the neck of the horse and read the tracks left by Evil Eyes. The *so-yá-po* moved fast. *Trying to run from his fate.*

"He knows we follow," Thunder Traveling to Distant Mountains said, peering into the trees.

"Yes." Wewukiye wished he could leave these mortals behind and turn into an elk. He would catch the man and... Revenge wrapped around him like wild berry vines, clinging, irritating, and igniting his anger. "I will go ahead and stall him."

Frog nudged his horse forward. "I will go with you."

"I can move faster alone." Wewukiye squeezed his knees, urging his mount forward. He would lose Frog and turn into an elk. He must avenge Dove's death.

Pounding of hooves and a hand grasping his mount's rope, stalled his thoughts and brought them both to a halt.

Frog's red face and round, angry eyes stalled Wewukiye from yanking his horse from the warrior's grip.

"You cannot avenge Dove by starting a war. Your feelings have been noticed by all. If the *so-yá-po* came to harm before Agent William takes him, we will all suffer." Frog released his horse. "We do this together."

Wewukiye turned from the man's watchful eyes. Frog spoke the truth. He wanted to harm the *so-yá-po*. He wished only for revenge. He swallowed the hatred and thought of Dove. To kill the man would not help Dove fulfill her gift.

He nodded and urged his horse up the canyon wall to get ahead of Evil Eyes by taking a shorter route. "We must travel quickly."

Frog grunted assent. Wewukiye led the warrior swiftly along a path he knew well from his travels as an elk. He slowed and pointed down. Evil Eyes moved through the brush below peering over his shoulder.

"We will get ahead of him and scare him back toward the others." Wewukiye urged his horse forward, working his way lower to get in Evil Eyes's path.

Wewukiye stopped his horse and spoke loudly. "Have you seen Two Eyes?"

The sound of an approaching animal stopped.

"He is said to be heading this way." Frog stated also with much volume.

"We will find him."

Crashing brush resounded in front of them as Evil Eyes turned around.

Wewukiye followed at a pace that kept them within hearing distance of Evil Eyes. Shouting in the White man's words and Nimiipuu drifted to them on the wind. Wewukiye smiled. Evil Eyes was caught.

He continued forward at a sedate pace even though his heart raced to capture the man who caused torment to Dove and her eventual death. Frog watched him. The warrior moved his horse ahead right before they overtook the party of Nimiipuu and White men surrounding Evil Eyes.

Wewukiye pushed his mount between Thunder Traveling to Distant Mountains and Agent William. Evil Eyes's mouth clacked shut, and his eyes widened at the sight of him.

"You will pay for the pain and death of a great Nimiipuu maiden." Wewukiye glared at Evil Eyes wishing him all forms of extended torture.

"We will get to the truth." Agent William waved a hand toward Evil Eyes. "Ollokot, lead Mr. O'Rourke's horse."

A weighted gaze drew Wewukiye from glaring at Evil Eyes. He turned his head and witnessed empathy and guilt in Thunder Traveling to Distant Mountains's gaze.

The realization Dove gave her life to save many more, didn't help the loss he felt. Her child would never grow up knowing the wonderful woman who sacrificed much to give her life.

He followed solemnly behind the procession moving at a trot back to the lake village. He wanted to feel empty, unable to go on, but the fire to prove Dove right and fulfill her weyekin kept him from charging though the others and taking the life of the evil *so-yá-po*.

Evil Eyes fought the rope securing him to his horse and shouted words Wewukiye had never heard. He believed them to be White man words, but they made no sense to him.

"O'Rourke, cork your mouth or I'll do it for you," Agent William said in a tone that meant business. But Evil Eyes responded in louder, surlier tones.

Agent William yanked a cloth from his pocket, knotted it, and shoved it in the man's mouth to staunch his angry threats. This show of authority made not only Wewukiye snicker but also several of the warriors.

They entered the village by the light of the half moon. Everyone gathered around as Agent William called for Dove's child to be brought forth. He took the infant from Springtime. Dove's daughter cried. Wewukiye stepped forward to comfort the baby, but Agent William nodded him away.

Wewukiye experienced the child's fear and unease. She needed her mother. *He needed her mother.*

Agent William blew softly in the child's face. Her small eyelids popped open. William made a show of looking from her eyes to the bound man's face. Evil Eyes stopped squirming. His brow scrunched as his narrowed eyes stared at the child.

Springtime relieved the agent of the baby, cuddling the child to her breasts. Dove's daughter would be cared for.

William walked over to Evil Eyes and yanked the cloth from his mouth. "Do you still deny the child is yours?"

"Where is that worthless squaw? Why isn't she out here accusing me?" He looked around. "Could it be because she didn't want you to know it was all her idea?"

Wewukiye growled and stepped forward his hands reaching for the man's throat. Frog and Thunder Rolling to Distant Mountains grabbed him.

Agent William raised his hand stopping the words flaming on Wewukiye's tongue.

"She's dead. And according to the man who did it, by your orders."

A wicked smile showed the man's tobacco-stained teeth. "You can't believe every sodgrabber. Who has dealt with the army for you and helped you stay in this valley?"

Wewukiye didn't like the way Evil Eyes changed the subject. "If the maiden liked your treatment why was she bruised all over and wishing to end her life when I found her?"

Gasps and whispers filled the air around him. Wewukiye didn't want to give up Dove's secrets but he saw no other way to trick this man into telling the truth.

"I told you she liked it rough. Couldn't get enough."

The lecherous leer on the man's face broke

Wewukiye's calm. He lunged forward, breaking free of the brothers and grabbing Evil Eyes by the hair. "Cut him loose. I want to settle this between us." He loomed over the man. Wewukiye witnessed the fear in Evil Eyes the instant the *so-yá-po* recognized him as the one who threw his rifle a great distance.

Evil Eyes's face paled. "Don't let him get a hold of me!"

Agent William stepped beside Wewukiye and peered at the *so-yá-po*. "Did you take Dove forcibly?"

Wewukiye yanked on Evil Eyes's hair, raising him off the ground.

"Yes. The damn squaw scratched like a wild cat." He stared straight at Wewukiye. "I'm glad she's dead."

Wewukiye grasped the man's neck in his hands.

No brother. That will not help the Nimiipuu. Sa-qan's calm voice stilled his actions but didn't lessen the rage eating his gut and searing his heart.

A wail rose from the group gathered round. Wewukiye spun to the sound and witnessed Dove's father helping her mother stay on her feet.

"You may give this man the Nimiipuu punishment for violating a woman. I will have him punished by his own people for the murder of Dove." Agent William handed Evil Eyes over to Frog.

Wewukiye stared at Thunder Traveling to Distant Mountains. Why would he allow William to take Evil Eyes to a White man's justice? He violated Dove and sent a man to kill her. He also told the Nimiipuu untruths and pretended to be their friend. All those reasons to Wewukiye meant Evil Eyes should be punished completely by the Nimiipuu, the people he injured.

"He has violated our people. How can you believe the *so-yá-po*'s laws will bring justice?" Wewukiye held Thunder Traveling to Distant Mountains's arm.

"We must live in peace with the *so-yá-po*. Agent William will make sure Two Eyes is punished. If we were to punish him, the White army would force us to leave." Thunder Traveling to Distant Mountains's eyes held sadness. "We must learn to follow the White man's rules. It is not easy, but it is necessary." He followed the procession escorting Evil Eyes to the whipping tree.

Evil Eyes's cries rang across the moonlit village. Wewukiye wished the man pain and eventual death for taking Dove's life, but he would not watch. He left the punishment to others. His aching heart wished only to cast his gaze once more upon Dove before he vanished into the lake and never sought another mortal.

Wewukiye entered the lodge where Dove lay. The sight of her motionless body and serene face dropped him to his knees.

"Would she want you to cry for her?" Crazy One placed a hand on his shoulder. "Should you not speak to your sister?" She drew him to his feet and tugged him out into the glow of the half moon.

His feet followed, but his heart remained in the lodge.

"Is this not what you need?" Crazy One motioned in front of her.

He glanced at the downed tree where he, Himiin, and Sa-qan spent many hours talking. Two women sat upon the log.

"Why are you taking me to see women? Where is Sa-qan?" Moonlight danced silver across the hair of one of the women. *His sister*. How many seasons had it been since he saw her in woman form?

But who sat with her?

His steps faltered. He did not care to converse with any other than his sister. She would not understand his loss, but she would honor it.

The woman beside Sa-qan shifted, and his chest

constricted in shock.

Dove slipped off the log and ran to him. He wrapped his arms around her but she wasn't there.

She laughed and his heart bounced around in his chest like a bird caught in a dwelling.

"How?"

He could see her but his hands slipped through her.

"The Creator has made me a spirit like you. Only I cannot regain my human form until they put me in the earth." She laughed again. "We will now be together forever."

If he could kiss her he would and never stop. "Without you, I thought my world would never be full of life again."

The flap of wings drew his attention. "Keep her well, brother." Sa-qan leaped in the air and soared toward the moon.

He searched for Crazy One, but she had disappeared as well.

"Would you like to see my world?" He held out his hand, she placed hers in it. He couldn't feel the weight or pressure of her hand, but heat raced up his arm, and they walked hand in hand into the lake.

He smiled and gave thanks to the Creator who had blessed him beyond anything he dared dream. His love for the woman entering his world brightened not only his heart but his future. He would never be alone again. Dove would be at his side forever.

Paty's list of Wild Rose Press books

Historical Westerns:
> *Gambling on an Angel*

Halsey Brother Series:
> *Marshal in Petticoats*
> *Outlaw in Petticoats*
> *Miner in Petticoats*
> *Doctor in Petticoats*

Contemporary Westerns:
> *Perfectly Good Nanny* (EPPIE Award winner)
> *Bridled Heart*

Paranormal Trilogy:
> *Spirit of the Mountain*
> *Spirit of the Lake*

To learn more about Paty:
www.patyjager.net

CPSIA information can be obtained at www.ICGtesting.com
Printed in the USA
239574LV00003B/2/P